P9-DWG-764

Losing Mr. North

ALSO BY ELAINE KAGAN

NO GOOD-BYES

SOMEBODY'S BABY

BLUE HEAVEN

THE GIRLS

Losing Mr. North

A NOVEL

Elaine Kagan

WILLIAM MORROW
An Imprint of HarperCollins*Publishers*

For information address HarperCollins Publishers Inc.,
10 East 53rd Street, New York, NY 10022.

HarperCollins books may be purchased for educational, business, or
sales promotional use. For information please write: Special Markets Department,
HarperCollins Publishers Inc., 10 East 53rd Street, New York, NY 10022.

FIRST EDITION

Designed by Jo Anne Metsch

Printed on acid-free paper

Library of Congress Cataloging-in-Publication Data
has been applied for.

ISBN 0-06-018474-4

02 03 04 05 06 QW 10 9 8 7 6 5 4 3 2 1

for Razi

Acknowledgments

The author wishes to thank her particular fraternity of law enforcement: Retired Lieutenant Jack Thorpe, Retired Detective Sergeant Tom Edmunds, and Detective Stephen Miller of the Beverly Hills Police Department; Deputy Andy Marsh, Detective Marston Mottweiler, Corporal Dennis Gray, Sergeant Randy Nixon, CSI Christian Dunlap, and Shelly Dumas of the Inyo County Sheriff's Department; and Officer Phil West and Sergeant Dave Lewis of the Bishop Police Department. Without their gracious generosity of time, expertise, and attention to detail, this story could not have been written.

Thank you to Marlene Thorpe and Irene Edmunds for the small peek they gave me into what it's like to be a policeman's wife.

Thank you to Ginger Barber, my steadfast cheerleader;

David Freeman, Dinah Lennie, and David Francis;

Razi, Carole, Carole I., Suze and Iva;

John Cassavetes;

always and forever, Bob Gottlieb;

and my dearest Eve.

Losing Mr. North

Rachel

IT BEGAN AS it always began—he called from the car. Eight-ten, already hot, already obvious that it would be a scorcher. Rachel blotted her lip with the back of her hand, dropped her toast crust on the *Los Angeles Times* front page, and picked up the phone. "I'm on my way, babe," Jack said, the rest of his words swallowed by crackling.

"What? Where are you?"

". . . said I just passed . . ." Static. ". . . ran into . . ." More static.

"You're cutting out."

"I'll . . . through the mountains . . ." The line went dead.

"Uh-huh," Rachel said, and replaced the receiver. She pushed at the edges of toast sitting on the newspaper, drummed her fingers on the table, and studied the house across the way—the sun was full on, hitting the white paint with a vengeance and causing a terrific glare. Jack was supposed to have come down last week; she had been waiting for the call. She took a swig of the cold coffee and ran her hand across her face. Okay, okay, no reason to get crazy, whatever it was that had held him up, he was on his way. Groceries first; he'd probably be in around three. She picked up a pen, scribbled across the margin of the newspaper: meat loaf—he loved meat loaf—pork chops, rib eyes to barbecue . . . maybe she should just order a whole cow. She tilted her chin into her hand—she'd have Carole over for the pork chops, Thursday maybe. Have the rib eyes Saturday, maybe ask Jack's nephew, Randy, to come over—Jack would like that. Rachel moved her cup across the newsprint, studied the wet coffee ring blurring the word *rib eye*. The dance of the meat, the monthly dance as if it were a period. She'd made lasagna once, vegetarian lasagna, and found him lifting up the wide noodles like a detective looking for the meat. "I am a detective," he'd said, "I can't control myself." "Very funny, Jack." The phone rang. If only she could figure out how to get him to eat chicken—disguise it. Rachel had a fleeting image of a girl chicken batting movie-star eyelashes discreetly beneath the brim of a hat with a veil. She sighed, then lifted the receiver. Jack said, "Hey," and the line went dead. She tucked one foot around the rungs of the kitchen chair, tipped it forward, and added Diet Pepsi to the list under grapes. Eight-twenty, plenty of time to do everything—if he kept his foot to the pedal, he couldn't make it in before three. She'd take her walk, change the sheets, the towels, go to the grocery store, work on the interview piece, water the front, call Burt's Plumbing to come and fix the damn sprinklers so she didn't have to water the front . . . hey, Jack could do it—maybe. Perfect timing. She wrote "front sprinklers" on another piece of paper with a question mark, pushed her finger against some crumbs, raised that finger to her lips. The phone rang, she lifted the receiver, and Jack laughed. "Mountains," he said, laughing, and again the line went dead. Rachel replaced the receiver. Damn car phone didn't work in the mountains and he knew that. Why was he so persistent when he knew it didn't work? She wrote strawberries, changed it to raspberries because she liked raspberries, changed it back to strawberries because he liked strawberries, pushed the chair away from the table, took the cup of cold coffee with her, and went up the stairs to get dressed.

Persistent, stubborn, grumpy. She put the cup on the green table by the window and yanked off the sheets. Yeah, grumpy. Actually stuck his chin out, crossed his arms over his chest like a warning, like a flagman on the road: Look out, lady; caution; beware. And set in his ways, inflexible for no reason, which was absurd. She was definitely going to make him eat chicken; she was not interested in watching him have a heart attack. Rachel sat down on the stripped bed, leaned over to lace up her tennis shoes, felt the dreaded little roll of flesh squash at her middle as she bent. She tied the shoes in double knots like she used to do for the kids, looked down at her body, studied the small, soft roundness that was obvious below her waist. One-twenty, not 116 anymore, no matter how she tried, 120. She pushed into the little roll of flesh with her finger as if she were pushing into pie dough, and then leaned back flat across the bed. Spreading. Forty-eight, she was actually forty-eight, not that she was going to say it out loud, but forty-eight and spreading like butter across bread. Bread, she'd forgotten to write bread, and she wasn't buying that jalapeño corn bread he liked. Talk about loaded with butter, talk about fat. She lay there, feet on the floor, eyes on the ceiling, bare back across the cool cotton mattress cover, wearing her ex-husband's faded shorts. Underpants and shorts and marshmallow tennis shoes, no top. Rachel studied the ceiling. She loved him; a little jalapeño corn bread couldn't hurt—maybe she'd buy a half. A jay was screeching in the back garden; her eyes went to the flash of hot purple bougainvillea across the side fence out the window; the phone rang.

She rolled over onto her stomach, slid forward, and grabbed for the receiver. "Hey," she said, "why do you try when you're in the mountains?"

Ben-oh said, "Hi, Mom."

"Oh, hi, sweetheart."

"Wassup?" he said. "Who's in the mountains?"

"Jack."

Silence.

"He's on his way down," Rachel said.

"Time to get laid, huh, Mom?"

She sat up. "Ben, don't give me any grief, okay? I'm not interested."

"Okay, okay. Sorry."

She took a breath, looked down at her breasts, realized she was talking to her son bare-chested. She rolled her eyes. "What are you doing up so early? It's not even close to noon."

"Very funny. I'm writing a paper . . . trying to write a paper. For Ennis. I hate him. Did I tell you that I hate him? Pretentious dick."

"You're writing a paper in the morning? You can't even walk in the morning. What's the paper?" Her head filled with a picture of her only son, sleepy Ben—nineteen, scrawny, tall, loose bony shoulders, deep brown eyes and matching stick-straight hair that flopped over his eyes in a kind of cowlick no matter what he used, basketball hands, matching feet, a sprinkle of freckles, the chicken pox scar over the left eyebrow, the earring, the tattoo—in her mind this image was superimposed over a picture of him when he was a toddler: all eyes, tufts of hair coming in like cactus, G.I. Joe pajamas, and the little down pillow Lady had given him that he carried everywhere, always covering his face with it when he slept. The pillow had not gone to college—it was in the hall cedar closet, covered in tissue paper, on top of the flannel sheets.

"He's making us compare the economic, uh"—papers rattling—"no, the ethics of the economy from the Roman Catholic perspective compared to the Buddhist perspective."

"When? Now?"

"Yeah, now, 2000, the beginning of the end of the world. I hate him." Something crashed in the background.

"What was that?"

"Oh, Becker's got a klutz problem. He is one." Rachel heard Ben's roommate laughing, a muffled something from her son that sounded like "fuff ooh" with his hand clamped over the phone, and the slam of a door.

"What's your room look like? Did you guys ever open the windows?"

"Very funny, Mom. Yeah, we opened the windows, we even emptied the trash. Actually, we threw it out the window."

"Good, Ben," she said.

The reek of old pizza boxes and beer and socks and sweat and boys and tennis shoes had nearly knocked her over the last time she'd driven up to school. She'd gone on the trip with her granddaughter, on a " 'venture," said the little one, the diminutive Sarah, who had Rachel's brown eyes and her sallow complexion but no roll around her middle yet. The defiant three-year-old Sarah, who already had attitude, who had held her ground in the doorway of the dorm room and refused to go in. "Unkah Ben's room stinks," she'd said firmly in her tough voice, tugging on Rachel's hand.

"So, listen, Mom, I need some, uh, money."

"Did you call your dad?"

"Yeah, I left a message with the Dixie princess."

Rachel tried to hide her laugh. "Ben, that's not nice."

"Yeah, makes her sound like a ship. So, he's in New York or something."

Rachel stood up. "You know, I heard they have phones in New York now."

"Mom . . ."

"Ben-oh, it is not my responsibility to put money in that account; it's your dad's."

"Yeah, I know, but . . ."

"Call him in New York."

"Jeez, couldn't you help me out here?"

"Nope. What's the money for?"

"Oh, you know, my life: books, food, sundries."

"Sundries?" Rachel ran her hand across her smile. "Where did you get the word *sundries*?"

"Sundries, as in drugstore. You know, toothpaste, deodorant, pens, et cetera."

"I know, but where did you get the word *sundries*?"

"I don't know. Lady, I guess."

Lady was Rachel's mother. It was Ben who had named her Lady. That *lady,* he'd said, referring to his grandmother, and it stuck. She became the Lady Rosenthal as if she had suddenly married an earl. Rachel shook her head and the other line rang. "Sweetie, I gotta go."

"Must be Jack, huh? What time is old robo cop due in?"

"Ben, let me know if you don't get your father."

"Yeah?"

"Yeah. I'll see what I can do." She hung up. Nine-twenty and she hadn't walked, she hadn't done anything, she hadn't even put on all her clothes. She scrambled across the mattress on her knees and picked up the other phone on the other side of the bed, Henry's old business line, the only thing that she still thought of as his in the house.

"Meet me in the street," Grace said.

"God. What happened?"

"I'm blue."

"Grace, I can't meet you in the street, I don't have a top on. And since when does blue qualify for meeting in the street?"

No answer.

"Grace, I have to change the sheets, walk, work on a piece for a German magazine, go to the store, make a meat loaf . . . did I say take a shower? Why are you blue?"

"Why are you making meat loaf? You don't like meat loaf."

"Jack's coming in."

A definite near ten seconds of silence and then Grace said, "Oh. I didn't realize it was a month." Just an edge of a tone of disapproval, just a tiny edge as loud as a trumpet blast.

"It's more than a month, it was a month last week. Why are you blue?"

"I don't know, just general blueness," Grace said. "Why didn't he make it in last week?" She hesitated and then gave a short, snippy laugh. "Interesting choice of words, huh?—make it in—and I'm not even the writer."

"Cute, Grace. Did Dickhead do something?" Dickhead was Rachel's name for Grace's husband, Dick.

"He doesn't want to sell the property in Napa."

"What does the lawyer say?"

"I didn't call him."

"Why not?"

"Too blue, *chérie*."

"Grace . . ."

"I know, I know."

They were quiet.

"What time is Jack due in?"

"Three, three-thirty."

"So I guess I won't talk to you."

"Of course, you'll talk to me. Don't I always talk to you? You can come for supper. How about pork chops Thursday night?"

"Ah, how soon she forgets her previous commitments when faced with hot sex. Aren't you supposed to go to some book-signing dinner on Thursday for some hotshot from New York?"

Rachel ran her hand across her face. "Oh, shit."

"Indeed."

"I'll cancel."

"You could always take Jack with you, he's such a hit with the liberals, so in demand."

Rachel watched the clock make its way to 9:30. The next thing she knew her daughter would call. That's all she needed—Ben, Grace, and then Dana, the three disgruntled members of her team. "Grace, do you need me to meet you in the street?"

"No, I'll wait until it's something important. I'll wait until I blow up Dick's truck."

Rachel laughed. "Is that the plan?"

"I'm just considering whether he should be in it."

"Are you okay? I've got time, really, I'll meet you." She pictured herself waiting in the foyer as Jack's car pulled up, still wet from the shower, wrapped in a towel.

"No, I'm fine," Grace said.

Rachel's eyes refocused on the blast of purple outside her window. "Have you noticed my bougainvillea? It's glorious."

No answer.

"Have another cup of coffee, have a poached egg with the yellow all runny the way you like."

"Yeah," Grace said, "just what I need, a poached egg. I've already had seven pieces of toast." She hung up with no good-bye; it was so Grace to just hang up with no words when she was through.

Rachel and Grace had been meeting in the street since before the babies were born. Well, one of the babies. When Rachel moved onto the block, Dana was five and Ben was one. And within the next five years came Grace's Amy. But meeting in the street had always been left for something momentous. In the eighteen years of their friendship, the up and down the block of their friendship, the countless dinners, hours of carpool, endless conversations, to meet in the street was set aside specifically for grief or joy: pregnancies; miscarriages; the murder at the end of the block, which was a terrific shock; and betrayals—nearly always done by Dickhead, except the day Rachel's husband, Henry, announced he had fallen in love with the Dixie queen. No. What had Ben called her? Princess, the Dixie princess. Henry would be pissed, but the name was perfect: the significant other was short and squat and moody, with wet blue eyes, ponderous breasts, thick ankles, and the most annoying Louisiana drawl that grew more cloying the longer she lived in L.A. And on top of everything else she was an actress. An unemployed actress who *went to class*. "That's her job, Mom," Ben-oh had said. "She goes to class more than I do. Dad ought to enroll her in UCLA." "She's not old enough," Rachel said. "Pissy, pissy," said her son.

Rachel slid off the bed. Okay, first a top and then the sheets and then the groceries. And then the sundries. She smiled. No walk. Put everything away, concoct the meat loaf before the shower because it takes a shower to get rid of the garlic and onions and tomato sauce smells under your nails. She'd get everything ready and then work until Jack got in. She would finish the piece for the Germans, she would start on the piece for *Allure*. She'd walk next week, when he was gone. She had better walk, she thought, pulling the T-shirt over her head, now that she was a forty-something-year-old single mom-grandmother with a paunch and a roll.

She missed Jack's next phone call, because she was pushing the shopping cart up and down the aisles. The jalapeño corn bread was a no, but the pork chops were a yes, because, after all, as far as Rachel was concerned, she was absolutely not a cook; she had mastered only three things: a roast chicken stuffed with lemons, penne with tomato, rosemary, and vinegar (she'd made that last month), and pork chops. Her pork chops were outstanding, even Dickhead said so. Chicken was out as far as Jack was concerned, not because he'd tasted hers, just because it was chicken. "But you haven't tasted *my* chicken." "It doesn't matter." "It's one of my best things." "I'm sure it is." "It's delicious, absolutely delicious."

His stance, the crossed arms over his chest. "Babe, what did I say? I don't eat chicken."

Her butt against the cabinet, she threw the lemon at him. He caught it. She pushed herself up with her hands and sat perched on the cold tile counter next to the kitchen sink. "Let me get this straight—you don't eat chicken because chickens are stupid."

"Correct." The corner of his mouth pulled up into a near smile; he positioned himself between her knees at the sink.

"Turkeys are stupider," Rachel said. His hands on her. "Turkeys tilt their heads back when it rains, with their mouths open, and they drown." She knew this stunning bit of information from a piece she'd done on turkeys for a Thanksgiving feature in *Good Housekeeping* years ago. His fingers up her skirt, rough fingers encircling the flesh of her thigh. "I don't eat turkeys either," Jack said, his face close to hers. She hit him with the dish towel; he kissed her. His gray eyes a blur, he lifted her T-shirt and her breath caught. With one thick hand grazing her nipple, Jack bent his mouth to her breast, Rachel pulled at his belt buckle; they wound up ordering in.

Sex with Jack. Heady. Intimate. More intimate than Rachel had ever had with any man. Staggering at this stage, this age—a rush of heat to the cheeks, a flurry of filthy thoughts, fantasies that should have been fulfilled years ago, freed and running loose in her head.

She played the messages after she'd carried in all the grocery bags. One from Woody, her agent in New York, about getting a no on the cellulite piece from *Cosmo* because some new, hotshot twelve-year-old editor there, who'd probably never even seen cellulite, thought it was too personal (did that mean cellulite was too personal or the piece?—she had to call Woody), and the other: "Hey, babe, I'm out of the mountains. The phone's on."

She circled the kitchen putting away the groceries while she listened to the ring of the phone in Jack's car, the particular ring of a cell phone which used to so offend her mother. "Don't call me on that," Lady had said, "driving around not paying attention like all the rest of them. You just call me when you get home." "Mom . . ." "You heard me," Lady would say, mumbling about the way it used to be as she hung up. Lady had preferred life when milk was delivered in bottles, the cream still at the top, and the operator gave a perky "Hello? Central" when you picked up the phone. Nowadays she had no idea what a telephone was, much less what you did with one. Lady Rosenthal spent most of her time in a wheelchair wearing too much lipstick and talking to people who weren't there. Highly paid round-the-clock "keepers," as Grace called them, tended Rachel's mother and didn't seem to mind when she thought they were someone else.

Jack answered. "Hey, where'd you go?"

"Groceries. Where are you?" She'd done the route; she knew both sides of that road in the mountains north of Bishop all the way to Beverly Hills—all seven hours of it door-to-door.

"Mammoth Lakes cutoff."

"You're making good time."

"Yeah, I should be there three, three-thirty."

Some of the strawberries were bad. No matter how many ways you turned the carton you could never see the ones they hid in the middle that were bad. They packaged them that way on purpose, Rachel was sure. "I got a turndown from *Cosmo*."

"What?"

"A turndown from *Cosmopolitan* on the cellulite piece." She ran a handful of berries under the faucet, then popped one in her mouth.

"That's because you don't have any cellulite. You're only supposed to write about what you know."

"I have cellulite."

"Hey, lady, I happen to be more familiar with your thighs up close than you are."

"You win."

Jack laughed; she smiled at the sound of it. "I'm glad you're coming down."

"Yeah?"

"Yeah. I thought you'd be here last week."

"Yeah, me too."

"But you weren't."

He didn't say anything. She stood there, a strawberry close to her lips, uneasy that she was asking, unable to stop the asking. "Jack, is something wrong?"

"No."

Something in his voice, something. "Jack?"

"What? Isn't this week good for you? You want me to turn around?"

"Of course I don't want you to turn around." She threw the strawberry into the sink. "You going to eat in Independence?" Her heart was doing this little dance up against her rib cage, a little rumba. Calm down, she thought.

"Nah, I'll wait."

"Hey, don't eat garbage."

He laughed. "You mean you don't think Burger King makes a good breakfast?"

"I mean you don't need eggs *and* potatoes *and* toast *and* sausage at that place outside of Olancha."

"You left out jam . . ."

"Jack, you're waiting to eat at that place near Olancha."

". . . and butter. What are you wearing?"

"Jack . . ."

"Rachel . . ."

She shook her head, put the milk in the refrigerator. "I'm naked. I went to the store like this. Nobody said a thing." She put the potatoes, tomatoes, and peaches in the sink. "I love you."

"I love you," he said, "but I may have to take you into custody for indecent exposure. Go lie down on the dining room table and wait for me. I'll be there by three." More crackling on the line.

"I thought you were out of the mountains," she said.

"I am."

"Oh, it sounded like . . ."

"I'll call you when I pass Jo's," he said.

"Watch out for the *Bessie*."

Jack laughed. "Yeah, maybe it will come and take me; I'll just sail away."

"Be careful."

"I'm just puttin' along, not goin' over sixty."

"Jack, your sixty is seventy-five to normal humans. Be careful."

"It's not like anybody's going to arrest me."

"Jack . . ."

"Yes, ma'am." And the line went dead.

Rachel's fingers were wet on the receiver; she put the phone down. He was a week late, but a week late didn't mean anything. *Is anything wrong? No*. That's what he'd said. She wasn't going to worry about it. She folded the grocery bags in perfect thirds and put them on top of the washing machine in the back hall.

The *Bessie* was the *Bessie Jo,* a steamship that was used to haul ore down from the Inyo Mountains across Owens Lake from Keeler to Cartago in 1882. Rachel learned that Jack knew everything about California and water; he probably even understood the movie *Chinatown*. Rachel laughed, she'd never understood the part about the water and the orange groves, and no matter how many times it was explained to her, her eyes rolled.

"It was too far to carry the ore all the way round," Jack had said, "and there weren't any railroads yet."

"What happened to her, the *Bessie*?" Rachel had asked on that first trip, gazing out the car window at the endless stretch of dry brown land that had once been water. "She sank," Jack said. "Before your Los Angeles took all the water from the valley and dried everything up." She reached across the back of the seat and patted his upper arm. "She's not *my* Los Angeles," she said, "I'm the one from Chicago, remember?" He didn't answer. She left her hand on his shoulder, her elbow cold against the upholstery. She studied his profile—the cheekbone, the line of his jaw—his big hands on the wheel. Broad nails, his skin tanned to a rich gold. The wind from the open windows was brisk and dry and icy, whipping her hair across her face; she pulled it back with her other hand. "You want the heat?" he asked. "No, I hate it." He looked at her and smiled. They didn't know each other that well then. Jack said the *Bessie Jo* would still come up sometimes; a puff of smoke out of nowhere and she would appear. "Sail right across that dry lake," he said to her. His eyes were like cut glass, pale gray as the sky against the range of mountains behind his head brilliant with snow, and her heart sank because she knew she was a goner. That hadn't changed, not in six years. He was rudimentary, a meat-and-potatoes man closed off to anything new, unsophisticated and loving it, and when she knew they would never work, when he crossed those arms and got stubborn or pissy or tried to get into it with her about her being a Democrat or a liberal or a marching feminist or anything that rattled his side, just when she knew everybody was right, that they were too different to ever make it and she ought to just face the damn music, he would say something like believing in a ghost steamship and she would lose ground. It occurred to Rachel that except for Dylan, whom she'd interviewed a few times, Jack North was possibly the most disarming man she had ever known.

She'd met him when she was writing an article for *Redbook* about battered women, about why they stayed, about why they could get drop-kicked across a living room and still be ironing the kicker's shirts the next day. "I find the majority of time it's economics," he'd said. Low voice, gray eyes somber, a frown of concern. He looked part lumberjack, part Greek god, and all cop: medium height, strong, with football shoulders, ruddy skin, and black hair—a thick tangle of it clipped and perfectly in place, a disconcerting spray of silver at one temple—a cleft in his chin. The spotless card he'd handed her from his powder blue shirt pocket read DETECTIVE SERGEANT JACK NORTH, BEVERLY HILLS POLICE DEPARTMENT. He looked like a Disney animated version of Prince Charming; all that was missing was a sparkle flashing off his perfect white front teeth. "Domestic violence falls under my table," he'd said, slipping his shades down and staring at her as if she were about to commit a felony. "Your table?" He cleared his throat. "Robbery and homicide, crimes against persons." "Oh," Rachel had said, "your table." She'd mumbled and scribbled it on her pad. When he'd held the chair out for her in the Detective Division interview room, she lost her footing, slipping into him, amazed at the solid bulk of a gun under his tweed sport jacket and his arm. Six years ago, the very day Henry had announced that he was leaving her for the Dixie queen.

Princess, Rachel thought, placing the red and green pepper slices across the top of the meat loaf in a layered motif. Hey, look at that; move over, Emeril. Her eyes lifted to the stove clock: 11:12. She covered the loaf with foil, let her eyes trail the countertops of her spotless kitchen, slid the baking dish into the refrigerator, and took the stairs up three at a time.

Henry had had the upper hand, of course, announcing that he wanted a divorce when she was sitting at her dressing table naked, still damp from the bath. Talk about betrayal. One could not fight fairly when one was naked and he knew that, the summa cum laude, but she damn well wasn't going to get up to cover herself. She squared her shoulders and lifted her chin in the mirror. "You're leaving me for another woman. Why don't you just have the balls to leave and be on your own?" She wasn't going to turn around either. If Henry wanted to ask for a divorce when he was behind her, he could just deal with her bare back. She had a great back, an evening gown back, he had once said. So much for loyalty. If he wanted to leave the evening gown back for a drawl with thick ankles, he could just go. In retrospect, she thought she had deftly handled the situation; she applauded herself on her restraint. No yelling, no throwing of lipsticks or brushes or jars of hysterically expensive face cream that were all well within her reach. "You want a divorce, go get one," she'd said.

Ending it had been a part of their reality for some time, a steady quiet panic since a cool February evening three years before. Henry had called; he was late, stuck in a meeting. They were leaving at dawn with the kids for Hawaii, and she could at least lay his clothes out on the bed for him, she thought, wouldn't that be great, get his things ready for him so he wouldn't be crazed. The photographs of him and the Dixie princess stuffed behind the electric razor in his dop kit were all it took—war was declared. The only thing missing in all that time had been the word *divorce,* and except for a little white-knuckle clutching of her hairbrush during his announcement, Rachel thought she'd managed it quite well. Then the disgusting scene that afternoon in front of the police officer—the detective sergeant or whatever he called himself—with Rachel losing it and slobbering like a drunk all over a bartender or some fool sitting next to you on the plane who tells you his life story.

"Hey," Jack had said, kind of patting her shoulder with his big paw, and she'd lost it, collapsing on his chest. Uniformed police officers walking up and down the hall outside of the interview room, motorcycle cops, black boots and helmets, peering in, and she's sitting next to him at a polished table peering at black-and-white photographs of black-and-blue women, where he was explaining something about how a sex crime could be anything from an annoying phone call to murder, and she could smell his aftershave, and it reminded her of her father, and she realized she was the same age her father had been when he died, and how she would like to give Henry more than an annoying phone call, and how she would have to begin again, when she'd actually already bought the dress for her eighteenth wedding anniversary, *and the shoes,* and this lump in her gut slid up to her throat and this horrific sob came out of her and her pen skidded off the pad. Jack North was her friend long before he became her lover, he was as close to her as Grace. Or Carole. And as far as lawyer stuff and kids and dividing the pieces of a wrecked marriage were concerned, he had the insight of a man's point of view, a most needed thing when one is trying to know what to fight for, what to give and take. If Rachel was fast and vocal, with a facade that she strived to keep coated with funny, Jack was the original man-of-few-words, uncomplicated in his plainness, direct and deep. Like a tree, that picture of him in her head hadn't changed in six years. A tree, a thick oak with thick branches and deep roots, and it worked, the two of them. If he was the tree, then she was the squirrel, and it worked. Most of the time. Maybe it was more difficult lately, maybe *testy* would be the more appropriate word. Irritable. Well, sometimes. Lately they got into it a little more. But there were the miles to contend with now, the separation of the miles since he'd retired and moved seven hours away to the middle of nowhere, and the lie of trying to pretend they were living some kind of regular life, the insanity of jamming some kind of pretend half-assed marriage into one week out of every month, and the looming reality that was rarely mentioned but was as dark as doom—the fact that Jack wasn't married to Rachel and probably never would be, the fact that Jack was married to Linda, and had been for thirty-five years.

Rachel dropped her panties and socks in the hamper, stepped into the shower, tilted her face up under the water, and closed her eyes.

The ring was gold and wide and had three tiny dirty diamonds at the top of the scroll. It was also too tight, his finger bulging around it like it was something he'd outgrown. "Twenty-eight years," Jack had said that first day, rubbing his hand across his black pants, "gonna be twenty-nine, come July." Rachel's thumb unconsciously went to the third finger of her left hand—the space left from her wedding band was pale and slightly indented. She had removed the thin circle of tiny diamonds that very morning six years ago and put it in one of her porcelain boxes to give to Dana. In time.

"Looks like I only made it to eighteen," Rachel said with a snuffling sigh.

"You want a coffee?" he'd asked.

The intimacy that had been established during her cry all over his chest was somewhat splintered now—swollen eyes and a damp powder blue shirtfront were about all that was left, and a cloud of embarrassment that drifted in the air between them. "I don't know," Rachel said, and he pushed back his chair and took her elbow. "Sure you do," he said. The cloud melted, moved to parts unknown.

Jack took care of her that first day, that stranger who resembled Prince Charming; he let her talk about her marriage, about Henry, intimate secrets that spilled from her like tears. He listened. Henry never listened, Henry went on. Henry demanded the front seat, the lead, the view closer to the window, the bigger wedge of pie, the cream on top, the last cherry, the captain's chair. Whatever was the best of the best and the most important, Henry demanded and Rachel had learned to give. She had learned to accept her place: next to him but a half-step back. "To the side," Rachel had said. "To the rear, ten-hut." Grace had said, "You were definitely behind his majesty, don't kid yourself." "No." "Oh, yes, sweetie, and you catered to it; you wanted all of us to be quiet when he was thinking, as if little old us could diffuse the king's recondite thoughts." "I didn't." "Oh, yes, you did," Grace had said when they'd met in the street to discuss the vacating Henry.

"Recondite?" Prince Charming had asked when she'd told him, those smoky eyes steady on her over his coffee and her Coke.

"Complex."

"Oh, yeah. Is he complex?"

"Oh, yeah." Rachel moved the straw through the ice cubes. "What's your wife's name?"

"Linda."

"That's pretty," Rachel added.

"Uh-huh."

* * *

"Linda," Rachel said now under the shower, tilting her head back to rinse out the shampoo. Linda of the homemade curtains, homemade batter biscuits, and homespun. The smell of apple pie, short ribs in the oven, sweet pots of herbs across the sill. Linda, who could make jam from picking the berries to pouring the paraffin, sew curtains without a pattern, and probably hook rugs. He hadn't mentioned rugs. Linda, who could put up siding. *That* he'd mentioned. Rachel had tried to conjure up siding—was it that silver stuff glinting at you on the highway from the side of barns? Linda, who rode horses and dirt bikes, who could race right alongside Jack. Linda, who could give giant barbecues for thirty without help. Linda, who probably had had her babies, sans even a lowly aspirin, squatting in a field. Cutting the cord with her teeth. Going in to do three loads of wash, finish stitching a quilt, and get supper, a five-course supper that would make Joël Robuchon proud. (Rachel had done a piece on Robuchon for *Gourmet*.) Linda, having the babies and going in to paint the house. Fix the roof. Hey, maybe Linda could fix the front sprinklers.

Rachel tipped her face up to the spray, reached for the conditioner. Linda, of the high-pitched voice with no trace of real accent except a soft drop of her *t*'s. Linda, who took a breath at the end of each sentence as if she were carefully selecting her words. Linda, who was eight years older—hooray! Linda, who had never had a career, who had never worked for a living, had no idea what that was. Linda, who had wispy dishwater hair that either hung limp below her shoulders or was teased and sprayed into a catastrophe that would be more suitable on a backup singer at the Grand Ole Opry. Linda, who had sun-baked skin, big tits, and was the exact same height as Rachel but topped her by sixteen pounds. Rachel had heard her voice, seen her picture, seen her handwriting; she'd even seen her last mammogram report. They both had calcifications on the left side; they both had brown eyes; they both had Jack.

Linda

IT STARTED JUST like always—he didn't come back home. Took off right after breakfast. By ten, ten-thirty, she was pretty sure—unless he'd gone to help Phil move gravel. Linda re-coiled the hose into a tight circle over the wrought-iron rack, tight the way Jack liked it, and wiped her hands across her backside. The roses had that mildew again, sneaking up across the buds. Of course, he could have stopped in to see about Mae Chapin's sagging porch. *Hey, Jack, you think you could stop and take a look at my pump? at my driveway? at my whatever-it-is that I need help with?* Everybody asking, as if that was all he had to do—drive around the county and fix things. For free. Linda whistled for the dogs, gazed across the bright blue into the valley, and released the edge of her lip from between her teeth. She ought to paint MR. NEIGHBOR-HELPING-HAND-HUSBAND on the side of his car, a picture of his face all lit up, all happy with himself. *Sure I can come by, Mae, sure thing.* All smiles and gray eyes, but he couldn't get around to doing something about the leak under her washing machine, could he? She jammed her hands into her pockets. The leaves would turn soon. You could feel that change in the air. Well, she could feel it.

She moved across the lawn as if she had someplace to go—across the lawn, into the kitchen—as if she had someplace real important to go. She poured a cup of coffee even though the machine had been off for more than an hour. Muddy, grounds floating; she lowered the cup from her lips and sat in the chair. The dogs studied her from the other side of the screen. Noon.

Linda slung one leg up and let it rest across the table. Picked at a piece of cuticle. Stared at the photographs of their smiling grandchildren pinned by fruit magnets to the refrigerator door: Emmie, Carey, Tony, and Patty Cake—lots of missing teeth, rotten haircuts, and Jack's smile. He wasn't helping Phil with gravel or fixing Mae's stupid porch—she knew where he was.

Linda lifted the other leg, pushed aside the remains of the breakfast dishes along with the coffee cup, and crossed her feet at the ankles. She knew; she knew yesterday. You could just feel it, and from nothing—it's not like there were clues. He didn't go out and get a haircut or buy a new shirt; he didn't do anything. But, there, see that, the set of his shoulders, the way he left his knife on the plate, the way he pushed back his chair, the way he looked at the top of little Emmie's head as she curled over her coloring book just scribbling away, his tone when he spoke to the boys about going on the bikes, his tone when he spoke to the dogs . . . something, nothing . . . and she had that feeling, and as much as she'd thought that maybe he wasn't going, she knew.

Linda moved her legs off the table and stood up. Time for Jack to go to L.A., to go get adored or whatever it is she does to him down there, Miss Rachel Glass, Miss Big Deal Writer, who writes trash for magazines.

Talk about how you could just spit. Jack, sitting in the car that first time, waiting for her outside Costco, and she walks up and surprises him, he's so caught up in what he's reading he doesn't hear, practically hits his head opening the car door. All stuttery, stuffing the slick pages of *Glamour* behind the maps in the car door, behind the map of Nevada, like she couldn't see. "How to Get Your Orgasm." Like he would read how to get an orgasm—like he thought she was some fool woman who didn't know which end was which. You push the cart through the aisles trying to come up with Christmas presents for all the babies and your husband says he'll be in the parts store and when you look for him he's all red in the face from his mistress's smut. Eyes down, not a word all the way home—"How to Get Your Orgasm" stuffed in the car door. Like she didn't know who wrote it, like she didn't know who that was. She took the magazine out of the car when he was in the bathroom and mashed it into the trash under the apple peels, under the eggshells and the beef bones. He knew better than to ask where it was. Like Linda had forgotten the name, like she didn't know as soon as it had started, like she walked around with a bag over her head. Six years ago come October, when they still lived in L.A. "Hello? May I speak to Jack North, please?" with one of those accents, know-it-all accents. "It's about a piece I'm doing on domestic violence, and I have a question and a deadline and I couldn't reach him at the station—could you have him call me, please?" It was so like Jack to give out a home number as if he were available 24-7, as if he were up for grabs, so like Jack. RACHEL GLASS, Linda had printed in big block letters on the blackboard next to the kitchen phone. RACHEL GLASS right after DOUBLE A BATTERIES, and off they went.

Linda stood at the sink, gazed out the window, and unplugged the pot. Six years. On the list of "someone elses" in Jack's life none of them had mattered before. Or all of them had mattered—at least to Linda—but none of them had held on. Not like this. None of them had had the persistence of Rachel Glass. Linda turned on the faucets and held her hand under the spray.

Six years of lies and you turn your head. It'll stop, you say to yourself in the mirror, and maybe you should cut your hair, it's too long, you know it's too long, and you only keep it that way because he says, "I like your hair long." Weeks go by and you think maybe, maybe, and then he's not home at six like he said he would be, he's home at nine, and you know from where. "You know, honey, how when you got a lead you got to push at it or it gets cold. Got to keep rolling," he says. A suspect, oh, yes, a suspect, a surveillance that went over his ten-hour shift, a lead, a clue, a something, a nothing. He was a cop, after all, what he did was important. "What is it, babe?" he would say, cool gray eyes measuring her from across the kitchen. Let it go, let it go. Pretend it isn't there, you say to yourself, but it's in front of you—this big, fat lie, this elephant sitting on the couch in the middle of your living room, just like they say, but you walk around it, and you don't start anything, waiting for it to go away. While you eat across from him, drive next to him, sleep with his hand thrown over your hip and his foot touching your leg, you wait and you pretend.

And sometimes something reminds you and the pretending comes hard. You're waiting to get a root canal and see an article about "Ten Steps to Perfect Thighs," but you don't pay much attention 'cause next to it is this recipe for a cookie called Creamy Delights, which you're gonna cut out with the little cuticle scissors on your Swiss Army knife, and the nurse says, "Mrs. North, you can come in now," and there's that name in front of you, practically knocks you out of the chair. Like it wasn't in your head already: Rachel Glass, like a bad dream. So you give up reading magazines—you sure don't need to read *People,* you can read the *Enquirer,* the *Star*—but it doesn't seem to matter. Just last month, the very week when he was down there with her, big Patty says, "Mom, come with me so you can hold the baby on your lap while they cut my hair," and right in the middle, while you're doing Itsy-Bitsy Spider, Patty says, "Hey, Mom, look at this, maybe it's okay to eat potatoes," and the words blur: "Carbs versus Protein—Who Wins?" by guess who. Clutching little Patty Cake to her breasts, nearly dropping her on the floor of the beauty shop with all that dirt and hair, the baby slipping between her knees.

Linda plunged the coffeepot into the water and stared at the left-over bits of floating egg. Little yellow islands. She had always loved geography, the pink and purple of the countries, brown mountains, gray borders touching blue and green water, the way the pieces fit. She turned off the faucets. She had been standing at this sink for thirty years. She let her fingers trail the water. That was the God's honest truth. The smell of bacon grease wafted up at her from the open coffee can; she turned her head. Twelve-twenty on the clock with the painted flowers he'd bought for her—the big surprise from him one morning all dolled up in a grocery bag with an old Christmas bow, like it was something she'd wanted, like it was something she'd marked in her catalogs. It was probably something Rachel Glass had marked in her catalogs. Linda pushed a piece of hair out of her eyes with the back of her wet hand. Rachel Glass probably didn't even look at catalogs; he'd probably put the wrong thing in the wrong bag. Or maybe he'd bought two clocks, one for both ends of the road. And maybe she should feed him all of Rachel Glass's articles, rip the shiny paper into tiny scraps and melt them into white gravy, watch Jack choke on "Carbs versus Protein" along with his chicken fried.

She'd thought maybe it was over, maybe something had happened with them and he wasn't going down there anymore. Just maybe, since she'd waited all last week for him to go. It was time for him to go, they both knew that it had been a month, not that either of them ever said anything. She wasn't about to start anything, but they both knew—every morning when he pulled out of the driveway she knew—but he hadn't gone, and it wasn't like there was anything special going on to hold him here. So she'd thought maybe it was over—that's what she'd been holding on to in her heart—that it was through. Fat chance.

Linda unwrapped the bread, stood at the counter with a center slice in her hand, and then thought about how she'd had French toast and bacon and eggs for breakfast, about how she'd caught a look at her ass in the mirror of Wal-Mart. Probably Rachel Glass had been out of town last week. Probably she'd been too busy to see him. Oh, yeah.

She dropped the slice of bread into the sink, watched it float around the water in the bubbles and scrambled egg. Once upon a time she was a cheerleader with a ponytail and a short circle skirt of tiny pleats and muscles in her thighs. She gave the slice of bread a little push. Once upon a time she was a size seven. She had pictures in a drawer, black-and-white snaps of her in midair, legs spread in a split kick, the pleats open and billowing above her underwear. Smiling. Arms high.

She maneuvered the bread through a treacherous patch of bubble icebergs. All she needed was a toothpick and a thin scrap of paper towel and she could fashion that piece of bread into a little raft with a sail. She would show Emmie next time. Once upon a time she could have been an inventor, she could have built boats, she could have been an anthropologist or a geologist, a doctor, she could have made things with her hands, once upon a time she could have been an anything. "What do you want to be when you grow up?" "Oh, Jack wants to marry me, but he doesn't want me to work, I'll just be a wife." A wife, a regular wife. She'd made a life around being a wife; it was a big job and she was good at it, a life around Jack, and then around Jack and the babies, and then the babies were grown and gone and it was supposed to be about her and Jack, only one week out of every month he was gone.

Linda pushed at the bread. He was probably late going down because he wanted to throw old Rachel Glass, make her worry. Maybe she was getting out of hand, maybe she needed some talking to. Iceberg, dead ahead, sir. Or maybe he'd decided he was through, maybe he'd put off going because he was getting his nerve up, going to tell her he was through. Linda laughed out loud. Knowing Jack, he'd probably just gone down a week late to throw the both of them off, make them both crazy. Linda pulled her hand from the water. Maybe he had driven away for good, decided to spend the rest of his years down there, thought about it for an extra week and made his move. She turned, her backside hard against the sink. Six years of it. How long was she supposed to go on?

At first she'd thought it wasn't true, but she was being stupid. Denial, they call it on the talk shows. All that noise in your head carrying on with yourself: something's going on; no, you're being silly; something's going on; no, it isn't; oh, yes, it is. Not that she'd asked him. Don't ask questions if you don't want to hear the answers—that's what her mother used to say.

She thought it would be over once they'd moved out of L.A. Too far away for all that slipping in and out, that "Hey, where were you?" when she'd realize he wasn't in the yard or under one of the bikes fixing something, and Mr. Innocence falling all over himself about how he'd just run over to the auto parts but they didn't have the bolt he needed or the screw or the throttle cable—when all along it was the screw and didn't she know it—slinking into the house afterward, and she could get dizzy from the smell of that woman's soap, or see that his hair was wet, or his face bright, or his step, which somehow in three hours since he'd disappeared and come back, had turned into some kind of strut. But then her mother got worse, and it was nearly time for him to retire anyway, and couldn't he do it early, a little less from the pension but "What the hell, Jack," she'd said, they'd get along, couldn't they just get out of there so she could be closer to home? "Okay, babe, okay," patting her arm, holding on to her when the doctor said it was in Mom's bones and who knew for how long, and she couldn't keep making the drive back and forth, and couldn't they just go? The drive, which made the game easier. You make the seven-hour drive to your mother and her dying and her smells and her sad eyes and your husband makes the drive to get laid by Rachel Glass. Seven hours for you, twenty minutes for him—Santa Monica into Beverly Hills—ten probably, the way Jack drove. And right next door when he was at the station, Rachel Glass's house was practically in the Beverly Hills Police Department's front yard. "Okay, babe," he'd said, "okay," and they'd emptied the little house where you couldn't *see* but could *smell* the ocean, U-Hauled everything worth taking up to the big house just like they'd always planned. All those years waiting for him to be done with bad guys and bullets, waiting to breathe easy, fall asleep easy, not fearing a phone call, a knock on the door to see them standing there, pasty faces waiting to tell her with their hats in their hands. Waiting to stop living in two places, go home to the one place where they would be happy when Jack retired, that was always the plan. "I don't want the girls raised in this hell hole," he'd said after Patty was born, and off he'd gone to find a place; he'd always hated L.A. "A place where we'll end up, babe," he'd said, his hands on her, looking out over a barren lot in the middle of California country, not where she could smell the ocean but in the middle of nowhere, which was what he wanted, in the middle of nowhere with nobody else around. Building the house piece by piece, whenever he could stash away enough—the foundation, a wall, the barn, her garden, a house overlooking a lake with miles of land on either side; taking the pictures, putting them in the album, putting her up there with the two babies and him down in L.A. Leaving her there while he went to make the money, get the bad guys, put in the years. Making the drive every other weekend. "What kind of a life is this you're living?" her mom had said. "You up here and Jack down there?" "It's for later," Linda had told them. They all thought she was crazy. Her driving, him driving, wedges of life like pieces of pie in a tin, and when the girls got older the wedges got bigger and so she'd bided her time. And when the girls left to have lives of their own, she spent nearly all of the pie down there with him. Waiting then for him to retire. Waiting, sometimes it seemed like she'd spent all of her life waiting. "Soon, babe," Jack had said, "soon we'll be together in one place. Who knew the *we'll* would end up meaning three? Me and him and the elephant in the living room. Table for three, please.

Linda looked down at her thighs, stared at the tight stretch of denim pulling across her stomach. She studied the dirty dishes on the table, three slick circles of syrup on the wood by her place mat, the stacks of newspapers on the floor under the windows, the piles of recipes she'd meant to get to, the basket of shirts waiting to be ironed. There was a big stupid spiderweb up in the corner where she kept the big pots—she had meant to stand on a chair and get that yesterday.

Three months to the day they'd settled in, three months to the day they'd moved out of L.A. and away from Rachel Glass, three months to the day that Linda thought it was over, that they were having a new life, he went out to breakfast one morning and didn't come home, didn't call till suppertime. She was making curtains, café curtains, couldn't keep the seams straight. He called finally, talked about how he'd gone to take a look at a bike this guy had, a detective, yeah, but out of Bakersfield, not somebody he knew out of L.A. "I'm in Bakersfield," he'd said, "think I'll just sleep here, head back tomorrow," and she'd stood there with her lips tight, her hand wet on the telephone, stood there with her heart hurting as if he had knifed her, as if he'd gutted her and all of her insides had slid to the floor. She held on to the chair and said, "Uh-huh." Didn't open her mouth, didn't say a word, not even when he came home, because, after all, to say anything was to say everything. Don't start what you don't want to finish—that much she knew.

She'd never finished the café curtains either, couldn't look at those stupid watering cans sprinkling across the material; she'd ripped it into shreds—$5.98 a yard in the garbage. Been with the man since high school; did she think she could go it alone? Somewhere along the way she'd lost the circle skirt with the tiny pleats, she'd lost the desire to be an anything, she'd lost the muscles in her thighs.

Linda went to the fridge and took out a Coke.

"What's goin' on with you and Dad, Mom?" Patty had asked. "Why do you put up with his shit, Mom?" Julie had said. As if they knew what it was to have given your whole life to some man. Turned it over as if it were nothing. Here, take my dreams, I'll raise the kids and be care of you, what more could a woman want? *Be care* of you: "Who will *be care* of me?" Patty had said when she was two. "Who will *be care* of me if you go?"

Linda took a swig of Coke, walked to the windows. The windows were bare except for the shade. "Where does he go every month?" Julie had said, all grown up now and snappy, glaring at her mother over little Emmie's head. The three of them in her kitchen making him a big birthday to-do, and Linda had spread the cobbler dough across the top of the peaches. "I'll do it, Mom," Patty had said, exchanging hands with her mother, pinching the edges, making a flower design with the knife blade just like Linda'd taught her so the hot juice had somewhere to go. "Where does he go, Mom?" Julie said again, with that tone just like Jack's. Patty's eyes lifted to her mother across the cobbler. Patty, her oldest, who loved her more because Linda favored her, always had since the day she was born. "It's not your business," she'd said to the two of them, and Jack had yelled, "Hey, Linda," from the garage, and she'd said, "Turn the pork chops over, one of you, and see to the gravy," and she'd left the room. Like the girls were the mother and she was the daughter, like she should explain. What went on in her house was between her and Jack. Their dirty secret. Their elephant. Their Rachel Glass.

There was dust on the sill. A streak on the glass, a baby fingerprint, probably from little Emmie's hand. She could hear the clock ticking; she took another drink of Coke.

He came home sheepish that first time; he'd been gone two days. Sheepish. Loving. Sorry. You can't be with a man for years and not know sorry. But not sorry enough. Two months later off he went again, just like before. Just took off as if she didn't exist, as if she wasn't waiting in the house, expecting him, looking to hear his car. And slowly it became a part of their lives again, Jack's coming and going; only this time he was coming and going to Rachel Glass, not to her. When he'd get back from a trip—that was how she thought of it in her head, a trip, as if he were a salesman on the road somewhere making a trip he had to, which was stupid but somehow gave her a little peace—when he'd get back mostly he'd just be testy, as if his having to make the trip was her fault. Carryin' on about her stacks of newspapers or why hadn't she paid bills when they were sitting right there, why when she cooked did she have to use every pot in the house, open every cabinet door just like she always had.

Linda touched the windowpane with her fingers, watched her prints disappear. A man doesn't make a seven-hour drive once a month if it isn't for love. Some kind of love. Some kind of something missing in his life, and she had to look to herself. Oh, yes, and she had, and tried to be something she wasn't, but that had only made things worse. Parading around in front of Jack like she was a hooker, like she was one of those girls hanging around Pineapple Hill in Van Nuys hoping to land her a cop; like she hadn't known him her whole life and had two babies and ins and outs and ups and downs, trying to turn him on, like a fool. Sitting with his paper, he hardly glanced up, and then when he did with that look, "Linda, what the hell are you doing?" he'd said.

Just like that and her in a nightgown that you could see through right after supper. Candles in the bedroom that she had put away before he could see. Like a fool. She was a fool. The two of them, two fools; she just hadn't figured out who was the biggest. She ought to call up one of those magazines that Miss Rachel Glass writes for, and write one of those tell-all articles herself—tell the real truth about what doesn't work trying to get your husband away from a whore. All those feminists with their talk about how women are supposed to be sisters. A lot of hooey.

Linda's eyes moved, then refocused on the screen door. Buddy wagged his tail at her, gave a little half-bark.

"Not now, Bud," she said.

One o'clock. She moved to the fridge, took out the plum jam, unscrewed the top. "It's 1:00 P.M. Do You Know Where Your Husband Is?" by Linda North. She took a tablespoon out of the drawer, lifted a spoon of thick jam into her mouth. She could write one of those exposés, tell-alls; she had plenty to tell. She took a big long drink of Coke, finished the can, the tin taste sweet and sickening in her mouth. Rachel Glass was no sister to anybody; she was a whore.

Ben

HE'D LIKE TO run Ennis over with his car.

Ben struggled with the last piece of cold pizza; it had sort of congealed itself to the box. Not that he had a car. Not that it would behoove him to run over a professor, the head of the religion department, no less.

Pizza looked kind of strange after a couple of days, and it would probably be smarter to nuke it, but there was a catastrophe going on in the microwave. Something Becker had exploded, a crusty splattering that actually resembled a Jackson Pollock, Ben thought. Chalk one up to art history, which was not something he would ever have taken, except he'd promised his grandmother, like a hundred years ago, before her mind had turned to mush. He chewed the pepperoni and thought about becoming premed. He could specialize in all the horrors that hit old people, find a cure for the rotten Alzheimer's and call it the Lady vaccine. Like Salk. That would be cool.

How much cardboard could you eat? He pulled at the stiff cheese stuck to the brown carton. Hopeless.

There was no way he could be a doctor. Even seeing his own blood made him woozy and then there was all the other sick stuff you had to do, like watch little kids die. No way. He had not forgotten the terror of the booster shot or that TB thing where they make a bubble under your skin. His pediatrician, old Dr. Pressler, was really little, with her glasses and her spiffy hairdo and her stethoscope bouncing on her chest, all five feet of her in those really high, high heels chasing him down the hall, trying to coax him out from under the table with the needle hidden behind her back. Sticking little kids, sewing up their heads when they fell off their bikes or people ran over them—no way.

He was still hungry. To find food would require going out, and if he left, the paper for Ennis would never be. Maybe Becker would return with provisions. He would think positively, he would meditate like Eve had taught him on Becker's return, his arms laden with burgers and fries.

Ben balanced the empty pizza carton on a stack of books and CDs. Hey, check it out, the tower of pizza.

He was all over the place about what he wanted to be. Not medicine, not law. His dad was a lawyer, an entertainment lawyer—talk about a non sequitur, as if law could be funny. A big joke, and so L.A. Had they ever heard of entertainment law in Arkansas or Idaho? Hey, man, who do you represent? The only acting moose in Boise: Bullwinkle.

He rifled through some CDs at the foot of his bed. He had to call his dad. What was the big deal about putting money in that account? Why did he always have to remind him?

Music was out; you can't be a musician if you sing like a buzz saw, and he'd given up the piano when he was, like, six. Torture. His mom had hired this gnarled witch to teach him; he couldn't concentrate on anything but this hair she had coming out of a mole near her mouth. Honest to God. Not exactly Cindy Crawford. She was Russian, gnarled and Russian and with that hair—no wonder he couldn't play the piano. She was like the cartoon version of the piano teacher from hell.

Okay, talk about concentrating. A first sentence, that's all he needed, a smart first sentence to pull Ennis in. Ben pushed at the stack of CDs and watched them fall off the foot of his bed. If he could only buy into being a Buddhist, the joy there must be in the knowledge that this life is fleeting, only a step on the way to being somewhere else. The only somewhere else he knew he'd like to be in was Maui. With Eve. On a beach. In a bed. A bed on a beach. Yeah. Drinking piña coladas.

Not that he'd ever been in Maui except that time when he was ten. He had attended the beginning of the end of his parents' marriage—at least that's how he thought of it in his head. Him and his sister, Dana, who was fourteen at the time and thought she was hot shit, and her friend Molly, who was a real pain in the ass. His friend Panzer, who was supposed to come with them, broke his leg in two places when that asshole from Harvard-Westlake kicked him playing soccer, and his parents wouldn't let him come. It didn't turn out to be Ben's dream vacation: Dana and Molly got to do everything, whining about how they were old enough to run around the hotel alone, and he got to sit around mostly watching his mom and dad go at it over cocktails. Or over breakfast. Or over snorkeling. To snorkel or not to snorkel: they could fight over anything, no matter how trivial. The fighting Glasses: that's how he thought of them in his head. His sister and even the pain in the ass, Molly, knew the score—the marriage was over; his parents were the only ones who didn't have a clue. It took them three more years of duking it out to come to the brilliant conclusion that they couldn't be in the same room with each other, much less in the same bed, and it was certainly no surprise to him or Dana when they had the big family sit-down to announce the *D* word. It was all he could do to not say What took you so long? Although Ben never got the gist of what the big deal was during those six glorious sun-filled days on Maui, it was definitely clear to him that it was a really big deal, as he watched his parents quietly cream each other until he got a sun rash and then some kind of throwing-up thing from a crab dish, and they made a joint effort to lay down their arms and take turns holding his head over the toilet bowl. None of which was going to help him with the ethics of the economy from the Roman Catholic perspective compared with the Buddhist perspective, and a first sentence that really sang.

Food was the answer. Food would awaken his brain waves and turn him into Norman Mailer Glass. Ben sat down in front of the laptop that was in his bed. He closed his eyes and visualized Becker returning, his arms laden with burritos and Cokes. Burritos or burgers—it didn't matter which. He moved some pillows, three books, and a tennis shoe, then read the only sentence he had. It was lousy, really lousy. Starting out sucked. If only he could have summed up the beginning of the semester in a couple of sentences and told it to his mom, she could have started him out. She actually wrote pretty good. He'd read some of the stuff she'd written before she'd sold out to the magazines, some short stories and some poems that were pretty good. Now she only wrote chick stuff: how to curl your eyebrows or whatever, how to get a guy. Worse, once she'd written this thing about chicks getting their orgasms. Thank God nobody he knew ever saw it.

Ben studied the sentence, then backspaced the cursor, obliterating each letter until the screen was blank.

So old robo cop was on his way down. Ben watched the cursor blink. He visualized Jack as a robot, half man–half techno being. He visualized his mother as a robo cop. He refocused on the cursor. He used to like Jack. Well, actually, he still liked him, but something about liking him was a mess. After all, the guy was married. Not exactly what you want for your mother, not exactly what you want your mother to do. And you'd think she would have thought twice, considering Dad had dumped her for the Dixie princess, which was another shocker, to say the least. Not that he'd thought his parents, the fighting Glasses, would stay together forever—you only think that when you're a little kid—but he never thought his dad would really leave his mom, who was kind of interesting being a writer and all and knowing a lot of stuff and being very verbal and intense and still kind of good-looking, for some fat would-be actress who was never going to make it and who didn't do or know anything as far as Ben could tell. And it wasn't like his father just fell for her in one of those middle-aged-crisis things and then came back home—he bought this cool place in Malibu and let her move in with him, and now he can't understand why Ben doesn't want to come over there and hang when he's home. It would be great, right there on the beach, with the sand and the waves and all, but along with the majesty of the Pacific Ocean he would have to stomach watching her fall all over his dad. She does this kind of breathy thing that his father doesn't seem to notice, but it makes Ben want to hurl.

Jack, on the other hand, isn't bad. He has a lot of stories, but he doesn't push them on you, he doesn't push himself on you, and he certainly isn't breathy around Ben's mom. You can see that he likes her, but it's not like the Dixie princess draping herself all over his dad. Jack has this kind of space thing around him, which is probably because he was a cop, which is kind of like being a cowboy, Ben thought. A gunslinger, which is the one thing Ben knew he'd like to be if it were still the olden days. He could have majored in cowboy.

Where the hell was Becker?

It's not like he wanted to be a cop. He could just see himself telling his dad. "Dad, I've decided to become a police officer"—oh, yeah. But it was something he admired, not that he'd tell anybody—everybody his age thought cops were lower than dirt. For Ben, it wasn't so much about the gun stuff; it was more about living on the edge. How many careers can you have where you put your life on the line when you go to work? But he couldn't really talk to Jack about it because he didn't talk to Jack about anything since he knew Jack had a wife. A wife that he lives with whenever he isn't with Ben's mom. Jeez. First off, it's hard enough to like the guy who comes after your father—confusing in the loyalty category, to say the least—and when she'd told him about the wife, that had kind of cinched it in the liking category, because how can you like a guy that you know is sleeping with his wife and your mother at the same time, even if he does put his life on the line? Or at least he used to.

Ben lifted the lid on the empty pizza carton and picked at the petrified cheese. Sometimes he thought it would be better if parents just didn't tell you anything, didn't fill you in on the details, because between that situation and his father with the dreaded Dixie princess it was easier to just not go home.

Talk about a laugh, the way grown-ups carry on about morals: Be careful with the girls, Ben. Be sensitive, Ben. Think about what you're doing with people's feelings, Ben. You'd think they'd think about what they're doing with people's feelings. Here's his very own mother carrying on with some married guy—does she even think about the wife?—and his very own father walking out on the three of them to live with a dumpy pinhead half his age, sailing out the door like he didn't remember that besides leaving his wife, he was also leaving two kids. I have to go, son. You have to? What does that mean—have to? Was somebody holding a gun to his head? As far as Ben was concerned, both of his parents needed therapy. Not that he didn't love them. He loved them, but he could certainly see where they needed help. If you studied to be a psychiatrist, did you still have to do the doctoring part with the sick kids? Ben wondered.

The door slammed. Ben looked up from the blank screen to Becker's grin. "Whassup, man?" Becker said from the door frame, his arms laden with pizza boxes and beer.

He had to tell Eve. Okay, so maybe he didn't have this meditation thing quite down yet, but he was certainly coming along.

Dana

IN THE OLD days she would have already called her mother—probably as soon as Jeff left.

Dana moved the spoon through the sugar. Okay, there was no reason to get hysterical: she would be clear and focused, she would weigh all the options, she would think it through.

Dana realized she was still stirring the coffee; she took the spoon out of the cup.

Okay, let's see. She settled herself in the chair, refolded the paper napkin next to the cup, and stared at the beige coffee blot on the white paper until it blurred.

Okay. She would get a job.

She refolded the napkin; the coffee stain was hidden on the inside fold.

What kind of a job?

The baby was singing to herself. She ought to just stop the afternoon nap, but it was the only peace she had and she had to think.

"Mommy?"

Shit. Dana sat motionless, the spoon in her fist.

"Mommy?"

If she didn't answer, maybe Sarah would just drift off.

The baby started to hum, Dana took a swig of the coffee. Sarah had left peanut butter and jelly crusts in a circle shape on the plate.

She would have to get a job, if they were going to split, if he was really going to leave and they were really going to split, and that's probably what would happen. She would have to put Sarah in an all-day nursery school and get a job, and what kind of a job was she going to get, since she hadn't finished college—which was what they were both going to tell her, her mother and her father were both going to tell her, individually and together, which was what they had said to her individually and together when she'd married Jeff three years ago: "Twenty years old. You don't get married when you're twenty years old in this day and age, cutting yourself off from your chances with just a year to graduate. What are you thinking, Dana, with your life before you" and on and on. She knew the litany—she knew it by heart—but she couldn't see herself pregnant during her senior year of college. She could have stayed in school, transferred from Northwestern to UCLA and finished, but she couldn't see herself pregnant in a cap and gown. Chicken, she was too chicken. Not that her parents knew she was pregnant, not when she married him, not at the wedding ceremony at least. And it's not like when she quit she was throwing away some big goal. To be a teacher was what every girl picked when she had nothing else. But that was rationalizing, she had to tell herself the truth. She was too chicken to have the baby by herself, too chicken to give it up, and too chicken to have an abortion. So she'd married him.

Dana ate one of the crusts.

She'd never had a big goal; she'd only gone to school because you were supposed to; it wasn't like she knew what she wanted to be. She chose Northwestern, her mother's school, because she couldn't have cared less where, or what, or anything. Drifting was how she saw herself. A leaf in the wind, very romantic. Like from the sixties—only not the marching-against-the-war part of the sixties, but the listening-to-Beat-poetry-and-drinking-coffee-in-a-black-turtleneck-and-pale-pink-lipstick part of the sixties. Or was that the fifties? Okay, maybe not quite that romantic but definitely adrift, definitely loose. And then Jeff. Coming down out of the sky and squashing her flat like a big foot. Good-bye drifting. One doesn't drift much when one is a mommy. And a wife. Don't forget the wife part.

She dunked another crust into the coffee. Peanut butter was so comforting, a return to when you were little, when everything went your way. Sarah was humming "Happy Birthday." It wasn't anywhere near her birthday—what a funny thing.

Dana knew she shouldn't have married him; she knew the day of her wedding as she walked down the aisle. She wanted to tell her dad; she wanted to hold on to his arm and ask him to save her, walk her backward up the white carpet and out of the Sunset Room of the Beverly Hills Hotel. Past the rows of people all dressed up, through the cloud of too much perfume, past the yards of satin ribbon and baby white roses, clutching her dad's arm back into the limousine like rewinding film.

But she hadn't asked him. She didn't have the balls.

He probably would have done it too, saved her. Her father's median age, she figured, was usually around eleven, but that was mostly in dealings with her mom or with his girlfriend, the cow—when it came to Dana or Ben, he could blossom into a total grown-up and soar. Like when the pony bit her butt at the circus, which was a total accident and certainly not the circus's fault, but definitely ammunition for her dad. It was only a bruise—the skin hadn't even been broken—just the shock of pony teeth at her backside, but her father went into gear, so much so that Ringling Bros. Barnum and Bailey and whoever bent over backward and cradled her into the arm of the circus for the three days they had left in L.A. She got to watch the clowns get dressed, put on their faces and noses and big shoes, and the trapeze people practice and fall into the nets; she stood in the sawdust to see the lion tamer work with the big cats—standing right next to the cages, she could actually hear them breathe, feel their heat, smell them. The biggest deal of all was that they let her ride in the parade. Wearing a red and yellow tutu, she wildly waved at the people from a red and yellow wagon that was being pulled by a red and yellow clown. She was five years old and so deliriously happy she thought she might explode. Her dad did that. When she got older she realized what it meant to be a lawyer, which was what her dad was—the circus was probably scared shitless that he was going to sue them—but when she was little all she could see was that her hero daddy made this dream come true.

She ate another crust.

She would have asked her dad to save her at the wedding if she could have, but she couldn't. All part of her chicken syndrome. She went through with all of it: her dad raising the veil and kissing her, handing her off to Jeff like a football, too many cocktails in the foyer while they picked up the white aisle and set tables for ninety-five, tiny potato pancakes with salmon caviar, beef in peanut sauce on a stick, her girlfriends in garnet velvet, her parents holding separate court—her dad with the cow, her mother alone—the dinner of chicken Marengo and baby peas and baby potatoes, and she was sure the baby would fly out of her into the toilet bowl, this unformed bit of secret baby trying to find a place for itself, ivory silk across the tile floor of the ladies' room, clutching the icy porcelain, the seed pearls across the bodice of the gown leaving tiny lavender marks across her breasts—trying to make her way back and forth to that bathroom without anyone realizing she was gone, in between the toasts, in between the dancing, the garter, the bouquet—she knew through all of it that it was a big fat mistake. Jeff was a mistake. She loved him, but he was a mistake. Her mother looked at him with slant eyes, the way they got when she knew something was up, said he was stuck on himself. It was true. Returning from one of her bouts in the bathroom, Dana, white as her wedding dress, wet under the silk, clammy, and her mother's hand on her arm, slowing her, facing her, feeling her head. "Are you all right, Dana?"

"I'm fine." Big smile. "Just excited."

The slant eyes of Rachel, all-knowing, some sixth sense she had when something was wrong with one of her kids. "I'm going to dance with Ben-oh," Dana tossed over her shoulder; her mother's gaze was steady on the back of her head as she made her way to her brother across the room.

She'd told Rachel right after they returned from the honeymoon, where she had spent most of the time sprawled across another bathroom floor. Puerto Vallarta, as seen from an aqua green tile toilet bowl. Jeff water-skiing, bringing her soda crackers back from the bar, singing the praises of the mariachi and the pool and the sky and the sun and the town and the food while she retched. He was bronze when they returned; she was pale yellow, or maybe it was more to the green.

"I'm pregnant."

In the middle of Saks in the middle of the shoe department, two words flying out of her mouth.

"Oh, Dana."

That was all Rachel had said for quite a while; she kind of stopped and sat down on one of the couches, and Dana sat next to her, and after a couple of salesmen hovered with their "May I help you?" they were left alone. Suited guys carrying boxes of expensive high heels circled them while they had a conversation that should have been had at home.

"How far?"

She could feel panic pushing its way up into her throat. "Four months." They both looked down at the front of her shirt. "I think I've thrown up everything I've eaten." Rachel took her hand.

"Is that why you married him?"

"Yes."

It was hard to look into her mother's eyes. "What do you want to do now?"

"Have the baby."

"Do you want to come home?"

"No."

"Do you love him?"

"Yes." It wasn't a lie; she did love him, just not quite enough. It had fizzled. She had no idea how such a thing could happen, but she knew it was true.

"Okay," Rachel said. Her mother's bravado, as if she had assessed the situation with all of its possibilities and knew what to do.

They sat there.

"I think we ought to buy some shoes." Rachel's confident smile and the warmth in her voice and Dana lost it, sobbing into her mother's chest in the middle of the Saks shoe department as if she were a child.

But Rachel did know what to do. She went with Dana to the doctor, was joyous with her when the nausea stopped, gave her a baby shower, was sweet to Jeff, was positive about Dana's decision, and bought dozens of sleepers with the feet in them, all of the baby furniture, a toy chest painted with jungle animals, and a rocking chair.

Dana finished the crusts, the last dregs of the coffee.

When Sarah was a month old, in a fit of bonding, her mother revealed the news that the reason Jack, the boyfriend, was always coming and going was that he had a wife.

Dana practically fell out of her chair.

She hadn't even been suspicious. So caught up in her own changes—away at school, then finding herself pregnant and throwing herself into marrying Jeff, leaving Chicago and walking down the aisle and practically nonstop into a delivery room. She hadn't even noticed that the relationship her mother was having was more than strange. Besides the fact that Jack was a cop—which was totally off the wall. And there was no talking to her. Her mother, totally sane, totally together, the one who could totally assess a situation and make a rational decision, had taken a crash off the deep end. She was having an affair with a married man. Her mother. If Dana had had an affair with a married man her mother probably would have smacked her. Rachel made the announcement and put the gates up. Dana pleaded; she used all the words: humiliating, embarrassing, appalling. She even swallowed the bile of the memories and reminded Rachel what it was like when it had happened to her, when Dana's dad had started to fool around. Because they didn't make it much of a secret, her parents, when her hero daddy fell in love with the cow. She was fourteen. She knew; she heard them. Her mother's outrage, her father's disgrace. It was loud.

It was upsetting just to think about it, to remember, but she thought about it and she reminded Rachel; she even used the old "put yourself in her shoes." She said everything she could think of. It didn't matter.

Dana got up, put the cup and plate in the sink.

To think that your own mother could do such a thing was more than confusing, and there was nothing she could do because there was no talking to her. So she stayed away.

There was no sound from the baby's room.

She never went over there when Jack was in town; she never called. She never asked about him, didn't refer to him, and when her mother mentioned him, she kept her mouth shut, or changed the subject, or hung up.

The baby was asleep in her new bed. Sarah had been adamant—no more crib—so they had granted her wish and bought her a big-girl bed. On her back, square in the middle, tiny and perfect—face flushed, wispy damp curls around the hairline, her eyelashes spread against the tops of her cheeks, her stuffed lobster tucked under her chin. The lobster's name was Crystal, and it was from her beloved Unkah Ben. Dana touched a curl, retucked the already tucked blanket, left the door ajar.

She had no friends her age who were mommies: They were in grad school. They were living in New York, sharing apartments and working as editors' assistants in publishing, rushing to Sag Harbor, drinking cosmopolitans, talking on their cell phones. They were living in L.A., sharing apartments and working as interns for theatrical agencies, rushing to Sundance, drinking martinis, talking on their cell phones. They were in the Peace Corps. They were in India teaching English, in Tokyo learning Japanese. They were having lunch at the Ivy at 1:15 on a beautiful Monday, pushing lettuce around their plates. They were not dunking peanut butter crusts into cold coffee and worrying about getting a divorce.

She washed the cup and plate.

Jeff was right: they shouldn't be together; they didn't care enough. But should she just give up? It wasn't like either one of them had fallen for somebody else; it wasn't like she was following in anybody's footsteps, no one was having an affair. But if the heat was gone before the ring was even on her finger, was there a point to beating the dead horse? And how could she already have a dead horse of a marriage at twenty-three?

It was hopeless; she had to talk to her mother. Rachel had this way of seeing into other people's madness, pursuing all the angles, and coming up with a plan. Except for when it came to her and Jack, her mother was terrifically smart. She needed her—Dana eyed the phone.

Maybe she could go back to school, maybe she could finish up and be a teacher. After all, she was ahead of the game, she already knew a lot of the ins and outs of coloring and Play-Doh and naptime. She knew about the joy of Cheerios.

Dana walked across the kitchen.

She knew about the reek of apple juice.

She would discuss it with her mother; she would tell her; she would ask her to go with her to buy the baby new shoes at Harry Harris and she would tell her there. Rachel would help her get a take on things, help her figure out what to do.

After all, it was a shoe store, and her mother was great under pressure in a shoe store. Dana reached for the phone.

Rachel

By 1:00, Rachel had deciphered most of her notes for the German piece on Maximilian Schell. She was down to debating whether she wanted to mention the *affectation*—the scarf that he wore always, so casually on purpose, thrown around his throat. Camouflage for a goiter? An unattractive Adam's apple? A deep fear of getting cold? Rachel watched the cursor gobble backward, eating up her paragraph on the mystery scarf—maybe it was best to rethink it. She leaned back in her chair.

By 1:00, she'd put pale blue sheets on the bed, the hysterically expensive ones she'd bought on sale, oversize towels in the bathroom, and deep red roses she'd cut from the garden on both night tables. She'd folded back the silk duvet in perfect angles on either side; all that was missing were chocolate mints.

By 1:00, she'd waxed the dining room table and put a cut-crystal vase of peach and white lilies on the coffee table in the living room.

By 1:15, she'd had a discussion with Woody in New York about cellulite—the piece she'd written, not either of theirs, although Woody was now very much into staying in shape with Pilates. Practically every female Rachel knew was into Pilates, some exercise with stretching and hanging and straps and God-knows-what that Rachel didn't even want to look at, much less do. "I'll walk, you Pilate," she'd smirked. "It'd be good for you, sittin' there all day hunched over your writin'," Woody had drawled. Since the Dixie princess, Rachel had withdrawn from anything that even resembled the South, except for dealing with Woody, who was definitely a New Yorker by way of southern belle. "Woodruff is a family name," Woody had said ten years ago over a cocktail table at the Carlyle and then, slyly leaning over her martini, she'd whispered, "not the Woodruffs from Atlanta, but nobody knows." Rachel had no idea who the Woodruffs from Atlanta were, but she was so smitten with the idea that there was a society where such a thing could be important that she fell for Woody right then and there. They decided to send the piece to *Mirabella* and *Marie Claire*. "Cover all the ages of cellulite," Woody said, "in one fell swoop." "One lumpy swoop is more like it," Rachel said, because part of her goal in life was to make Woody laugh. Make anybody laugh was probably more like it. If she had it to do all over again, she would try stand-up, but it seemed silly now. Of course, there was *that* . . . there was age, the dreaded middle age and all that came with it—divorce, night sweats, divorce, hot flashes, divorce, mood swings—perhaps a divorce-menopause monologue. How droll.

By 1:30, she'd written two paragraphs, walked away, plumped up all the sofa pillows in the living room, come back and read what she'd written, and cut it with the little scissors on the computer task bar.

By 1:30, she'd talked to her daughter. "Come with me to buy the baby new shoes, Mom."

"Oh, honey, I can't."

"Oh." Definitely disappointed. "You working?"

"Yeah, and Jack's on his way."

Hesitation. Louder than static, louder than crackling. And then a breath, "Mom?"

"What?"

Two words, and a red flag flew over the airwaves while they both regrouped. The tone in Dana's voice that she flung around like a shawl and the warning in her mother's voice—the "What?" of *back off.*

Another breath and Dana said, "I just wondered, did you ever meet that guy whose wife died? The one Carole said was so nice?"

"Nope."

"Why not? I thought you were being open."

"Just didn't. What's the peanut doing?"

Dana exhaled. "She was having a nap, now she's just pretending to be asleep, singing to herself under her blankie."

"A chip off the old you-know-what. You okay?"

"Mm-hm."

"How's everything with you and Jeff?"

"Okay."

A down okay, not a good okay, Rachel could tell. Most of the time it was not all right between her daughter and her daughter's husband; most of the time Rachel wanted to smack Jeff for the way he pushed Dana, but it was not her place to do the smacking; most of the time she even managed to keep her mouth shut. "You can't live your children's lives," Lady had told her when Dana had married him. At twenty. Rachel had tried everything she could think of to stop her from going through with it except lock her up. "You won't change her mind," Lady had said.

"Why won't I?"

"Because no one ever does."

Rachel looked at her mother.

"I couldn't fix yours and you can't fix hers," Lady said.

"Did you want to fix mine?"

Lady smiled. "Of course."

"Mom?" Dana said.

"Yep."

No more tone, all gone. "I love you."

"I love you too, sweetheart," Rachel said.

Vulnerable, Rachel thought, when she put down the phone. Sad. Was that what she was hearing? Sad about her own life or sad about Rachel and Jack? Hard to know. Dana didn't like Jack, didn't like anything about him, besides the situation. "He's a cop with a cop's mentality; he's a Republican, a conservative; he can't hold his own with you, can't measure up; he's never seen anything, done anything, never been to New York or Europe, or Mexico, or anywhere, and doesn't want to go; he's never read anything or wants to know anything; he's closed; he lives in a vacuum; Mom, he carries a gun. What are you doing with him? You should be going out with guys who are right for you—what are you doing with him?" And after hearing it once, Rachel made it clear that she didn't need to hear it again. She was not interested in dating; she was only interested in Jack. She told herself that love had no logic, and she was not obligated to explain.

Maybe Dana needed her. She looked at the phone, contemplated calling her back. Maybe she was projecting. She'd see her as soon as Jack left.

By 2:00, Rachel had met Grace—not in the street; she'd walked to her house, where they'd sat on Grace's front steps so Grace could smoke.

The quiet of a Beverly Hills street in early afternoon: one gardener's blower, one ecstatic carpenter bee in the lavender roses, one car making a lazy turn at the corner of Elevado and Elm. Grace squinted her eyes at the horizon. "Do you remember when Amy and Ben-oh were little? When they raced their tricycles right here?"

"Sure I remember."

Grace took a deep drag of the cigarette she wasn't supposed to be smoking, cupped her other hand above her eyes like the bill of a baseball cap. "God, it's hot."

"What about when the kids were little?" Rachel asked.

"I was happier then . . ." Grace took another drag, waited. "You're not agreeing."

"You drank then, Grace," Rachel said.

"Yeah, I know. I was thinking maybe I'd have a brandy. A gin and tonic. Something icy with a sprig of mint." She sighed. "Remember whiskey sours? I loved whiskey sours, I especially loved whiskey sours, and brandy, a shot in my coffee on a crisp day, a cold beer on a hot day." She took another drag of the cigarette. "Did I say gin and tonic? I was happier when I drank."

"No, you weren't."

"I think so."

Rachel moved to the lowest step, stretched her legs out in front of her across the warm sticky grass, and leaned back on her elbows, tilting her face up to the sky.

"We could sit by the pool," Grace said. "We should get in the pool; the air is like fire."

"I have to go home. Are you going to go through with it this time?"

"What? Get a divorce?" Grace put the cigarette out on the sole of her sandal. "Today? I don't think so; I have to get my color done at four."

"Grace?"

"You just want everybody to be divorced." A trace of anger, or was it just irritation? She turned to Rachel. "Yes?"

"Why do you stay with him? What are you waiting for?"

"I don't know. A sign from above?" Grace shook another cigarette from the pack and held on to it. "Ah, we wives who would rather be wives in a dismal failure than venture out on our own . . . didn't you write about us? Don't you remember? 'For Better or Worse and Usually Worse—Women Who Stay No Matter What'—*Allure,* last year. I don't believe you mentioned in the article that you followed me around with a pen." A look at Rachel. "Not everyone has your balls, *chérie*. When a husband says he's got the hots for somebody else, not everyone says, Go pack your bags, baby; get the hell out; adios."

Quiet, a beat of quiet, and then Grace said, "And speaking of adios, why is Dirty Harry making his pilgrimage from the wife a week late? Oops, excuse me, Dirty Jack."

"I don't know."

"Ah, a change in the routine. Did he mention it?"

"No."

"Ye plot thickens. Do you think he's flown the coop? Left the missus with the cows and chickens and vamoosed to live with you in the splendor of Bev Hills?"

"Grace . . ."

"What?"

A long look at each other.

"No, I don't think he's flown the coop."

"What would you do if he did?"

Rachel didn't answer.

"I see," Grace said. "Well, it's good that you have that all worked out." She pushed her hair behind her ears. "I think you should be especially careful, people have been known to do damage to husbands when the Santa Ana blows." She leveled her eyes at Rachel. "Does Mrs. North know where Mr. North keeps his guns?"

Rachel turned her head.

Grace raised her shoulders and sighed. "Okay . . . what time's he coming?"

"Three, three-thirty."

"Ah, by five you will have gotten laid. By five I will no longer have gray roots and you will have gotten laid." She flipped open the lighter. "I haven't gotten laid in a long time. Dickhead has already given at the office by the time he gets home. Not that I'd let him touch me."

"Grace, get a divorce. Go through with it."

"Only if I can have a whiskey sour." She put the cigarette in her mouth and lit it, cupping her hand around the flame as if she were in the middle of a windstorm. "And a brandy," she said, eyeing Rachel. "No. Two."

To be the *other woman* when your best friend has been battling the *other women* since she said "I do." To be the *other woman* when your very own husband left you for one. Shaky ground. Insanity. Rachel sat at the computer, her hands resting on the cool keys. Did she want everybody to be divorced? Lonely? She ran her hand across her face, got up, and paced the room. Why did Grace stay? Why did Jack's wife stay? Was he coming down late because he'd flown the coop? That was a good one not to think about. Would she have ever left Henry if Henry hadn't left her first?

Rachel stood behind her chair and watched the computer cursor blink. She didn't want to write about Maximilian Schell's dirty scarf, or Jennifer Lopez's tips for perfect abs, or the ten best concealers, or where to get previously owned Manolo Blahnik shoes—which meant still expensive and now used. She didn't want to write about any of it. She went into the kitchen, opened the door of the refrigerator, took out a bottle of water, and had a long drink.

Did she want everybody to be lonely?

She'd fallen into Jack. Needed him was more like it. All that crap with Henry and the timing was right. Ripe. But she was lonely long before Henry made his announcement. Lonely in a marriage, a lonely husband and a lonely wife silently sparring from opposite ends of the house. Rachel wondered if that's the way it was with Jack and his wife. She didn't ask; well, sometimes she asked but he didn't always answer—there were certain things Jack wouldn't talk about, certain subjects where the door was closed. Six months ago he'd stopped wearing his wedding ring, and when she'd asked him why, he'd said he just wasn't wearing it, and when she'd pressed, he'd given her one of those looks. The look of "you don't want to get into this." The invisible rules of what you asked and what you didn't, what you pushed and what was better left alone. Like why he hadn't come down last week, like what was in his head.

The cool air from the open fridge felt good. The Santa Ana had started her number; there would be a stretch of breath-stopping days, stifling, burning, dry days where the brutal wind would come up over the mountains, lie low in L.A., and mess with people's nerves.

She had fallen into Jack. And then she had allowed herself not to remember he was married. She'd ignored it, like a gift she had given to herself, and then she'd gotten all tangled up in the ribbons, and it was too late to throw away the box. Rachel smiled at the thought of Jack in the box. Too silly. She chugged the rest of the water in the bottle. It wasn't funny; it was low. She was as low as the Dixie princess if the truth be known. Well, it was known. Friends and family who knew there was a Jack also knew of his . . . what? His encumbrance? His complication? His problem? His what?

"He's *what*?!" Ben-oh had said, his jaw dropping like a cartoon character's.

"Married," Rachel had said again to her son. Three years ago, one soft June morning, she'd told him, when it was gray and cool and he'd finally emerged from his room right before noon.

"Married?" His hair was sticking up like it did when he was a baby; it still did that when he first woke up. Like a big sweet rooster, he'd gaped at her. "My mother is having an affair with a married guy?"

Rachel poured too much milk over the cornflakes too fast; it sloshed out of the bowl onto the countertop; she reached for the sponge.

"Hello? Mom? I'm standing here."

She'd sponged the milk, took a second to sponge the milk, then turned and looked at her boy. Wired and gaping eyes, sleepy no more, naked except for his boxers, skinny chest so innocent, bare feet big and wide on the black and white tile floor. She handed him the bowl.

"What are you—crazy?" he'd said.

She didn't answer.

"What is it—some kind of midlife-crisis thing where people go batshit?" He shoved a big spoon of cereal into his mouth.

"Do you want a banana with your cornflakes?"

"Do I want a banana? Very funny, Mom. You're the one with the banana problem."

"Ben."

He scowled at her. "What? Hey, I'm not the one."

Downing another spoon of cereal, he'd moved to the side counter and slid himself up onto the stool. Bony wide shoulders, the long honey back hunched over the bowl and spoon; he shook his head. She put a glass of fresh orange juice next to his hand; she touched his hair.

"Jeez," he said, his mouth full of cornflakes, "old robo cop's married."

Rachel didn't say anything.

"Did you know he was married when you met him?"

"Yes."

There was a small smudge of milk at the side of his mouth. "Jeez, Mom."

Rachel just breathed.

"Great," Ben said, chewing. Scorn in his voice; she had never heard that sound coming out of her boy. "So, does the wife know?"

"Yes."

"She does?" Mouth open, incredulous, he shook his head again. "How do you know?"

"I know, Ben."

"What? Did good old Jack tell you?"

Rachel thought about taking a drink of his orange juice but stayed where she was. She also thought about running out of the kitchen but stayed where she was.

"How do you know he's not lying?" The crunch of cereal. "It's not like you can trust some guy who fools around, you know."

She didn't say anything; she was not going to get into it with him at that level, not now. Maybe not ever, and certainly not now.

"So, like what? She knows and it's okay with her?"

"I don't know."

"So, where does he say he is when he hangs out here?"

Why had she decided to tell him? Where had she come up with such a daft idea?

"Good-bye, honey," Ben said over his shoulder in a big-guy voice, a Jack-imitation voice, "just call me at Rachel's if you need me."

There was the possibility she might throw up. "Okay, Ben, I didn't tell you about this so we could discuss it; what I do is not your affair."

"Ha," he said, "great choice of words, Mom," and drank the entire glass of juice, his eyes lowered so that he didn't have to look at her.

* * *

"What do you say when you come down here?" Rachel had asked Jack from the sink.

He looked up from the newspaper. "What do you mean?"

"Where do you say you're going?"

"I don't say anything."

The water was running behind her; she held the coffeepot in her hand. "You mean you just drive away?"

He looked at her, then down at his hand on the table, then up. "I just drive away." A pause, a few seconds of silence, only the water running, a car in the street, a horn. "She knows where I am."

"She knows?"

"Yeah."

"What do you mean she knows? She knows my name? My address?"

"Rach . . ."

"You mean you told her?"

"No."

"So how does she know?"

His eyes were cold. "I'm telling you, she knows."

"She knows you're coming to me when you leave . . . when you leave and you don't come back after a few hours."

He didn't answer.

"You just drive away and she knows."

They stared at each other across the kitchen, her back to the sink, his chair at the table, orange blossoms in the window behind his head, and she turned around and counted the scoops of coffee, one, two, three, four, right into the pot. He wasn't going to talk about it. And what was she going to ask? Was she going to fight for Linda? Whose side was she on?

Rachel did not expect her children to understand; *she* didn't understand, and she did not want to discuss it with them; she just couldn't deal anymore with the lies. Is Jack going to move in? Why not? Hey,

Mom, what's up with you and Jack? Well, uh, let's see. . . . She didn't want to lie anymore, so she'd told them the truth.

"Jack is married," she'd said, first to Dana and then to her precious Ben-oh, feeling her arms tighten around herself, swallowing the bitter bile of vomit as she saw disgust in her children's eyes. How much should we tell our children? How much constitutes a big fat mistake?

By 2:30, Rachel had turned off the computer and gone upstairs to get dressed. Or undressed. She was not going to ponder guilt when he was on his way; she was not going to assess the situation or consider why she continued, why he was late this month, why she wanted to be a part of such heartache, what she wanted out of it, or what she thought there would be in the end—Would he leave? Did she want him to?—she was not going to allow herself. She would enjoy, and furthermore, she was going to surprise him, be waiting for him draped across the dining room table like he'd said . . . like a . . . harlot.

She laughed out loud, a grown woman in a relationship that wasn't brand-new, moving hangers of lingerie in the middle of an afternoon; a silk slip with thin straps, a low V at the breasts, ending right above her knees, black. He liked her in black. Rachel turned, ran her hands through her hair, and studied her face and body in the mirror. A forty-something-year-old harlot—oh, please. White? He also liked her in white. She turned, caught herself in profile. She couldn't do it, it would be laughable—sitting around waiting for Jack in heels and a slip. She lifted her shoulders, eyeing her small breasts. Waiting on the dining room table, no less. Red? She had that red thing with the slits. The curve of her stomach, the pale olive of her skin. It was a long drive, he'd be tired. He'd probably rather have a sandwich waiting on the dining room table, a roast beef sandwich with too much mayonnaise.

"You're my harlot," he'd said when he'd found her in the bedroom the last time, just five weeks ago, the last time he'd been in L.A., "my hussy." There was longing in his eyes as he reached for her. "God, look at you, Rach." It had been that way with them from the first.

A Tuesday afternoon, a quiet Tuesday afternoon some six years ago; Dana and Ben were in school. It was raining, coming down fast and hard in sheets—another day of rain, another night—it seemed like it had always been raining; Grace had been carrying on that they should build an ark. Rachel was writing a piece for *Marie Claire* on eyebrows when the electricity went off, and it didn't occur to her that besides no computer and no lights and no refrigerator hum, no electricity also meant no pumps—two pumps in the back garden kept the backup of rainwater from coming into the house. When she casually opened the kitchen door to watch the rain and saw the water rising steadily up the steps—garden tools and old tennis shoes floating in what an hour ago was a bricked-in patio and now resembled a small lake—Rachel's mouth fell. She ran out and started bailing with a bucket, then realized the futility of one small woman with a bucket; she might as well have been using a teacup. Rachel ran back inside to call for help. Soaked and shaking, dialing the plumber, or should she dial the fire department, and there was Jack—on the other line and then in her backyard with a generator—she had no idea where he got it; she had no idea of anything except he was there. His shirt and sport jacket and pants plastered wet against his skin, he pulled an extension cord from the pumps to the gennie. To save the day, Grace said later, like some white knight, missing only a sword and a horse. It had been five months then since they'd met, five months since she'd interviewed him for the piece on battered women, five months since Henry had left—a handshake here and there, some small hugs, hours of conversation, nothing more. She could talk to him, really talk to him, and he could listen and sort it out; he had this extraordinary knack of cutting through the bullshit to the reality and making things clear for her. She had come to rely on him, need him—oh, she had come to need him, but she didn't want to say that to herself—it wasn't anything, don't be silly; they were just friends. Friends on the floor of her office pulling at their wet clothes. Friends in a frenzy of mouths and hands, wet wool, wet hair, wet cotton, wet fingers, the small of her back and her ass raw, red, scraped, bruised, hard against the wool carpet, his smell and his tongue and his mouth, his body, she couldn't get enough, she couldn't slam into him close enough, she couldn't get her breath. In the middle of an afternoon, a quiet Tuesday afternoon in the rain, on the floor of her office, as if she were someone else. With Jack it had always been that way. Shocked from the first that she could be so brazen, shocked now. When it came to Jack, Rachel was everything she had never been. Wanting him, thinking about what it would be like, thinking about what he would do to her, what she would do to him until she ached.

She tried now to get a good look at her backside, angling her head to peer over her shoulder. Not bad. A little fuller in the hips, perhaps, a little thicker in the waist than when they had first begun, but not bad.

"Nice Jewish girls are not hussies, Mr. North." Just five weeks ago, the last time he'd been in—she had called him in the garage, actually called him on the cell phone, said she'd needed him upstairs. To fix something, she'd said. Needed him, she'd said.

His stride across the room, pulling her into him, rough hands cupping her ass, her breasts hard across his shirt buttons, the rake of stubble, his hands, his fingers, his mouth, his mouth. "Nice Jewish girls are not harlots," she'd breathed into his skin. "Are you absolutely sure you're Jewish?" Naked, she had been waiting for him, posed in the bedroom, astonished with herself. Naked except for high heels, standing there, her face hot, flushed. "Rach?" he'd yelled from room to room. "Hey, where the hell are you? What am I supposed to fix?" Her nipples hard when she'd finally heard his foot hit the bottom stairs. Wet, already wet when his bulk stopped motionless in the bedroom doorway, her heart slamming, "Me," she'd whispered, "fix me," and he'd crossed the room. The worst writing, she'd thought later, drivel, absolute drivel. "Fix me"—how could she say such a thing?—she should immediately send herself to writer's jail. Needs. Rachel Rosenthal Glass with needs. Astonishing.

A fast shower to wash off the heat. She wasn't going to think about it. Body cream and perfume. Not about Grace or her kids or what people thought. She wasn't. Her hair was a crap shoot—dark and chopped short, it dried where it was. Not about Linda or guilt or what she was doing. The red. Why was he a week late? She wasn't going to think about it. Claret silk, draped low and soft across the bodice, slit up the thighs, and high, burgundy strappy sandals that she'd bought once and never worn. Jack and her, that was all she was going to think about—Jack and her, and now. Rachel pulled the cloud of soft red silk over her head, adjusted it around her body, and slipped into the shoes. She stood in front of the mirror.

A Jewish hussy, perfumed and primed. A Jewish harlot in the raw. Three-twenty in the afternoon and she was about to become the centerpiece on her own dining room table. Waiting for a man to ravish her. Centerpiece. Oh, Lord.

Grace

SEX. THAT'S WHAT they all think, that it's sex. Women are fools.

Grace leaned closer to the makeup mirror, lifting the waves off her forehead.

It's not just sex.

The gray at the top of her head was coming in like a skunk's streak—strong and wide—and at the temples, and, look at that, sprinkled practically through the whole right side. She took a deep drag of the cigarette. Pathetic, the whole thing was pathetic.

Sex is just the cover, the catalyst that begins the dance.

Grace gently pulled the skin at the sides of her mouth up toward her ears. An old geisha. There was no way to do it, no matter which surgeon, no matter how much money, when you lifted the skin and tucked it, your expression changed around your eyes.

It wouldn't matter anyway.

Sex, they think, and youth. My husband left me for a younger woman—how many times had she heard that?

She took another drag and blew the smoke toward the open window. Her eyes circled the pool, following the low hum of the lawn mower. Taki was cutting the grass—a small bent man, back and forth across the expanse of green, a pattern of wide stripes left in his wake.

And if you pulled up your face and your neck and your tits and your ass and your everything, you would still be old. And it isn't about being young anyway, it's about being you.

Taki's shoulders were so stooped—too many lawn mowers too many years. Did he kiss Mrs. Taki good-bye each morning and then pull off the road somewhere in his neighborhood and lure young Japanese maidens into his truck? Was he fucking them in between the flats of geraniums and sacks of rose food?

She studied the chaise longues in a row around the blue water, the plump green cushions and thick peach towels waiting to be used. The same pale peach as the tender hibiscus and a young woman's throat. And even if you were young, when you were young, when she was young and beautiful and taut and fresh and stunning, in love with Dick and he was in love with her, falling all over himself to have her, it still wasn't enough.

Grace took one last drag on the cigarette and put it out. It isn't about young.

Dick had fooled around from the very beginning. Crazy about her, crazy for her, and still he fooled around. She was young then, young and beautiful. It isn't about young.

She turned from the window to her face in the glass.

A fresh look at themselves through new eyes—oh, baby, talk about a thrill. That's what it is, that's what they need, and sex is just the beginning. Grace had long ago figured it out.

Sex and then the acknowledgment, which leads to the appreciation and the adulation, and he topples, a slow slide, a bit of a struggle, but he's eating it up, and he loses his place in the glory of it, the beating heart, the anticipation, and loyalty fails. Faithfulness goes out the window, and he falls. She's got him. This new woman looks at him and it's everything—reinforcement, rejuvenation, rebirth—new love for his lonely heart, new hope for his lost dreams, new heat for his tired cock, and there's no stopping it now. He's a new man. The irresistible high that comes from new eyes starts with a fuck, always that, always the fuck—the dance of the flirtation for as long as it lasts and then the fuck—the guy in the office and the girl on the next floor, the orthopedic surgeon and the nurse, two strangers taking an art class—it doesn't matter—simple, trite, predictable—and it's only a coffee and it's only a cocktail and it's only a breath away from the "hi, honey" call. "Hi, honey, I gotta finish this." "Hi, honey, I'll be late, go on without me." "Hi, honey, I gotta go to Atlanta." "Hi, honey, the meeting went on forever; sorry I missed your call."

It's after the fuck when you've got the real trouble, when you've got to watch your step. The gratification that comes from the thrill of this indulgent renaissance becomes their drug, more than hair dye, a face-lift, a trip to the spa. He thrives on it, then he survives on it, and that's it, you're out. You've lost your place. You can't give it to him. No matter what you lift or tuck or prune or pull, no matter if some genie pops out of a goddamn bottle and takes you first-class to the fountain of youth. It's still you behind the nip and tuck—old eyes, old girl, your same old eyes looking at him, not new.

Grace dabbed cream and concealer on the soft flesh in the lavender hollows under her eyes.

That's when you make your choice. That's when you decide how you want to deal with it. Sit in it or move on.

All men fool around. And some women think it's about how far, but what's worse—the fuck or the flirtation? There is no way to measure the bigger hurt, the larger betrayal. It's what you do after, it's how smart you are about holding on—if that's your choice, to hold on, because if you're smart, you can.

Dick rebounds off each woman and begs to come home. Home to her and her mind and her smart mouth and after the first couple of bouts of pain and rage and humiliation Grace made the choice. Why give up her security, her checkbook, her meal ticket? She wasn't interested in kidding herself, she wasn't about to start anew. She didn't have the heart for new adventure and she didn't have the guts to take a walk by herself. Sell the house and split everything and go out on her own. Get a job? She hadn't had a job since she'd married him, since she was in her twenties—get a job now? Four chairs for you and four for me, divide the silver, the pension, the stocks. What for?

Grace poured moisturizer into her hand.

She had searched her soul during all of the in-between times and she knew that what she was doing worked. She was set, she had what she wanted, holding on to Dick worked for her, she wasn't about to let go. She knew how to reel him in. She could feign reconciliation with the best of them, look at him and pretend. Pretend she believed the promise. She would not point out previous promises—what for?

Blush to the apples of the cheeks, line the eyes with a smudge of taupe pencil, a little mascara, soft red against the lips. She would lift the gray and lift her spirits with a walk around Neiman's. She would buy a dress, a beautiful dress. She would let him take her to dinner. She would listen to his self-reproach and accept his guilt. She knew how to do this, she had done it before. She would lower her eyes at his shame, weep at his remorse, and let him touch her hand. She had been married a long time.

She would let Dick back in—back into her house and her bed because it worked for her; she had long ago figured that out.

Grace lifted the stopper from the perfume bottle and tilted a few drops of the cool liquid at her throat.

And the way Grace figured it, so had Mrs. North. If Rachel thinks that Jack North will ever leave his wife and come to her, she's a damn fool.

Linda

RACHEL GLASS WAS the first as far as Linda knew. Not the first time Jack had someone else, but the first time he'd fallen in love. If that's what it was, and she thought so—love. Linda pulled out of the driveway, adjusted the rearview mirror, and watched the shape of dust rise behind her exhaust. The first time he'd had someone else was in 1975. Nineteen seventy-five, after that thing with the gun, and in some ways it had been a relief. Not because she wanted to think of Jack with someone else, because she didn't, she hated it, each and every time he had somebody else she hated it, but that first time was different because she'd been waiting for it to happen since she'd walked down the aisle. It had always been clear to her that Jack would cheat. Clear as a bell.

Linda's eyes slid from the road back to the mirror and she took in her face and her hair. In 1975 they'd been married for ten years and maybe he'd had someone else before then, but she didn't think so, and maybe she should get color in her hair, finally, dye it bright red or bleach it platinum or maybe a deep, rich brown. Mahogany, like in the Clairol ad, instead of gray-beige-yellow, which is what it was, a beige blur. A beige flyaway blur. Linda's eyes refocused on the road. Who was she kidding? She'd only seen her that one time, but she saw how the light hit it—it wasn't in a Clairol ad—Rachel Glass had mahogany hair.

Well, look at that. Mae Chapin must have hired some construction crew—what does it say on the side of that truck? Marin Brothers—to fix her porch. Linda tapped the horn and waved; Mae turned, but it was too late to see that it was Linda; she waved to taillights and a cloud of dust. Linda pushed the accelerator, took the curve down from the lake with maybe a little too much speed but what the hell, and it pleased her to go too fast. It's not like Ralph Crawley or Charlie Eckerts would pull her over and give her a ticket; after all, she was still a policeman's wife—even if he was retired.

Linda held the wheel steady with two hands and kept her foot to the gas. She knew Jack would cheat on her from the very beginning. Everybody knew. He was pretty. Prettier than she was. Much. Always had been, always would be, even her mother had said so, and even back when he married her and she was limber and young and at least, she thought, cute, she saw how people looked at him first and then looked at her, then back to him, always back to him as if he were lit up or had an outline, a black Magic Marker outline, as if she were just a beige blur. Maybe she'd always been a blur. Mom said she was vague. What a terrible thing to say to a child—she didn't even realize how mean it was until years passed. She would never say that to Patty or Julie. Not that they were blurry, they weren't; but just because a person doesn't always have the precise words to say at the precise moment doesn't mean she's vague. That was the trouble with words, fast didn't always mean accurate. Linda thought of it as having step smarts. Sometimes she wouldn't know what to say when Jack said something; she wouldn't have a comeback or get exactly what he had said—the all of it, it wouldn't be filled in totally—and then when the moment was over and she'd be leaving, walking down the steps, she would get it, it would come to her in a rush, and she would know what she should have said—too late to say it in the moment, but not necessarily too late to say it at all—you had to bide your time, you had to pick your moments. She preferred to think of it as thoughtful, not vague. Her grandmother Stella said she didn't have gumption, which was a laugh because it certainly took gumption to stay married to Jack. Linda moved her foot on the accelerator, raised up in the seat some, and straightened her back.

When she'd married him she was nineteen; when she'd met him she was fourteen. With braces. And big tits. It seemed like she'd always had big tits. Linda perched her elbow out the open window and slowed down as she approached town.

He'd transferred into her class, her school and her class; he had been sent to live with his aunt in Bishop. Banished was the word he used. His parents had been married and divorced when he was little and were both on their third spouse—Jack had gotten into more than one scuffle with his mother's new husband so he'd been sent to live with his aunt. Of course, Linda didn't get any of this information until later; all she knew was that he was the new boy. Mr. Kopit, the teacher for ninth grade, who had also transferred in that year and was way too sophisticated for Bishop—his previous job had been for a prep school in Montecito where a year's tuition cost more than a car—was a firm believer in his own version of etiquette. "Miss Layton, do you want to help us out here with the answer?" "Yes, Mr. Kopit." And she could feel the new boy's eyes on her as she went to the board.

"Hey." He was behind her in the line at the cafeteria, cutting in to get a piece of chocolate cake. He was terrifically good-looking and she hadn't expected him to speak to her and she was trying to figure out how to say something back without letting her braces show. He had four milks on his tray, spaghetti red with meatballs, bread and butter, three puddings, and now the piece of cake.

"Hey," she said back. It could be done; you just had to kind of adhere your upper lip to the wires on your front teeth. She probably looked like a chipmunk, but it was worth it. It occurred to her that your lips only went up when you said *e*'s; if she could just think each sentence through and keep away from *e*'s. . . .

"What's your name?" He grinned; she didn't.

"Linda." So far so good, she took a red Jell-O.

"Mine's North. Mr. North, exactly."

She could feel the smile pulling.

"Just Mr. North, yes, ma'am, that's what I'm called."

"You don't have a first name?"

"Nope."

"I see." Shit. How could she say "see"? She bit her upper lip, gave her tray a little push.

"So, Linda Layton, would you like to go to the game?"

Her lip was unsticking; she couldn't help it.

"I mean, excuse me, MISS Layton, would you like to go out on Saturday night with MISTER North?"

Mr. North, who was out of town now visiting his girlfriend. "Mr. North, we're going to have a baby. Mr. North, I love you. Mr. North, what do you want for supper? Mr. North, get your feet off that spread."

Tony would be done with football practice at five; she had twenty minutes to swing by the Wicki Shop and pick up hamburger and buns. Tomorrow she would be more productive; she would put new liner paper on the kitchen shelves, get that cobweb, throw away stuff. But now she'd surprise Julie and drop Tony home with stuff for supper, but she wouldn't go in. No reason to subject herself to anyone's asking "Where's Jack?"—especially not her daughter, especially not with her knowing he'd just been gone. Linda pulled into the Wicki Shop parking lot, killed the motor, and got out of the car.

"Hey, Linda," Marge said from behind the register. "Marge," Linda said. Two pounds ought to do it and eight buns, each of the boys would have two . . . was two enough? Maybe three pounds. And potatoes, no, Julie probably already had potatoes . . . tomatoes would be good . . . nice beefsteaks . . . and . . . "Hey, Linda, where's Jack?" Linda looked up from the stacks of hamburger meat into Charlie Eckerts's badge. "Hello, Charlie." "Ma'am," he said. "Ma'am, my foot," Linda said, clutching the package of cool hamburger meat up against the front of her shirt. "I have to pick up Tony at football," she said, and turned.

Charlie walked with her to the potatoes. Big black sheriff boots next to her dirty Keds. Jack had worn a uniform like that once upon a time before he was a detective, but it was navy blue; Beverly Hills was dark navy blue. Charlie was an Inyo County sheriff; they wore green and tan.

"I saw him play last Friday," Charlie said, popping the top on the can of Coke he was holding, "your grandson; he's pretty good."

"He's wonderful," Linda said, balancing four potatoes on top of the package of hamburger meat, the stack reaching the top of her breasts.

"Burgers tonight, huh?" Charlie said.

Linda didn't answer; she reached for a tomato and one of the potatoes rolled off the stack and bounced to the floor. Charlie went for it. "You want a basket?" "No, thank you," she said. Why did she feel like screaming? He held out the potato and for a fleeting second, she thought he was going to put it back on the tower propped up against her; she thought Charlie Eckerts was going to reach out with an Idaho potato and touch her breast. "So, where's your old man?" he said, and Linda took the potato and she could feel her face get hot. "Home," she said as she turned, lying to him as she turned.

Charlie was behind her. "Is he going to race Saturday?"

Linda dumped the potatoes and ground chuck in front of Marge at the register. "Hamburgers tonight, huh?" Marge said. Linda nodded, opened her purse. "I made hamburgers last week," Marge said, "but it's really not good for your cholesterol." She shook her head. "Fish, that's what they say . . . fish, fish, fish, and Walter hates fish. 'You can't make fish taste like a rib eye, Marge; leave me alone.' " Marge sighed heavily. Linda pulled some bills out of her wallet. "I try," Marge said, gazing at Linda. "Do you like fish?" Linda didn't answer. "Not me," Charlie said. He leaned against the checkout counter, took a swig of Coke, and handed Marge a clean folded bag out of the stack. His gun clunked against the gum display. "Thanks," Marge said, her eyes taking in all six feet three of him as if he were something good to eat, as if her very own husband, Walter, wasn't right there in the back of the store somewhere—probably unpacking tomatoes, which Linda realized she hadn't gotten. There she was with potatoes and Julie probably already had potatoes; hadn't she decided that when she came in? Marge gave Charlie a ridiculous look that she must have thought was sexy—did the whole world revolve around sex? And then she remembered where Jack was, and she remembered the type across the page—"How to Get Your Orgasm"—and the color of Rachel Glass's hair, and she could see her own face in the rearview mirror as if she were still in the car and the way her skin was loosening on either side of her chin, and it was all she could do to not throw the money across the counter instead of drop it into Marge's fat hand.

"Is he going to race Saturday, you think?" Charlie asked again.

"I don't know, Charlie." She handed Marge the cash and scooped up the bag.

"I'll call him, I guess," Charlie said.

"Mm-hm, I gotta get Tony," Linda said, and practically ran from the store.

"Wassup, Grandma?" Tony said as he got into the car. Sweat and mud and the particular tang of end-of-the-summer grass got in with him. He slammed the door. "Where's Jack?"

"Since when do you call your grandfather by his first name?"

"He told me I could. Is he home?"

Linda took off too fast, which caused the Honda to skid on the dirt at the edge of the football field, go into a little half turn, and kick up a lot of dust.

"Cool," Tony said.

She resisted leaning her head against the steering wheel, banging her face hard against the steering wheel. She resisted crying out loud.

"He's gonna take me out on one of the bikes."

Linda felt her heart heave. "Tonight?" How could he take Tony out if he'd gone to L.A.? Damn it, Jack, how could you promise him and then drive away?

"Tomorrow after school," Tony said.

"Oh." Linda pulled onto the road.

"I don't have practice on Tuesdays."

Linda took a right and started up the hill. Was he going to call Tony and tell him he couldn't take him? And then Julie would know and she'd start in . . . lies begat lies . . . and couldn't he just have waited until next week . . . and couldn't he just stop going there at all . . . or hadn't he gone? Had he told Tony he'd take him because he really hadn't gone to L.A.? It's not like she knew; it's not like she could get ahold of him; even if there was an emergency she had no idea where he was. Well, she could call Rachel Glass; if push came to shove, she could call him there but that would only be if somebody died. . . . It wasn't like she didn't know the number; it wasn't like she hadn't called every now and then, which was mortifying at this age to think you would call somebody and then hang up . . . hear Rachel Glass say "Hello?" and put the receiver back on the hook. As foolish as driving down there that time, spending half the night parked down the street from her house, watching Jack's car in her driveway, as if the car were going to do something, as if she were seventeen years old. . . .

". . . and I'm old enough," Tony said.

Linda turned to her grandson. "What?"

"I'm old enough," Tony said. A piece of hair fell over his eyebrow; she took her hand from the wheel and pushed it back off his face. He let her.

"Old enough for what?"

"To race. After all, I'm gonna be fifteen."

"Your grampa said you could race?"

"Well, sort of, so could you talk to Mom?"

The hair as black, the eyes as gray; it was uncanny how the grandchildren looked more like Jack than even Julie and Patty, especially Tony and Emmie, the eyes especially. Little Patty Cake was the only one who looked a little like Linda and probably only because her hair was sandy—what hair she had, which seemed to Linda to be very thin even for a baby's, not that she was about to say anything that would upset Patty, who had waited so long for a baby. Julie had been pregnant practically from the time she got her period, and Patty had had the hardest time—miscarrying, miscarrying, and miscarrying. Linda was certainly not about to say that the baby's hair looked thin.

"She's kinda wacko about it," Tony said. "You think you could come in and talk to her? Tell her you think it's okay?"

"I don't know if I think it's okay."

"Oh, I thought you said . . ." Disappointment cloud, dead ahead right across the face, the face that looked so like Jack's. Linda's eyes drifted off the road and onto the mirror; she lifted her hand and pushed back the flyaway hair that was blowing across her cheek and nose.

"Grandma?"

"I can't come in today, Tony, I have things to do."

She had nothing to do, nothing. She heard his body shift in the seat. She wasn't going to think about it, and she didn't look at him, kept her eyes front—the sky was deepening, not dark, after all, because it was only September and only twenty after five and even still warm, but you could feel the change—well, she could—that thrill of autumn, her favorite time. She loved September and October; the fall always felt like a new beginning to her, another chance. Most people probably felt that way about spring, but she didn't; it was always the fall. Football and leaves turning and you needed a sweater, she loved that, how you suddenly needed a sweater and what that meant.

She turned into her daughter's driveway. "Take the bag with you, honey, it's hamburger."

"Okay, okay."

"Tony?"

He looked at her reluctantly; children were so obvious when you had let them down. Like Eeyore in *Winnie the Pooh. It's all right,* he says, *I don't need a birthday party, it's okay,* but his heart is breaking, his lip all stuck out like that. "I'll call your mother tomorrow about the racing. Okay?"

All smiles again; it took so little.

"Thanks, Grandma," he said, and he was gone.

In 1975 Jack was working as a patrol sergeant on an early night watch. Evening, a beautiful Beverly Hills evening, with the sky all stripes of pink and blue, maybe five o'clock, maybe five-thirty, and he gets a call about a forgery suspect who shows up in a Bank of America building right on Canon and Wilshire, trying to sell some hot coins; important coins worth thousands, or hundreds of thousands, important coins from Russia or Persia, a country Linda couldn't remember, the amounts she couldn't remember, only what happened could she forever remember in minute detail. The sixth floor of a high-rise glass-and-metal security building smack in the middle of Beverly Hills, which should have been a piece of cake. Jack didn't say a piece of cake; she'd heard that later, when she was sitting with Suze in Frankie's in Culver City, two cops near their table relating the story and the young one, the rookie who still had pimples, says to the other one, "a piece a cake." Jack takes the call and arrives on the sixth floor of the building in uniform and is shown in by the security guard, who then leaves. And the two guys who are supposedly buying the coins, but who are really plainclothes, they leave too—"stage left." That was how Jack put it when he told the story, as if it were only a play or a movie, only make-believe, as if what had happened was not real. "They took off like they were supposed to," he would say when he told the story, "stage left. And I say to the guy, 'Let me see your identification,' because I've already seen photos of the guy and I know it's him."

The guy gives Jack New York ID, a New York driver's license, but it's plastic, laminated or something, which is not right, because it was paper back then, a certain kind of paper, but this is laminated and it's new, and he hands Jack a new Social Security card in the same plastic.

"And I knew," Jack says with this gleam, and he straightens his shoulders as he finds himself at this part of the story; he straightens his shoulders and sits high in the chair. "And that's when," he says, "I made my tactical mistake." He takes a second, his face set. "See, I knew he had a gun on him."

"How did you know?" Whoever is listening always asks the same question at this exact place—"How did you know?" "The hair on the back of my neck stood up," Jack says with an evil grin, and then he shrugs. "I don't know; you just know when a guy's got a gun on him . . . you just know." Everyone who's listening to the story nods as if he knows what it means to feel a certain something when a crook has a gun on him. Jack takes a moment for this to sink in. "So, I say to the crook, 'You got a gun on you, don't you?' That's what I say, which is my mistake, and the guy hops back a full step. I mean, hops, you know, back like a dancer, like a full step, and draws a gun out of his jacket and holds it on me and says, 'Hold it.' 'Hold it, hell,' I say, and I draw my revolver, but he's already got his gun on me and he fires."

"He fires," he tells Linda that night as she sits across from him at the kitchen table just like night after night, every night, when he comes home and she says, "If you want to eat, tell me; tell me about your day."

"And he fires," Jack says, "the gun pointin' right at my head; he fires."

And she looks at him. Her breath stopped in her chest and she's holding on to the table apron hard, but he can't see that, and she looks at him as if it's all okay.

"And it clicked," he says. He takes a second, his eyes on hers, and then that slow smile, and he says it again, both of them caught as if they're frozen in a painting. "It just clicked," he says.

One bad bullet, he found out later, one bad bullet; the guy had one bad bullet in the gun and all the rest were good. One bad bullet at close range, and if it would have been one good bullet, Jack would have been dead. So you sit at the kitchen table and you say to yourself, he's okay, look, you see, he's okay. It's over, it's through, because after the shock that the bullet hadn't done its job, after the shock that he was breathing and not bleeding, Jack threw the guy to the ground, cuffed him, and the backup came and they did what they do. So you put the plate with the warmed-up spaghetti in front of him and you say to yourself, it's over, he's okay, it's through. Because it's not like you have a choice. You are a cop's wife, and you're not going to put your fears on him. The truth be known, she'd never gotten used to it. Never. Somewhere inside of him he believed that he was one of the good guys that was supposed to save the rest of the good guys in the world from the jerks. And she went along with it. Because she had to. Because she loved him. Out of her control, she'd say to herself, you can't get crazy, it's out of your control. You are a cop's wife and you do what you do. File it, you say to yourself, you see he's okay. So you stand up, you touch his hand, that's all you do, and your mouth is dry and you stand up and wipe your palms on the sides of your pants and touch his hand. "You want bread," you say, "to push the spaghetti?" because that's what you do.

In 1975, after the bad bullet, which was what they called it—"Tell the one about the bad bullet, Jack" that night after the bad bullet, he didn't come home right away. He went with the boys to the Crown House, a bar on Santa Monica Boulevard where they used to hang out, Beverly Hills's finest—just across the line from where Beverly Hills officially ended, which they referred to with a laugh as out of town. To debrief, which was what they called it then, which was to get tanked up, unwind, collapse, renew. That's where it happened, Linda figured later, that very night when Jack started with the first someone else. After the scare, when he was ripe for someone to hold him and tell him he was okay, alive and okay, and there she was. Not that Linda had been given the chance to be the one, because she'd had no idea what had happened, she was home dealing with two kids, how could she know? And then the weeks after that there was more to know than the scare and the story, like the dull pain after the dentist that's a low hum in your jaw, or the smell of a dead rat in the wall that you can't get to and nobody smells it yet but you. You know it's there; you smell it. There's someone else. Your husband is cheating; your husband is fooling around, the hum and the smell say, and you know.

There is no reason to know, no earthly reason. He still comes home pretty much on time, although a cop's life pretty much gives a man opportunity to cheat: the crazy hours are one of the things you have to adapt to right from the start, and the fact that he's parading around out there in a uniform, which makes him prey. A handsome guy is even handsomer in a uniform and especially with a badge and a gun—the handsome hero saving the world from bad guys always turns heads—and it's not like he was working east L.A. with the dregs of the universe, but right in Beverly Hills. Beverly Hills, where every other woman is a beauty, where every other woman spends her day getting her hair done and her nails and her everything—nannies to take care of her children, maids to take care of her house, time on her hands. Linda knew about the notorious morning coffee breaks, when a cop leaves the station for more than coffee and a doughnut: Beverly Hills wives with fancy houses and fancy cars and fancy husbands and a not-so-fancy cop she keeps on the side. Beverly Hills was the land of temptation, and Jack was probably the best-looking guy on the force. She knew all about it; she lived with it—the only thing higher than the divorce rate for police officers was the odds for fooling around, but she also knew it hadn't happened yet, and then suddenly she knew it had.

He still came home pretty much on time—okay, maybe ten minutes here, maybe ten minutes there—he's not where he's supposed to be, but it's nothing, and he still makes love to you pretty much the same, maybe not with the same enthusiasm, but you chalk that up to you, because how can you keep yourself looking the way you should what with two children to do for—but everything else seems to be pretty much the same. And you know this man, you've been married to him for ten years, loved him since you had braces, and there's no reason for you to think he's cheating, no earthly reason, no sign, no fights, no flag going up. Nothing. But suddenly you know.

"Women know," her friend Suze had said then, "always. That son of a bitch, Jerry, him and that Anna—who looked like a fireplug; let me tell you, there's no accounting for taste—and how many times had I gone over there to pick him up. 'Hon, will you pick me up?' he says to me. Been in that office with the two of them and he looks at her and she looks at him like all those times, and my feet suddenly get cemented to the floor because all of a sudden out of nowhere like there was a whistle, like someone whacked me over the head with a bat, I knew." Suze's blue eyes were slits as she took a drag off her cigarette. "Women know, baby, women know . . . *always*"—she blew the smoke out hard across the table—"it's a gift from God."

And Linda had laughed, a little laugh slipping out into all that crying all over Suze's kitchen, crying and telling her while the kids played "cave" under the table, her Julie and Patty and Suze's Dylan breathing on her legs under the table, sticky little hands on her calves and her knees and the reek of cold lamb chops and apple juice, and this little laugh came out of her to think that God would do such a thing. As if knowing your husband was cheating on you could be a gift. A heartbreak, a humiliation, and a gift. As years passed and names were added to the list in Linda's head of the "someone elses" in Jack's life, she decided that whether she agreed or not it was a gift, Suze had spoken the truth—a woman always knew. You could ask any of them. You could take a survey: go up to a woman in the grocery store while she's squeezing cantaloupes and say, "How did you know?" and the woman doesn't even have to stop squeezing; she'll get this look in her eyes, even if she's still looking at the cantaloupe and not at you, and she'll say, "I just knew." Any woman, every woman, it was true. You could do an article about it for a magazine. No, Linda could do an article. "It's 1:00 P.M. Do You Know Where Your Husband Is?" followed by "How Did You Know Your Husband Had Someone Else?" another masterpiece by hotshot writer Linda North. If she was the writer and Rachel Glass was the . . . what? The mom, the grandma didn't count, because Rachel Glass was a mom and a grandma too. If she was the . . . what?

Linda pulled into her driveway, cut the motor, and let her head lean back against the seat.

Okay, what if the tables were turned, if they had to trade lives? Linda could live in that big house down there in Beverly Hills with the elms and the palms and the roses, the brick front walk and the truckful of gardeners; Linda could drive that shiny little blue BMW with the top down and go have mahogany put in her hair, and Rachel Glass could live up here and finish the café curtains and do the basket of ironing and sit in the dark of the driveway and look at the sky. *First star I see tonight, I wish I may, I wish I might, I wish my wish comes true tonight.* She'd seen Rachel Glass that morning, that stupid morning last April when she'd driven down in the night. Right after the business with the wedding ring. Jack, wiping his hands, walking in from the garage and the skeleton of a dead bike, pieces of it cluttered on top of her washing machine, lying in a bucket of solvent, strewn across the fenders of her car. "Linda"—busying himself with a rag, eyes down—"where's the GoJo?" Jack's square hand scooping a dollop of the orange goop cleanser as she held out the jar. "I gotta go get gaskets." "Where's your wedding ring, Jack?" Dismayed, flustered. The disappearing wedding ring that had lost its place in a jumble of bike parts. As if she could believe such a thing, a wedding ring that hadn't slipped in thirty-four years, slipping into the trash of old gaskets and spark plugs. And she'd said, "You didn't lose it, you took it off," and he'd said, "No way," and she'd said, "You took it off; what are you doing?" and he'd held his ground. And nobody said anything for an hour and then the slam of his car door, tires on the gravel, and he took off. Took off the ring, because she knew he'd taken it off; Ms. Glass probably didn't want to see that wedding ring, that hand with that wedding ring touching her. He'd taken off the ring of their covenant, her husband, then taken off for Rachel Glass. Linda had walked the house. Room to room, all day and part of the night, walking, Buddy at her heels, until she couldn't take it, couldn't stay there, and after midnight she was on the road.

Sunrise, birds singing, the sprinklers coming on across the rectangles of green, across the perfectly trimmed hedges and edges, and Linda slumped in her car. Dawn brightening the sky into a silky blue and yellow, children being backed out of driveways with slicked hair and backpacks and lunch boxes, soft Spanish gibberish out of uniformed maids walking dogs, pushing strollers, the soft slap of Nikes pounding the pavement as willowy Beverly Hills women in designer pastel sweats and dark glasses ran the mile. Linda sat forward to study the crease the armrest had left across her cheek and up into her eye and down into her mouth, and why had she done it, followed him, driven down in the night to prove nothing; she knew where he was. She was not about to knock on the door, to face him, to face the outcome, and Rachel Glass came out of her house.

The front door slid open, and the woman took about five steps down the brick front walk. Little. No, not little, thin, with a quick step. Alive. The sun hit her hair as she bent to pick up the newspaper, short curls of rich mahogany falling across her cheek, her forehead, and Linda heard her own intake of breath. Sitting forward in the seat, hand at her throat, the edge of her left breast and her ribs crushed against the steering wheel, she realized she'd been holding her breath. Rachel Glass was wearing a robe, a peach silky short thing. One slender arm extending, reaching for her newspaper, the robe opening in a V across her chest and above her knees. Rich lady legs all the way up into the silk, all the way down into the bare feet that moved across the red brick into the wet grass. She looked like a dancer, Linda thought, like the tiny ballerina circling at the top of the tinkling jewelry box her mother had bought her that one Christmas, circling and circling in the tiny mirror even after her cousin Midge broke it and the music stopped. And Rachel Glass pulled the blue plastic wrap from her newspaper, raised up, and looked right at Linda's car.

Neither of them moved.

A tiny diamond in the woman's earlobe caught the light; she paused for a few seconds, then bent her head to the newsprint, turned slowly, and returned to her house.

Linda started the motor and drove the seven hours back as if someone were chasing her, stopping only once to use the bathroom and get gas. Gas that she pumped for cash, cash that she'd taken from the envelope she kept hidden between the dish towels in the kitchen, because she didn't want Jack to see a charge slip, to know she'd done such a thing. And for what? To see his car in Rachel Glass's driveway?

As if she needed proof; she knew where he was. She had no idea if Rachel Glass had seen her, there was no way to know, there was no one to ask. *First star I see tonight, I wish I may, I wish I might, I wish my wish comes true tonight.*

Linda sat in her parked car in her own driveway for maybe five more minutes, her eyes on the sky. She tried to figure out what her wish was and then she got out of the car. It was six o'clock and sitting there was ridiculous—it occurred to her that maybe a woman knew when her husband had someone else the same way a cop knew when a crook had a gun on him—but it seemed too hard to put it together to work into the article she would never write because she wasn't the writer, was she? And besides that, it was six o'clock and she had to feed the dogs.

Rachel

IT WAS SIX O'CLOCK. He'd distinctly said three. "Three, three-thirty." Distinctly. Rachel dialed his cell phone again; she had already dialed it maybe a hundred times.

"Message C.O. 20, welcome to AT&T Wireless Services," the voice said. "The subscriber you have called is unavailable or has traveled outside the coverage area. Please try your call again later. Message C.O. 20," the voice said.

Rachel slammed down the receiver and got up from the chair. She paced the downstairs, went into the kitchen, got another glass of water, drank it, slammed the glass hard against the sink. Hey, wait a minute, there is no reason to be this crazy; he's just late. She walked back into her office, her eyes circling the room. *Please try your call again later.* She hated that voice, that pompous son of a bitch of a voice. She took the stairs up two at a time, moved through the bedroom. *Traveled outside the coverage area.* She sat on the foot of the bed, chewed on her lip between her teeth. *Mammoth Lakes cutoff. I should be there three, three-thirty;* that's what he'd said. She remembered dialogue. She was a writer, for godsakes; she certainly remembered dialogue; she'd been interviewing people for years.

Her eyes on the bougainvillea but seeing only the green freeway sign with the white writing, she stayed quiet for maybe thirty seconds, perched where she was. *Mammoth Lakes cutoff.* She'd seen that; she'd been there; she knew where that was; following Jack's taillights in her BMW, the top down. "What's up there?" her cell phone to his cell phone. "A lake, dopey." Laughter and Rachel said, "I mean, is it pretty?" "I'll take you up there sometime," Jack said. *Mammoth Lakes cutoff.* They'd never gone. *Mammoth Lakes cutoff.* Rachel frowned. Static, she'd heard static; she was putting away the groceries, 10:30, 11:30, putting away the groceries and there was static, but he said he'd already been through the mountains. *Mammoth Lakes cutoff,* that's what he'd said.

Rachel got up, straightened the duvet where she'd sat, ran her hand across the soft wrinkles, straightened her back, her shoulders, and studied the duvet until it blurred. She moved to the front windows, eyes on the street. Six o'clock, hot September six o'clock, all quiet on the western front, all serene and soft like a Monet. Jack was never late.

She went into her dressing room, sat in front of the mirror, saw his face behind her, over her shoulder in the glass. "He's a looker, I'll give you that," Grace had said from the beginning, "the epitome of macho man-dom, lean and mean and gorgeous, a Marlboro man." Rachel studied the framed color photograph of her and Jack beside the mirror, the one taken in Santa Barbara with the ocean behind their heads. Blue ocean. *Traveled outside the coverage area.* Where the hell was the coverage area*? Three, three-thirty;* that's what he'd said.

Of course, he had to set the camera on a tripod with a timer every time he took their picture; it wasn't like they went anywhere with friends. Couples who play together, take trips, take each other's pictures are usually married, each to the other, not to someone else left at home. *The subscriber you have called is unavailable.* The only friends they had were . . . well, Grace came over sometimes to eat, but only because she was lonely when Dickhead was gone—she really hated Jack, it was clear that she hated him, clear to Rachel, not clear to Jack. And Carole came over sometimes or invited them to her house, but

Carole would go along with anything if Rachel needed her to, if Rachel liked something Carole would go along. And, of course, there was Randy, Jack's nephew, who enjoyed a visit, steaks on the barbecue, too much red wine, he'd bring a girl, they'd play some poker, but it's not like he had a brain, it's not like you could have a conversation with Randy about anything that required a mind, and like Grace said, "Let's call a spade a you-know-what. What kind of a guy can be friends with the aunt and the uncle *and* the uncle's girlfriend? What kind of a guy is that?" And there was always the fact that Jack was married—to tell or not to tell—because to divulge that part of who Jack was meant getting someone else involved, some friend, some acquaintance, some person you thought you wanted to have dinner with when Jack was in town; to tell the truth was to take on that person's disapproval—better to stay away, better to be alone—so when Jack was in L.A. they were nearly always alone. As if she had two lives—one with Jack and one without. *Hey, who is that guy who mysteriously slinks into town to see you?* Rachel studied her face in the glass. He wasn't easy, not with her friends anyway, her life, her acquaintances, people in her business—writers mainly, people on the fringe of the entertainment business, newspaper people, aware, sophisticated people—he was far from open, he was not available to anything that smacked of liberalism, anything that wasn't Republican and conservative and everything that Rachel didn't believe in but shut up about. *Who is that guy who comes down here? The one you see once a month?* She had taken him to an Authors' League dinner once and he'd practically had a fistfight with some guy over a racist remark, Jack's racist remark, and when the guy called him on it—well, it was the last time she had tried to mix Jack into her other life. *Oh, you know Rachel, she can't meet us next week. The mysterious Mr. North will be in town.* "You're my mysterious Mr. North," she'd told him. "You bet I am." *The subscriber you have called is unavailable.* Where the hell is he? What the hell is going on?

She went back downstairs and circled the dining room table, moved into her office, tripped over one of the strappy high-heeled sandals she'd left toppled at the side of her desk, actually lost her balance falling over it, half sat, half fell to the rug. *I'll call you when I pass Jo's.* Why hadn't he called when he'd passed Jo's? Why doesn't he call now? Jack doesn't do this; he doesn't do this; this isn't what Jack does. She let her head drop and ran her hands across her face.

Of course he does it to Linda, doesn't he? He has it in him to do this; he does it to Linda all the time. Doesn't say he's leaving, doesn't call when he gets here, doesn't call sometimes for two, three days. "Don't you think you ought to call her? Don't you think you ought to let her know that you haven't crashed somewhere by the side of the road?" His eyes on her across the bedroom, across the pillows on the bed, and she thought, Wait a minute, what the hell am I doing? The whole thing was ludicrous—the girlfriend is telling the man to call his wife?—insane.

Rachel's eyes flew around the room. *Crashed somewhere by the side of the road.* Okay, okay, you do not have to take everything straight to the bad. What is it?—superstition? Jewish guilt? There's a logical explanation, he'll walk in and tell you and you'll laugh.

Rachel stayed where she was on the rug, her back cold against the wall of warm stucco, cold when it was probably still in the nineties at ten after six; it was ten after six; *I should be there three, three-thirty,* he'd said, and it was ten after six and the house was warm, the windows all open, but she was cold and her hands were trembling; that's what that was, it was kind of shocking to see that she was trembling; she'd never seen trembling up close. She put her hands under her arms, under her breasts, the sides of her breasts, held on to herself, arms around herself in a kind of hug.

Ten after six and the carpet scratched at her through the silk slip, sitting in a red silk slip, oh, God. This was all so silly. Jack, call me. How could you make me worry; how could you be so insensitive?

Rachel took a breath, a deep breath, held on to herself and took a deep, deep breath. Okay. Okay. Okay.

He's gone somewhere. "Hey, I'm gonna stop off and see Randy"; "I'm gonna stop off and look at a bike"; "I'm gonna stop off because I have . . . a flat tire"—that's it, maybe he had a flat tire. A flat tire, oh, that's good. A flat tire, two flat tires, four flat tires, car trouble, maybe car trouble. Fabulous car trouble. But why wouldn't he call if he had car trouble, if he had a flat tire and was going to be late, why wouldn't he call? *Three, three-thirty.* She was biting a hole in her lip; he'd say, "What the hell did you do to your lip, Rach?" kiss her, hold her, laugh at her fears; where was he? She could taste the blood.

How could you make me worry? When Dana had started driving, when Ben had started driving, she wanted to throw herself across the front door, not let them go. "Don't make me worry, you understand? You're going to be late, you call me, I don't care what time it is." "Okay, Mom." Intense, looking at them. "Don't *okay* me, I'm dead serious. If you're not going to be home when you said you'd be, call me; don't ever make me sit here and worry about where you are, conjure up horror stories and make myself crazy. . . ." Ben-oh's smirk and tone at the madness of mothers: "Okay, Mom, okay, jeez, chill." Shades of a Dorothy Parker short story—please let him call, please let him call—oh, God, where was he? Goddamn it, Jack. Her eyes circled the office; she got up. Stop it, just stop it; do something. What are you going to do?

Rachel moved into the dining room. Her hand trailed across the round pine table as she circled. *I'm naked. I went to the store like this. Nobody said a thing. I love you. I love you, but I may have to take you into custody for indecent exposure. Go lie down on the dining room table and wait for me. I'll be there by three.* Three, not ten after six, not six-thirty. She remembered dialogue; she was a writer; she remembered; she knew. Rachel went to the phone, dialed. Grace answered on the second ring.

"Hello?"

"Grace?"

"You got me"—a breath—"God, it's the crush of evening. Did you run out of ketchup for the meat loaf or have you lost interest in Dirty Jack?"

"Grace . . ."

"What?" She heard it; she heard the fear; her voice changed. "What's the matter?"

"He's not here."

"What do you mean?"

"He didn't show."

"What?"

She wanted to beat the receiver against the wall. "I mean he's not here; he never got here; he isn't here."

"You mean he's late."

"No."

"Rach . . ."

"He's never late, never. He said he'd be here by three. Three, three-thirty." The tears caught her out of nowhere; she buckled; the sobs caught her out of nowhere. There was no reason for all this drama; he was only a little late. "He doesn't answer the phone . . . I feel like something terrible . . . oh, God . . ."

"Okay, wait a minute. Something came up, he got waylaid, he . . ."

"What? What could come up? Nothing came up . . ." Yelling, angry, yelling and sobbing like a child.

"I'm on my way up," Grace said, and the line went dead.

She ran. Rachel stood in the open door and could hear Grace before she could see her, Grace's breathing as she ran. "Okay, okay," she said, pulling the door shut behind her, "you're hysterical, you're overreacting. Did you have a fight?" Grace bent over at the waist, hands on her knees. "Don't mind me; I'll get my breath back any day now."

"He said he'd call when he passed Jo's; he didn't."

"Who's Jo? Start at the beginning."

Taking her time, taking the moment to present the information so she would be understood, looking at Grace calmly, explaining calmly, taking her time. "He calls every couple of hours on the way down, from the cell phone in the car."

"Okay . . . and he didn't?"

"No, he did; he called to say he was on his way around eight and then he called again when I was at the store."

"And you called him back?"

Rachel nodded.

"On the car phone . . ."

"Yes."

". . . and he answered."

"Yes."

"Okay."

"Okay."

"And everything was perfect."

Rachel nodded.

"Hunky-dory. I can see you were anticipating his arrival by your stunning outfit. Is that a slip or a nightgown?" Rachel inhaled, gave no other response but an inhale and a slow shuddering rush of air out, and Grace mumbled something unintelligible and shook her head. "You haven't talked to him since then?"

"No."

"What time was that? God, I feel like a cop; I feel like Jack; I feel like I'm on *Homicide*. Is that still on?" She watched Rachel bite her lip. "Okay, listen to me: his battery went dead and he forgot the thingy to plug it into the lighter and he doesn't want to stop to make the call; he'd rather keep going so he can get to you; he's hysterical to get to you so he doesn't stop."

"Then where is he?"

"Uh-huh . . ." Her eyes on Rachel. "Okay, he had to stop and do something. He went to see this Jo guy."

"Jo's a place, not a person, and if he stopped to do something why didn't he call? I did all this, what you're doing. I've been going over it again and again since four."

"Okay, let's have a drink."

"Grace . . ."

"Okay, okay, water. Can I at least have a water?"

Rachel followed Grace into the kitchen. "He's never late," she said to Grace's back.

"Car trouble," Grace said, and took a glass out of the cabinet. "Car trouble and he's in the middle of nowhere and his phone won't work. Come on, you're a writer. So, what does he do?"

"Uh . . ." She shrugged, frowned. Grace glared at her. Rachel shook her head. "I don't know . . . he . . . walks?"

"Okay . . ." Grace filled the glass with water and took a big drink. "So he's walking"—she exhaled, patted her lips with her hand—"there's Jack walking"—she gestured, her fingers moving like the tiny legs of a puppet—"he's . . . walking . . . walking, and he'll be here tomorrow . . . say around three . . ." She looked at Rachel. "Three, three-thirty, a day late, no big deal."

Rachel sat in a chair at the table.

"You want some water?" Grace asked.

Rachel shook her head.

"You've definitely lost your sense of humor."

"Yeah."

Grace collapsed into a chair across from her. "What do you think happened?"

"I don't know."

"I know you don't know, *chérie,* but it's clear that besides losing your sense of humor, you've lost your perspective. What do you think happened? Really. Where do you think he is?"

She had no idea. She had no idea at 7:15 when she convinced Grace to go home. She had no idea at 7:30 when she poured herself a large vodka and orange juice. She had no idea at 7:45 when she pulled off the garnet slip and pulled on a T-shirt and jeans. She had no idea at 8:00 when she found herself weeping at the sight of the foil-wrapped uncooked meat loaf on the refrigerator shelf. She had no idea at 8:15 when she found herself sitting on the sink chewing a piece of last night's chicken; two pieces, one in each hand. Or at 8:30 when she poured herself a second drink. She had no idea any and all of the times when she listened to the voice tell her: *the subscriber you have called is unavailable.* Jack could be hurt; he could have had car trouble; he could be walking down a dark road. He could have changed his mind and gone back home; he could have decided that he was finished, that he could no longer do this dance, and he'd driven in the opposite direction for the last time and she would never see him again. Or maybe he'd driven in a third direction, maybe he'd left both of them. Maybe he had a third woman in the middle somewhere and she'd shot him. No, tied him up, drugged him, desperate to keep him there, couldn't stand the fact that he barely had time to see her, what with Rachel and Linda, what with the going back and forth, there was hardly any time left for her. Jealous, in a fury, she'd tied Jack to a chair, barricaded the doors, would keep him kidnapped there until they were all too old. Or maybe something had fallen out of the sky while he was driving, that's right, a big something had crashed out of the sky and smashed through his windshield and cracked him on the head and now he's suffering from amnesia and walking around in *Random Harvest,* and Rachel circled the living room, moved through the hall and back into her office and stood once more, rigid, in front of the telephone, fingers pressed hard against her forehead, thumbs in her temples pressing hard. Rachel had no idea where Jack was at 9:00, but somehow she knew that if he was okay, he would have called her; she knew that more than anything. She picked up the phone.

"Beverly Hills Police Department," the voice said; a woman's voice, oh, it was a woman's voice, soft and kind and unexpected, and Rachel broke, swallowed hard, tried to breathe.

"Beverly Hills Police Department," the woman said again. "Hello?" It was impossible, the whole thing was impossible. Opening the can.

"How can I help you?" the woman said.

Rachel put down the phone, slumped in the chair.

"Do people know about us?" she'd asked him. One of those treasured Sunday afternoons: his eyes on the hockey game and she was working her way through the *New York Times* and she thought how nice it would be if they had friends. She could invite them to dinner, make salmon on the grill. No, steaks. Jack wouldn't eat salmon—where was her head?

"Hmm?"

She had her feet in his lap; she pushed at his middle with her toes, rattled the paper; Jack frowned.

"Jack?"

His hand circling her foot, he turned his head. "Huh?"

"Do people know about us?"

"What people?"

"I don't know . . . people."

"No."

"No one?"

"No . . ." he said quietly, rubbing her foot, looking at her, then, "Steve," he said.

"Steve?"

"Yeah." His thumb working her instep, he turned back to the hockey game.

She knew who Steve was: a cop, Jack's ex-partner, Steve Thorne; they'd worked together for years.

"You told him?" No reaction. "What did you tell him?" Nothing. He kept his eyes on the game, his hand on her foot, but his eyes on Luc Robitaille or one of those guys who was flying down the ice after a puck or something. "Jack?"

"Rach, I'm watching this."

"I see that."

He turned to her, a little anger thing going on in the eyes, the gray eyes moving over her, cold. "What is it?" He pushed the clicker and the TV went off.

"I didn't say you had to turn it off."

"What do you want to know?"

And her heart quickened or something in her chest. Why was she doing this? What was it she needed? She hardly had enough time with him herself. . . . "I just wanted to know if anybody knew."

"Knew what?"

"That we're, you know . . ." The writer who lost her words; what had she begun . . . ?

"You want people to know I'm having an affair?"

"I just . . ."

"What?"

She pushed back against the arm of the couch, tried to straighten herself; his fingers were tight around her foot.

"Do you want me to get a billboard on Sunset?" he said. "A sky-writer? Jack loves Rachel. Is that what you want?"

What did she want—did she want to bring the whole thing to a head? Now on this Sunday, sweet Sunday, is that what she wanted now? "I'm sorry . . ." She tried to pull her foot out of his grasp. "Jack?"

"What?"

"That hurts."

He let go, as if he didn't know he was holding her foot in the first place, he released it, turned his head away. "Steve knows," he said, "that's it."

"Okay," she said softly. Her heart was banging around in her chest and she felt something, what did she feel? "I'm sorry," she said again. Afraid. That's what she felt—fear.

He looked at her. "You want to do this?" he said. "You want to open this can?"

Fear. White fear. No, gray, like his eyes. She loved him; did she want him to leave Linda? Put the cards on the table; just the facts, ma'am. Did she want Jack to choose? She moved to him, turned herself around and up into his lap and his arms and kissed him, didn't answer the question, kissed him and clung to him to smother the fear. She'd never brought it up again.

To ask to have friends was to ask to have a life, a real life with one house and one woman, no back and forth. To ask to have friends was to ask to be a couple, not a couple with an extra wife, extra woman on the side. . . . Let it ride, something inside her said, don't make waves, kid, let it ride. She'd never brought it up again.

Rachel swiveled in the chair, wrapped her arms around her middle, and turned slowly around. Did she want to open up this can?

She'd talked to Steve Thorne twice when he'd picked up Jack's phone when Jack was still at the department, before he'd retired; she'd seen him once. Jack was working something two blocks away and he'd surprised her, knocked on her door. She was writing in her robe; she'd stopped with the morning coffee to check what she'd been working on the night before, and found herself still in front of the keys two hours later, lost in what she was writing, in a black silk wraparound robe and red socks, nothing else. She went to the door like that and there he was.

"Pardon me, ma'am, Beverly Hills Police. We got a call that you were parading around in your underwear. Would you like some assistance getting dressed?"

He'd stayed three minutes; he'd just been around the corner and figured if she was home, he'd say hello. Steve Thorne was waiting in the car. Around Jack's shoulder, as he pulled her to him, she saw the man in the car. "What are you doing answering the door in your bathrobe?" "Your friend is watching," she'd said into Jack's neck, and later he'd told her that the man was Steve Thorne.

Steve Thorne who was married. Linda and Jack used to go out to dinner sometimes with Steve and Mrs. Thorne. Rachel swiveled the chair at the desk. Couples. Mr. and Mrs. Thorne, Mr. and Mrs. North, *Mrs.* North. Maybe Jack had gone home. *The subscriber you have called is unavailable or has traveled outside the coverage area.*

The ice had melted in her drink; you could see the water floating on top of the orange juice, a meltdown of an eighth of an inch. *Hello, Steve? This is Rachel Glass, I live on Elm*—oh, yes, that would help, that would place her, Rachel Glass on Elm . . . for God's sake—*Hello, Steve, this is Rachel Glass. I'm so sorry to bother you, but Jack was supposed to come down today, and he called a few times from the road this morning and said he'd be in by three, but he hasn't gotten here yet and I . . . Rachel, yes . . . Uh-huh . . . Rachel Glass, you remember? . . . Right . . . Jack's girlfriend . . . Yes . . .* Her fingers were back against her mouth; she didn't feel them fly there, but there they were. How could she call Steve Thorne? Jack would be furious. *What were you thinking, Rachel?*

It was twenty to ten. It was twenty minutes to ten, for God's sake. What was she supposed to do? Wait until dawn? The dawn comes up like thunder. *The subscriber you have called is unavailable or has traveled outside the coverage area,* the voice said. "An' the dawn comes up like thunder outer China 'crost the Bay!" Rudyard Kipling said.

It was a quarter to ten. She was frightened. Rachel picked up the phone and opened the can.

Steve Thorne wasn't on—would she like to leave a message on his voice mail? Rachel's mind flew, tried to settle, tried to sort. "No, thank you," she said to the policewoman, but she didn't hang up. Couldn't.

"Can I help you?" the policewoman said.

"I . . ." Rachel ran her hand across her face and picked up a pen.

"Is something wrong?" the policewoman said.

Do it, just do it, like the Nike ad. "I've been waiting for someone, someone who was scheduled to arrive around three-thirty this afternoon, and they haven't gotten here yet and it's nearly ten."

"And you're worried."

"Yes."

"And you feel you have reason to worry?"

"Well, this isn't something they would do . . . not call to explain."

"I see. Well, lots of things can happen to change people's plans. How were they coming?"

"By car." Rachel scribbled on the pad, drew loopy overlapping circles and then J, A, C, K.

"Do you know the route?"

Every inch of it, oh, yes, she could see every inch of it: gas stations, towns, snow on the mountains. "Yes, I know the route."

"Well, if it's on the freeway system, you could certainly call the California Highway Patrol."

"The Highway Patrol," Rachel repeated, pen poised.

"To check for accidents," the policewoman said.

Oh, God. Rachel didn't move, didn't breathe; the policewoman continued, "But things come up, you know, all the time. Is it a family member?"

A family member. "No, he's a friend." God, what was she doing, what was she saying, *a friend*. That was a good one, just a friend.

"I assume you've called his family to make sure nothing changed his plans?"

Well, no, not exactly . . . well, no, how could I . . . Rachel couldn't speak, she said nothing, couldn't get the words out, no words.

"Have you called his family?" the policewoman said.

Nothing.

"Do you know the number?"

Did she know the number? Oh, yes, she knew the number. Rachel said nothing, stood up quietly, and replaced the receiver on the hook.

Julie

HER FATHER WAS in deep shit. Julie scraped the remainder of congealed supper off the plates into the trash. He had no right to tell Tony he could race, no right to even talk to him about it without first discussing it with her and Brian—Tony was their son. She took a knife to a hardened glob of ketchup. Where does he get off pulling that shit? That king-of-the-world attitude like he does with her mother, like everything is up to him.

Will you look at that—what is it with Emmie that she never eats the meat? Little chewed-up bites of hamburger hidden under everything else on the plate. What did she eat? The bun and nothing? The kid is living on milk.

"Mom?" Carey behind her. "What does it feel like when you have a headache?"

"Why?" She put the knife and plate into the sink, wiped her hands on a dish towel, and felt his head. "Does your head hurt?"

"Sort of."

"Go get the Tylenol."

She pushed her knuckles into the small of her back. The next thing you know he'd tell Carey he could race too. Goddamn it. She could be sitting with her feet up if she wouldn't have had to take the time to have a fight with her son. She could be in the bath; she could be in the bed, the kitchen all cleaned, the lights off; she could be sound asleep. And she was going to tell him, he could just take that king attitude and shove it where the . . .

"Mommy?" A little hand clutching her thigh.

"Emmie, sweet Jesus, what are you doing up?"

"We're done with the story."

"You were done with the story a long time ago. Where's your daddy?"

"Sleeping in my bed. I covered him with all my animals."

"Your animals?"

"He was too big for just the dwarfs."

"Mm-hm." Julie crouched down on her heels to listen.

"He didn't fit in green blankie; he stuck out all over."

Her eyes even with her daughter's, she cupped Emmie's little pointed chin with one hand and ran the other through the child's thick black curls.

"I have hair just like Grampa's."

"Yes, you do."

"Black as ebony," Emmie said in a high spooky voice, "skin white as snow."

"Right you are, Miss Snow White," Julie said, crushing Emmie to her chest. "It's time to go to bed."

"I wasn't Miss Snow White, I was the man in the mirror." Emmie said, kissing her mother's ear. "Daddy was making snore sounds."

"I'm sure he was."

"I put two bears on his head but you could still hear. Was Tony bad?"

"No."

"Did you grind him up?"

"Did I what?" Julie yawned.

"She means—is he grounded," Carey said. He handed his mother the Tylenol bottle. "He's in his room all pissed off."

She stood up. "Watch your mouth, buddy."

"What's the matter with that?"

"You heard me."

Emmie kissed her mother several times on the knee, little kisses through her panty hose; she still had on her panty hose, her dress and her panty hose from work—maybe she should just stay dressed for work tomorrow. Would anybody in the crummy office of Gilcrest and Jakowski notice if the supervisor of Accounts Receivable was wearing the same thing?

"Mommy, did you grind him?"

"No, I did not grind him. I just told him he couldn't race."

"Why not?" Carey said.

"Because it's dangerous."

"But Grampa taught him."

"It's still dangerous." She shook two Tylenol tablets out of the bottle into his hand.

"But Grampa said . . ."

"I know what Grampa said. Take those." She handed him a glass of water.

"He's too little to race," Emmie said.

"He is not."

"Carey, take the Tylenol."

"Too little," Emmie said in a singsong.

"Not."

"Mommy said, I heard her, Mommy said."

"Carey," Julie said.

"Is too." Emmie glared up at her brother, egging him on.

"Emmie, that's enough."

"Is not," Carey said, smirking at his little sister.

Julie gave Carey a look; he swallowed the tablets, made a face. She bent down, scooped up Emmie, and took the glass out of her son's hand. "Bedtime, folks." She carried Emmie out of the kitchen and down the hall. She was too tired to have a bath; she'd fall asleep and drown—Brian wouldn't hear her, he had animals on his head. She adjusted Emmie on her hip. "Did you brush your teeth, Carey?"

"Mom, I'm not a baby."

Emmie kissed Julie's nose, little kisses across the bridge of her nose and into one eye.

"Sweetie, wait a minute."

"I'm kissing you. I'm a very good kisser, Grampa said."

"Grampa, Grampa."

"Grampa is my Prince Charming," Emmie said, burrowing her face into her mother's hair. "I'm gonna marry him when I'm a big girl."

"You can't marry your own grampa," Carey said.

"I can too."

"You're nuts; you don't know anything."

"Carey, let her be," Julie said.

"You can't marry your own grampa."

"Grampa said I could." Her lip curling down and the sobs catching her, she began to wail into Julie's neck.

"Sweet Jesus," Julie said.

"Mom, that's cussing."

Emmie's little body heaving. "Go brush your teeth, Carey."

"I did already. I told you."

"Well, do it again!"

"No wonder I have a headache," he said. He kicked the door of the bathroom open, went in, and slammed it closed behind him.

"It's okay, baby," Julie said to Emmie, "it's okay. You can marry your grampa if you want to."

The room was dark except for Emmie's Snow White lamp, a small glow of yellow light. Her husband was asleep on his back, snoring, still wearing his Burt's Plumbing uniform, the sleeves rolled up, the white T-shirt that was mostly filthy showing at the open buttons at the neck. His feet were still on the floor in huge work boots; the rest of him from the knees up was spread diagonally across Emmie's bed, the Spot book in his hand. He was indeed covered. A menagerie of toys lined the tops of his arms and legs—stuffed bears and bunnies and dogs and cats, even a large garish yellow chicken—the seven dwarfs, Emmie's favorites, were crushed together in a mound on his chest. Two bears sat on Brian's face: Brownie was balanced on his forehead, tush down, legs and paws across his closed eyes, and Stinky was sitting on one cheek and ear. As Brian exhaled, the little plush paws of Brownie raised up and down. Julie nearly fell. There was no way to get a camera, no way to record this except in her head, and she was caught, not only by the rising laughter but by the extraordinary sweetness of the gesture, which made her want to sob. Or maybe it was because she was so tired. She stood there, swaying with Emmie, staring at the sight of her husband covered by stuffed animals.

Emmie sagged in her arms—a hiccup, a holdover sob, a few snivels, and she was gone. The weight nearly toppled Julie; she lowered the child to the bed. Emmie rolled over with a whimper, her nose planted firmly in the side of her daddy's upper arm, and Julie took three steps backward and collapsed into the rocking chair. Brian's arm went up and around his daughter; two bunnies and a stuffed puppy fell to the floor without a sound.

Julie felt herself undo, loosen into the cushion of the rocker like someone had let go of her strings. She leaned her head back, her stockinged feet planted directly in front of her on the cool floor.

She hadn't spoken to her father in over two months. Nobody knew that; nobody knew what was going on except Brian, but not really, because although she had confessed to him that she'd said something, she'd left out the details. She and her father had been in the same place twice since they'd stopped talking—once at her mom's birthday, and once at the Labor Day barbecue. There was no way to get out of either and they were both at his house. They had kind of danced around each other both times, didn't speak directly to each other, didn't look directly at each other, just danced around, and the only one who seemed suspicious at these two occasions was her mother, but that was only in the way she had looked at Julie; she hadn't said a word and, of course, her mother was big on keeping her mouth shut, swallowing her feelings and giving you that optimistic smile—which pissed Julie off even more.

The only sticky part was when she'd somehow ended up standing next to him for the birthday photo. The particular smell of his after-shave, his hair goop, the sight of his broad hand on her mother's shoulder—and her eyes had filled. She'd wanted to hit him, but she didn't look at him, just bent around him to kiss her mom.

Julie rocked quietly in the chair.

It was hard to know the boundaries. She was thirty-three years old with three children of her own and maybe Brian was right, that what her father did was none of her business, but somebody had to say something and it certainly wasn't going to be Patty, who fell right into their mother's footsteps and never opened her mouth.

She'd left work that day for what she'd said was an early lunch and then a doctor's appointment—neither of which was true—and she'd waited for him at the last stretch before town. She knew he was on his way back from L.A.; she knew that sound in her mother's voice, the lie sound was how she thought of it, when she'd asked where was Dad, and she knew his schedule; it was routine by now—out of town on a Monday morning, back in town on the Monday after that.

At the last curve as you slowed before Bishop proper, she pulled her car off the side of the road next to the Best Western billboard, where he would spot her for sure. She knew how he left for anywhere before dawn, she'd grown up with it, countless arguments when she and Patty were kids—"Five? We have to leave at five in the morning when it's still dark? Jesus, Mom, talk to him." She counted the hours from L.A. to Bishop, figured when she thought he'd left, when she thought he'd get here, she was only off by twenty-four minutes. The Ford Explorer slowed when he saw her Chevy wagon, when he saw her leaning against it; 395 was quiet, right before noon and quiet; he let a semi pass and then a single car and then he hung a U, pulled up behind her, got out. The tiny frown of concern, the quick step, the physical presence of a take-charge guy, her dad. Once a cop, always a cop, in command.

Julie rocked softly. She realized she was unconsciously moving the chair to the rhythm of Brian's snores. There was a piece of her that thought she probably couldn't get out of the chair. Maybe Brian would carry her to bed the way she'd carried Emmie, once she got the teddy bears off his head.

She'd been wearing a new dress that day, a new dress that she'd bought in Lake Tahoe at a fancy shop that had cost too much money, but she thought it made her look real good so she'd bought it anyway. Black, with an A-line skirt, kind of a flare, actually, like something she'd seen in a magazine, and she wouldn't have been wearing it that day if she'd planned what she wound up doing, but she hadn't planned; it was when she'd talked to her mother, called to talk to her dad and gotten her mother and heard her stall. Heard her lie. "He went to Bakersfield." "Oh? What for?"

"I don't know," Linda said, "something about a bike. I have to go, honey, I'm supposed to meet Angie Saniger."

"I thought you couldn't stand Angie Saniger."

"I can't. I mean, I can when I have to and I have to."

"Why?"

"Julie, I don't have time. I'll call you when I get home."

Fast, clipped, breathless; Linda hung up.

It was the lie voice that drove Julie to wait for her father at the Best Western billboard by the side of the road. The lie voice that fueled her, filled her with such anger she thought she would spit—that her mother had to do such a thing, that her father put her mother in a position to have to do such a thing—because that lie was a lie for him, always for him, everything for him, to protect him, to make sure he looked good. The way he looked when he got out of the car and walked the few steps to her side.

"What's the matter, kid?" His hand on her arm, the hand that taught her how to tie flies, how to shoot, how to play poker, the hand that turned the pages of the book when she was little and he'd read her a story, her little hand on top of his, circling his knuckles round and round with her little fingers—she shrugged it off, ever so gently she shrugged that hand away.

"What are you doing, Dad?"

A half smile. "I'm going home. What are you doing?"

"Where were you?"

His expression didn't change; he didn't answer, just gave her that little smile. The smile she used to love, the smile she craved and waited for, waiting in the driveway for Dad to get home. She was his favorite, his tomboy, his sidekick, and he was her best friend. Patty wanted to stay home and play dollhouse; Julie wanted to go with Dad. She recrossed her arms in front of her breasts, her backside hard against the car; she was not going to cry. She wasn't.

"Why are you doing this to Mom?"

"What do you want, kid?"

"I want to know what's going on."

"I'm coming back from Bakersfield where I looked at a guy's bike."

She was the only girl member of the famous Pescatores. All the rest of the dads and dumb boys had thrown a fit, but he had insisted that she could fish. She could tie a hair's-ear nymph fly; she could lay a dry line under a hanging birch and tease a speckled rainbow halfway into her waders—he'd taught her all of it, and she'd showed them—she was a first-class angler, just like he'd said.

She looked at him. "You're lying. You weren't in Bakersfield."

"Watch yourself, kid."

She was always closer to her father. Patty was just like her mother, and she was just like him.

"What do you do every month in L.A.? Why do you go there?" Gray eyes steady on her, but she held her ground. "You have a woman there, don't you?"

He took a moment, or maybe it was an hour, or maybe it was just the time it takes to inhale—he didn't move, just took that moment staring at her and then he dropped his eyes and turned. "I'm going home."

"Dad, don't do this."

He never said another word. Got in his car, started it, pulled out onto 395, made another U-turn, and took off. Hadn't spoken to her since. And she hadn't spoken to him either. She was so thrown by the intensity of the moment she could hardly get back in her car.

And now he thought he could just bypass her when it came to Tony, tell him he could race without asking. Did he think she was like her mother and would keep her mouth shut?

She got out of the chair, walked quietly to the sleeping Brian, and took the bears off his head. He sighed in his sleep; she touched his cheek with her fingers and whispered his name. She helped him disentangle himself; together they covered Emmie. He stumbled down the hall to check Carey and his headache and Tony and his anger; she went back to the kitchen, finished the dishes in record time, made herself a cup of decaf, sat down at the table, and dialed her dad.

Linda

BY 6:30, SHE'D had supper—in front of the television; she didn't turn it on. Meat loaf, leftover meat loaf sliced cold in a sandwich with pickles and mayonnaise, ketchup on the other side. On white bread. Not store-bought; thick slabs of white bread that she'd baked for Jack the day before, the day before she knew he was leaving. Again.

Who cared? What's the difference anyway?

She'd also had a bag of potato chips. Sour cream and onion. And a glass of milk. And then some Dr Pepper for a little taste of sweet, just a taste, but what did it matter anyway? Was Jack going to give up Rachel Glass if Linda lost ten pounds? Fifteen? Twenty? Maybe she should just cut off a leg.

Linda pressed her fingers against some meat loaf crumbles left on the plate. How much could a leg weigh? There was probably no way to know. No way to know how much a leg weighed, no way to know if Jack would ever give up Rachel Glass. Buddy got up from where he was sprawled under the coffee table, lumbered over, and sat in front of her, giving her the eye. She fed him the little pieces of meat. He licked her fingers and slid back down, let his paws slide out in front of him pushing at the rug. Bella stayed where she was by the front door, asleep on her back, legs against the wall up in the air. Bella was too old to make the walk for meat loaf; she would wait for whatever showed up in her bowl. Linda ran her finger across a blob of mayonnaise on the plate and put it in her mouth.

By 7:00, she'd watched the news. Not that it mattered. What did she care about what was going on in Washington or Kosovo or wherever it was flooding or tornadoing or they were blowing each other up with missiles and guns? What do you really care about that isn't your own? You forget it as soon as you turn off the TV, as soon as you scoop the ice cream into the bowl.

By 7:10, she'd had vanilla ice cream, not in a bowl, four teaspoons standing at the open freezer door. Well, four and a half.

By 7:30, she'd washed the dishes, all of them. The ones from breakfast, the ones from supper, everything she'd let pile up in the sink. She'd washed down the table, sponged the sink countertops, straightened the chairs. By quarter to eight she'd eyed the ironing, let her eyes glide over the recipes waiting to be clipped; by five to eight she'd discarded the idea of doing anything that felt like a chore. By five to eight she'd moved to the bookshelves in the front room, pulled out a photo album, and settled on the couch. Buddy padded across the rug, did his slide step in front of her legs, collapsed flat, resting the bottom of his muzzle on the top of her Keds.

She wasn't afraid of the quiet; she'd spent lots of quiet evenings alone. When they were living in two different places, when the kids were little and he was down in L.A. most of the time, she'd never been one to go where they were invited if he wasn't going to be home. It didn't matter to her to go without Jack; she'd just rather stay home. Even when she was down there with him, and he was a detective, and he'd have to go out on behalf of the department, cover for the chief or the second, because there was nearly always a member of the BHPD invited to what went on in town: cocktails for the Canadian prime minister, a reception for the queen of England—she'd gone to that one; it was at the Beverly Hills Hotel, and Queen Elizabeth was much better looking in person than she was on the news, not that she'd gotten that close to her. She'd told the kids all about it: how you ate sherbet in between the courses and all the different forks and spoons and wines, until her head was floating, because she thought it was just going to be one of those stand-arounds but it turned out to be a sit-down. But most times Linda stayed home. She wasn't like Jack, a people person; she didn't fit. Suze could drag her around the better dress department at Saks Fifth Avenue and gussy her up, but she still felt like Daisy Mae. Jack, on the other hand, looked like one of them. She always thought that's why they asked him to cover, because he could pass for a movie star. He'd always said it was because they lived close, Santa Monica being closer to Beverly Hills than where most cops lived, which was the valley, but Linda was sure it was the way he looked.

She positioned her back against the pillows as if she were cozying up with a juicy book and opened the album to the color wedding photograph of her and Jack. The phone rang.

"Hello?"

"Hey, Linda. So, how were the burgers?" Charlie Eckerts said.

"Good." Linda made a face at Buddy. Well, it was her own fault; she shouldn't have picked up the phone. She should have let the machine get it; where was her head?

"So," he said, "did you have French fries?"

"Jack's not home, Charlie."

"Oh? No?"

"No, he went to take Tony for a ride."

"Oh."

"You want him to call you?"

"Oh, sure. Later. I want to talk to him about Saturday."

"Okay," she said.

"Okay," Charlie repeated.

There was a lull. "So, did you have French fries?" Charlie asked again.

"No, broccoli—salad and broccoli."

"Poor Jack," Charlie said, laughed, and hung up.

Lies.

She closed the album and left it on the arm of the couch. More lies.

By 8:15, she'd had vanilla ice cream again, not in teaspoons in front of the open freezer door but in a bowl. With crushed pecans. And chocolate that she'd melted in the microwave, a piece she'd found all labeled in the freezer, Christmas chocolate that she'd used last year to bake that fancy French cake that looked like a log.

By 8:30, she'd gone round the channels with the remote but nothing had roped her in. How many times could you watch *Casablanca*? How many times could you hear Bogart say, "We'll always have Paris . . ." and see the look on Ingrid Bergman's face when she realizes he isn't getting on the plane, he's giving the transit letters to Paul Henreid instead. How many times could you listen to Claude Rains say, "Rick, this could be the beginning of a beautiful friendship . . ." and see him throw the bottle of Vichy water in the can, and what was she doing lying to Charlie anyway? *He's gone to L.A. to be with his mistress; could he call you back next week?* That's what she should have said. Lying to save face. Lying to a policeman like all the people in *Casablanca* did, and, of course, the policeman in *Casablanca* lied too, wanted the young bride to sleep with him for the transit papers, and if it wouldn't have been for Humphrey Bogart she would have, that was how much she loved her husband, her groom. Linda sat with the empty ice cream bowl in her lap. Buddy was waiting to lick it, waiting patiently; she put it on the floor.

She would have slept with Claude Rains to get the transit papers for her and Jack. She would have. Linda watched the dog lap away all traces of chocolate on the side of the white dish. She still would. Well, that was the problem, wasn't it? She still loved Jack.

By 9:00, she'd gone outside with the dogs. Sat in a lawn chair, just sat. It was warm and balmy; on the news they'd said it was hot as blazes in L.A. The phone rang; Linda didn't move.

L.A.—City of Angels; city of whores was more like it. Rachel Glass probably had air-conditioning; all whores had air-conditioning, after all. The phone rang again. Would Rachel Glass have slept with Claude

Rains for the transit papers? Hey, it was backward, wasn't it? In *Casablanca,* Ingrid Bergman had Humphrey Bogart *and* her husband, she was the one making the choice. This time it was Jack. Jack had the two of them; Jack got to be Ingrid Bergman in real life. Leave it to Jack. Of course, there were extenuating circumstances: the husband in *Casablanca* was a hero; he stood for something—an underground hero fighting for the Resistance—and he had to win; the hero always wins; the cards are on his side. The phone rang again. In real life Linda was Paul Henreid, the husband.

Buddy took off after something, fast, across the lawn and into the dark at the end of the property. Linda stood up. But she wasn't a hero. The phone rang for the fourth time, and the machine clicked on; she couldn't hear it but she knew it had. She wasn't a hero; she wasn't anything.

"Buddy?"

She whistled. What cards did she have on her side? Bella followed Linda's eyes into the darkness; watched intently for maybe thirty seconds and then gave way to the ground.

Linda went in and pushed the PLAY button on the machine. "Hey, Mom, where are you?" Julie said. "I should have called earlier to thank you for the hamburger, but I had this whole thing with Tony and I need to talk to Dad about this bike crap. . . . I *do not* want Tony racing. I don't care what Dad says, I don't want it. . . ." Her daughter took a breath, sighed. She must have had a real wingding with Tony; you could hear the leftover anger in her voice. And exhaustion. "I'm sorry, it's not your problem; it's between me and Dad. So, okay, have him call me, uh, it's nearly ten."

Linda reached for the phone to call Julie and it rang. She picked it up without thinking, as if her hand had a mind of its own, and then she was stuck. "Hello?"

"Hi, Mom," Patty said.

Oh, Lord. "Oh, hi, honey. Can I call you back? I'm watching *Casablanca*."

Hesitation. "Haven't you seen it a million times?"

"Uh-huh. Did you need something? Can I call you tomorrow?"

"Can I talk to Dad?"

"He's out with the dogs."

"Oh. Well, tell him to call me tomorrow, will you?"

"Sure. Okay, I'm gonna go, I don't want to miss the end." Linda put the receiver back on the hook.

Once a month she lied. Her small part in aiding and abetting—lies. Once a month she participated in Jack's carelessness, his slow destruction of their life. Nails in the coffin. That was how it seemed to her.

Linda opened the door for the dogs—Bella meandered in slowly; Buddy raced in with his dirty tennis ball firmly clamped in his jaws. The image of Linda's wedding photo floated in front of her, only in silhouette, the two of them black on white and now a target stapled to the cardboard and metal device, running on the wire forward and backward across the firing range. Jack in his cop stance, the new cop stance, the weaver stance, dominant foot back, two hands in supported position on his nine-millimeter, taking aim. She knew. She'd been there; she'd watched him shoot. The marriage moving from left to right; draw and fire.

And she was a part of it; she could not call herself a victim, she'd seen enough *Oprah,* listened to enough *Dr. Laura;* she was an accessory to the crime. *And what do you do when he comes back after seeing his honey?* Nothing. *You don't tell him it's over? You don't open your mouth?* No.

She had in the old days. A phone number, a receipt, a scribbled name, a word, a slipup, oh, the tiniest omission and she became a detective married to a detective. You had to stick with it; you had to take your time and stick with it, because you knew it was true—and eventually he would see that he was cornered. She would accuse and he would deny. Then he would admit and she would be shattered. Followed by the promises, the groveling, the acceptance, the negotiation, and the reprieve. Interspersed with the Bloomingdale's buyer, the paralegal on Hill Street, the character actress, and the OR nurse. It took its time; it took its toll. Linda got tired.

Dr. Laura would probably hang up on her.

By 10:30, she was in the bath. Down and into the steaming water, cold tile against her back, the luxurious slide into the hot, steaming water, under, feeling her hair spread from the sides of her head, floating out from her face like seaweed. Submerged. Free form. That's how she felt when he was gone, when he was down there in L.A. with her. Floating, suspended, as if she were off the ground, hovering, waiting. It wasn't like Linda was with him all the time; it wasn't like they did anything exciting, went anywhere exciting; it wasn't like they had an exciting life. After thirty-five years of marriage sometimes you don't even talk. Linda sat up and pushed the wet hair back from her face, the water from her eyes. Yes and no and how'd it go and do you want ribs for supper and I'm going to the store and could you bring me a soda when you get up and where are the keys. She looked down at her breasts, slid lower, nipples skimming the shimmering water; she put her feet on the hot and cold. It wasn't like she was attached to him, but when he was gone she just didn't quite know how to be.

How long had it been since she'd put polish on her toenails? Orange polish, that's what she liked, orange. She reached for the soap. Buddy came like a bat out of hell into the bathroom, skidding on the throw rug, just missing the hamper and the sink. The tennis ball in his mouth, he sat at attention by the side of the tub. "No, Bud," Linda said. He eyed her, waited, gave a little whine. She didn't look at him. He left the bathroom, tail down, the ball still in his mouth. Linda circled the soap around the washcloth.

The third time Jack took off for L.A. and didn't come back after breakfast and didn't call for two days, she'd put all of his clothes outside. She had. Folded the shirts in stacks, the arms of the sweaters tucked neatly inside the crease, pants over the hangers, the socks in rolls—all of it spread across the picnic table, the barbecue, the chairs. His leather jacket, his blues (that he could still get into from when he was a rookie, which pissed her off, since she couldn't get into anything that she'd bought even last year), his two suits, four sport jackets, good slacks, his sweats, jeans, T-shirts, his gym shoes marching behind his loafers marching behind his dress shoes marching behind his work boots, his good boots, his cowboy boots, in step with what Patty used to call "Daddy's cop shoes"—black and brown oxfords with thick soles and laces—his ties slung over the backs of the chairs moving softly like flags, it seemed to Linda, like going to the fair. Belts in coils, baseball hats, the bills bent just so, handkerchiefs—Jack always carried a white handkerchief just like his dad—his navy down jacket, his down vest, his yellow slicker, and his cashmere scarf, the one she'd gotten him for his fortieth birthday, when they'd gone to dinner at the Cock 'n' Bull on Sunset and she'd had too much wine, and he had to stop the car, pull over, because she thought she was going to throw up. And his gloves. Driving gloves and work gloves and the soft caramel leather ones he'd gotten from the kids. And his jewelry box. Not that there was much in it—a couple of old tie clips, some shirt studs, a pair of gold cuff links he'd gotten from Steve and Irene Thorne when he retired, which didn't make any sense because he didn't have a shirt with French cuffs, the good watch he hardly ever wore unless it was somebody's birthday or a wedding or a funeral, his ID bracelet from high school that he'd given her when she was seventeen. All of it in neat piles, as if she were setting up for a yard sale; she could have put little tags on each and every item, negotiated like they did in dusty countries where they wore turbans and robes. *Oh, no, that was his father's. Oh, yes, he got that from his children. Oh, no, I'm sorry, but that's at least three dollars; it's very old.* An antique. No, vintage, that's what they said now.

Linda ran the soapy cloth over her shoulders.

But then it had rained. She'd carried it all back in, everything. Back and forth, the screen door slamming with each trip. At first she'd just watched the clothes from the window, watched it coming down, flattening everything. Rain dripping off the baseball cap bills, bouncing off the toes of his good shoes.

Linda resoaped the washcloth and washed under her arms.

She'd put everything back in the drawers wet—the shirts, the sweats, the sweaters, all smelling like wet lambs—he'd never said a word.

She scrubbed her knees, her toes, her heels, her ankles. When they were first married, Jack had taken the washcloth, lathered it, and washed her as if she were a child. On his knees at the side of the tub, bent over her body. So loving. Each and every part of her with such care. She didn't know people did that. She had cried. Things were different now.

She leaned forward, turning on the hot, rinsing the washcloth. People don't do those things after they're married a long time. "Does Your Husband Still Give You a Bath? Has Your Lovemaking Gone to Pot?" the third article in a series by Linda North. She turned off the faucet, leaned back, spread the hot terry cloth flat across her chest. It felt good, like someone had their open hand on her. Not that they didn't make love, because they did; Jack still had a passion for her, she knew that; you can't kid yourself about somebody having a passion. But it was routine. And there was no way she could turn it into something else, entice him as if she were new and fresh and someone else; she would lose if she tried to compete. She didn't have to read some article to figure that out. Like that game they'd played with the kids where you had to say what color a person was, what kind of food. "Their essence, Carey," Tony had said with a smirk to his brother, and Jack had said, "Essence, huh?" laughing—across the kitchen from her, downing a glass of water, his T-shirt damp and splattered with car oil, a piece of hair across his forehead like one of the kids. She loved to look at him, still loved to look at him. "Macaroni and cheese," Jack said, wiping his mouth with the back of his hand. "Who's mac and cheese?" Carey said, looking up from the tower he was building on her kitchen floor. "Your grandma," Jack said, "that's who." Macaroni and cheese. Comfort food. She knew. The good old light in the window, the warm hearth, that's what she was to him. And Rachel Glass was probably some fancy French dessert or that Moroccan thing that she'd seen in *Bon Appétit* with the dough and the powdered sugar around the chicken. Of course, the Moroccans used pigeon. Not that she would, because it sounded horrible, but it was probably delicious. Lobster, very expensive lobster. Or sushi. Not that Jack liked raw fish, but, oh, she knew the gist of it. Who wanted macaroni and cheese when they could have the taste of something new and thrilling? You only want macaroni and cheese when you need to feel home.

She had slept with only one man. One man only. Her husband. Her one and only husband who was having an affair. The phone rang. Linda sat up; the washcloth slid into the water, cool air hitting her chest, her breasts. It was nearly 11:00; she'd already talked to the girls—who would call now? She put her hand on the rim of the tub, pushed herself up, got out, reached for the towel. Three rings and it stopped before the machine got it; it stopped. You couldn't even have a bath.

She stood there, waiting for it to ring again. Probably Charlie. She slid the towel around her legs, her knees, her arms, her stomach. No, Charlie wouldn't call this late. She wrapped the towel around her middle, tucking one edge into the fold, sarong-style. Dorothy Lamour. And what was she going to say to Charlie tomorrow? Her feet were wet; she reached for another towel. Maybe she just wouldn't answer the phone tomorrow. Maybe she'd go someplace, take a trip. She'd never done that—alone. Maybe she wouldn't be home when Jack got back. Maybe she'd stay away longer than he did. Linda rubbed at her hair with the dry towel. She could do that. Maybe he'd drive up and walk into a cold house, an empty house. "Hey, Linda, where are you?" walking from room to room. "Where the hell is she?" Jack would say. To no one. She eyed herself in the mirror. Maybe she'd drive to Las Vegas, pick up somebody, have an affair.

Linda laughed out loud; the towel around her middle fell to the floor.

Cesarean scars. Cellulite. Fat. Fat chance that she would ever cheat on Jack. She couldn't be with another man. She wouldn't. You'd think her anger would have squashed her love, but it hadn't—she still loved Jack and he still loved her, Rachel Glass or no Rachel Glass. She knew that in her heart. "I love you, babe," he'd say, and give her that look. She knew. The phone rang; she took off after it, colliding into Buddy, fur and paws, and she tripped and he whined, but she got it, picked it up right after the second ring in the bedroom on Jack's side of the bed. The clock on the nightstand flipped the red numbers up into a perfect 11:00. News at eleven, Linda thought, and why did she suddenly feel better? Silly and naked and damp and breathless but not so sad, not at this moment, nearly laughing. "Hello?"

"Linda?"

"Yes?" She didn't recognize the voice, a woman's voice she didn't recognize. Buddy dashed into the room, like the chase they had played when he was a puppy, skidding around the door frame. Linda smiled and held out her hand. "Who is this?" she said.

"Linda," the woman said again, but not a question this time, just her name, just *Linda,* and then she stopped and Buddy barked; she caught the fur of his neck in her fingers. "Who is this?" Something, a chill, probably because she was naked, running around naked, cold.

"Rachel Glass," the woman said.

Rachel Glass and, oh, her heart heaved, Rachel Glass calling her house at eleven, Rachel Glass and Jack, and she must have let go of the dog as he jumped, knocking her backward, tumbling her backward, his nails leaving red rake marks across her bare flesh.

Jack broken in her head, on the gurney of an ambulance, sirens and lights and gray, or from a heart attack, at the foot of the stairs, or behind the wheel, a wreck, a blowout, across a table, in Rachel Glass's bed, dead, dying, shattered, smashed, hurt, bloody—Buddy's tongue across her nose, tail wagging, Linda pushed him, smacked him hard away from her, a whimper from both of them as they fell.

Naked, clutching the fur of the dog and the phone across Jack's pillow, the shock of Jack's aftershave on the pillow slip, the sound of that woman's voice, and Linda fell.

Rachel

I'LL MISS YOU," he'd said, "but I have to go." Two years ago, when he'd announced he was going to retire, leave L.A. "I have to do this, Rach."

"Hey, talk about being geographically undesirable," she'd said as a joke, a bad joke, into his chest where he couldn't see her eyes, where he wouldn't see her face shatter, holding on to him, her face burrowed into that place at the bottom of his throat. He'd been taking off his shoes: big, silly oxford shoes with thick crepe soles; she'd made a lot of jokes about those shoes. Bent at the waist, sitting on the foot of her bed, untying the laces, and she was sitting next to him pulling off her boots. The lush of a sweet afternoon, the quiet, the two of them taking what they could get, talking while they undressed, getting undressed in the middle of the afternoon because they only had an hour and a half. Sometimes an hour and a half, sometimes twenty minutes. Before Jack had retired, Rachel had rarely had him for whole days and whole nights; they took what they could get—an afternoon here, a morning there, a couple of hours on a Thursday in between. And it was ill-timed, perhaps, impulsive, oh, a hasty move on his part to tell her then that he was going, to tell her at that moment that he was going, but perhaps he was lulled by the comfort of the moment, the two of them so natural, so easy together, because they were easy together, and somehow it spilled from him in that ease, that warmth, and out of nowhere, his hand on her arm, his frown, his voice guarded and gentle, he told her he was retiring, leaving L.A.

It wouldn't be bad, he'd said, only six hours, seven, he'd said, if you kept your foot to the pedal, he'd said, a piece of cake. "I'll come to you; I'll come down whenever I can."

She couldn't imagine. "Come down for how long?"

"Days . . . I don't know. I'll work it out; I'll come down."

"But where will you say you're going?"

"I'll work it out. I love you."

"But, Jack . . ."

"Rach, I promise. I'll never leave you for too long; I'll come down."

He didn't have a plan then, she knew that later; he had no plan. He didn't want to give her up so he said he'd work it out. And she believed him. Or she went along with it because what else was she going to do? She wasn't ready to end it. No. Sell the house and move in closer proximity to wherever he was going? No. Madness. Give him an ultimatum? No. Not then. Ever?

Rachel sat motionless in the dark.

She had never given Jack an ultimatum. She'd just let it go on, one week into another, one foot before the other, another month, two, six, until it became a routine. He retired; the department threw him a party that she didn't get to go to; good-bye, good-bye, I love you, and he drove away. Standing in the street watching the taillights, like in one of those country songs. It took him three months to work it out, three months of phone calls and promises until he came back down. He stayed two days. It took him two months the second time to come back. He stayed five days. And little by little they settled into a routine—he settled, she settled, and *she* settled, the three of them settled for whatever this was.

Her clock was really loud; she'd never realized. Rachel lifted her head from her hands; she could feel the finger marks, red finger marks the length of her face. She sat back in the chair, the creak of the chair in between the ticks of the clock—midnight—she stood up. Her legs weren't shaking now. She walked into the dark kitchen, stood at the sink, turned on the tap. Yellow lights through the window painting the garden, glossy lemons in the moonlight. She cupped her hands under the cold water; she felt very old as she stood there looking out the window at the dark and the light. Very old and very tired, as if she could shatter like a china cup.

What time did he leave and what time was he supposed to get there and what that all meant. In words now like type across a page, black type spelling out the horror across the crisp white page. The words that had never been said, the in-between-the-line words, like the looking-the-other-way. What time did he call and what did he say and what that meant to the other woman on the other end of the line. Who hung up. After the details, after the cold facts hit her like the cold water in Rachel's hands. After Rachel had said, "I don't know what to do," Linda had said, "I do," and the line went dead.

Rachel had sat with the phone in her hand listening to the disconnect, the photograph fuzzy in the developing fluid and then coming clearly to life in Technicolor to go with the black-and-white words; Linda, with all of her edges now, all of her lines, her wrinkles, the sunbaked skin, the extra weight, the dishwater hair, all coming into focus now, no longer soft. Linda, of the golden batter biscuits and homespun. Linda, who could put up siding and ride horses and dirt bikes and make curtains and jam. Linda, who knew what to do; Linda, who was calling someone; Linda, who would find out what had happened and where he was. Linda, Jack's wife.

Rachel lifted her hands, drank some of the water, let the rest run down her neck and her shirt. Wet cotton against her breasts, rivulets of water like fingers against her skin. She had cried; Linda hadn't. She had known something was wrong for hours; Linda was just getting the news.

"What time did he say he'd get there?"

"Three, three-thirty."

Quiet, breathing. Was it her breath or Linda's? Whose intake of breath did she hear?

"When was the last time he called?"

"Around ten-thirty, eleven this morning." After she'd gone to the store, she was thinking, when she was putting away the groceries like she'd told Grace, like she'd gone over it again and again in her head, but she didn't say that to Linda, just stood there clutching the phone, answering the questions as Linda asked.

"Was he at a gas station?"

"No, he called from the cell phone."

Quiet, a beat of quiet, and then Linda said, "The cell phone?" and Rachel knew then that the cell phone had been a secret. Jack had never said the cell phone was a secret, that he hid it; why hadn't he said? Silence, both of them thinking, both of them adding it up in their heads. Of course, now what did it matter? Now that the can was open, what did it matter what came out?

"He didn't call again?"

"No."

"Did you try to call him?"

The wife knowing that the girlfriend had a way to call her husband, a way the wife didn't have. "Yes," Rachel said, "but he didn't answer; he hasn't answered all day."

The dog whimpered. Rachel could hear a dog; she knew there was a dog, two dogs. She'd seen their pictures in front of the house: huge white things with big black noses and big black eyes. Great Pyrenees mountain dogs or great mountain Pyrenees dogs, beautiful, huge. She knew what the house looked like—a ranch house from the suburbs—rough gray stone and splintering wood. Not beautiful, Rachel thought, not beautiful like the dogs. Winter, spring, summer, and fall—Jack with the wraparound throwaway camera. "Hey, Rach, want to see the house?" Look at the snow, look at the blossoms on the pear trees, look at the dogs. "Hey, Rach, take a look at this," he would say, pulling the snapshots out of his back pocket where they had curved to the shape of his butt.

"I called the police," Rachel said. Linda's breath, definitely Linda's breath across the wire, "and they told me to make sure he wasn't still home."

"Well, he's not."

Hard, hurting, cold, scared, and now it was both of them, both of them scared. "I know, I mean, I had to make sure. . . ." Quiet. Rachel's hand wet on the phone; she had to do this. "He would have called," Rachel said, "he wouldn't do this . . . not call."

Broken now, but not crying. "No," Linda said, "he wouldn't do this, no."

"I don't know what to do," Rachel managed to get out.

"I do," Linda said, and hung up.

"You're out of the loop," Grace said. "You're out of the loop now; it's up to her, Rach, go to bed." The air was still warm, her skin was still cold—cold, icy arms. "But how will I know what happened? If he's okay? How will I know?"

"You won't."

Rachel turned off the water, crossed the dark kitchen, the dining room, flipped the lights off in her office and down the hall.

"You're not the wife, you're not the next of kin, you can't do anything until someone calls you, which will probably be tomorrow. . . . Of course, my expertise is based on whatever Ed McBain wrote for the Eighty-seventh Precinct, whatever Scudder did in all of Larry Block's books before Scudder drank himself out of his badge, but it's got to be the same in real life"—Grace spoke in a rush and inhaled, not breath but cigarette—"whatever is procedure, that's what they'll do now."

She wasn't the wife; Rachel knew she wasn't the wife. What was the point of Grace's bringing that up now?

Grace exhaled again into the telephone, a long exhale. She was smoking in the house at midnight, which meant either Dickhead wasn't home or she was hiding downstairs, smoking in the kitchen, blowing the smoke out of the window so he wouldn't know, which ordinarily would have gotten a rise out of Rachel, the whole thing would have gotten a rise out of Rachel; she would have asked, she would have gotten into it—*Why are you smoking, Grace?*—but she said nothing, she had nothing left; she was riding on empty from the moment Linda had hung up.

"She'll have to file a missing persons," Grace had said.

"A missing persons?" Her pulse in her ears. *I'll miss you, Rach, but I have to go.*

"Well, he's missing, isn't he?"

No words; there were no words. Could a pulse be that loud?

Grace inhaled, exhaled. "He's not here, he's not there—that's missing, *chérie—n'est-ce pas*?"

Missing. *I'll miss you, Rach, but I have to go.*

I'll miss you, he'd say on the mornings that he would leave, the once-a-month mornings when he would leave to make the drive back home. *I'll miss you* was the last thing he'd say. Backing down the driveway, his hand raised, watching his hand disappear as he turned the corner at the end of the block.

I miss you, she'd say every day when he called. *I miss you, Jack. I miss you too, Rach,* every day.

She had changed hands, her fingers too tight around the telephone. An exchange of places. Linda, the wife, would file a missing persons; Linda, the wife, would know everything. Rachel, who was out of the loop, would not.

"Go to sleep," Grace said. "Try to sleep."

"Sure."

"Do you want something? A Valium?"

She shook her head.

"Rach?"

"No."

"Do you want me to come up?"

"No."

"Call me in the morning when you get up. Call me if you hear anything. Call me if he calls."

But she didn't think he would, Rachel could hear that; Grace didn't think Jack would call. She knew something was wrong; she just didn't want to say it. To say it out loud—more type across the page—to say it out loud was to accept the possibility that it could be so. The click of the lighter, Rachel could hear that too, the flip and click of Grace's lighter as she hung up the phone.

There would be no sleeping, Rachel thought, no sleep for the wicked. No, it was peace. *No peace, saith the Lord, unto the wicked.* Isaiah.

Rachel grabbed hold of the banister. Oh, please, God, help me; please let Jack call.

Patty

IT WAS AFTER midnight; why was she rolling around? Patty turned over, away from Kevin, fixed the blanket so that it covered her shoulder, gave her pillow a push. It was probably just as well that her father was out with the dogs when she'd called. She rearranged her legs, the left leg on top of the right, and then changed them back again. A perfect example of what Mike had told her about thinking things through—and she hadn't or she wouldn't have called. Until tomorrow.

She sighed, lifted her cheek, smoothed the pillow slip, and resettled. What was that thing she'd read—about how there's a way you can relax each part of your body one piece at a time, starting with your feet. Or was it starting with your head? Oh, for goodness' sake, by the time she did her whole body the baby would be trying to get out of the crib.

How had she expected to talk to her dad with her mother sitting right there? It was the fact that Kevin wasn't home, that's why she'd gone ahead and called, not waited until tomorrow. What a stupid move. If she kept thrashing around she was going to wake Kevin—which would also be a stupid move.

It had just been such a shock to see him.

Why didn't she just get up? She could read; she had a stack of books from the library; trying to keep yourself still when you want to turn over is torture.

You do not expect to run into your father when you're doing something bad. No, not bad, she hadn't done anything bad, it was just something she didn't need to discuss with anybody; it wasn't like they were hiding or anything. She wasn't going to do anything bad, she wasn't stupid, and she didn't even know if her father had seen her; he hadn't called. She'd raced back home to see if he'd left a message so she could erase it, but there was nothing there.

A cup of coffee, that's all it was, and there was nothing bad about meeting Mike for a cup of coffee. Really. She was allowed to have friends, wasn't she? A new friend, a man friend. Wasn't she allowed to have a man friend in her life? Really—she was an old married woman, a mother—what was the big deal? She just wished she would have seen her dad before she'd met Mike for coffee rather than after so she could have discussed it with him—whether she should say something to her dad, mention it—because wasn't it better to say, *Hey, Dad, I saw you in front of the mini-mart down in Big Pine; isn't that funny? Did you see me too?* Because wasn't it better to bring it up before he did, before he said something to her mother like, *Hey, I saw Patty down in Big Pine. What was she doing in Big Pine?* and then her mother would call and ask her what she was doing in Big Pine, and then what? And wasn't it better to say something to him before he left a message on the machine that Kevin would pick up—*Hey, kid, I saw you in Big Pine today*—that wouldn't go over so good. *What were you doing in Big Pine?* Kevin would ask. If it wasn't for a message from her father, he would never ask her where she was. She saw a movie once on TV where the man and wife ate this beautiful supper and asked each other about their day. It was wonderful. She didn't even remember what the story was about or the rest of the movie; she only remembered that scene. Fat chance with Kevin; he never asked her anything.

She turned onto her back.

What could she say she was doing in Big Pine? Visiting Pamela Jean would have worked if Pamela Jean hadn't moved down to L.A.

She wondered if she'd mentioned to her mother that Pamela Jean had moved. No, that wouldn't work anyway—Kevin knew. And it wouldn't be good to say one thing to her mother and another thing to Kevin. Not that they talked a lot, but still.

Mike would have known what to do; he was so smart about things, insightful, probably because he was so well read. She usually only read fiction, sometimes a biography about a woman, someone she admired, like Eleanor Roosevelt, and once she'd read a book about Clara Barton, who was the first nurse, but Mike had probably read everything. Being a teacher and all, coming from someplace important. She couldn't imagine; she'd never even been to New York, to the Bronx, which was where he was from. The Bronx. It sounded so exotic. He said it wasn't, but still. The Bronx, Bishop. Really.

She was a hick. Well, she was. It didn't matter if she tried to keep up—being from New York and being from Bishop, California, certainly isn't the same thing. She hadn't seen half of what he had.

She was a thirty-year-old hick with a baby, finally a baby after all these years, and a husband that she'd had all these years, and it was clear to her now that she'd married too young. Before she'd found herself; before she even knew who she was or what she might be. She hadn't even thought about it—where she could have gone, what she could have done.

She could have gone to New York, to the Bronx. She probably wouldn't have, but still. She'd never even thought about it. Like she wasn't allowed to think about it, wasn't supposed to. Just stay put, marry Kevin, don't go looking for any dreams. Not that she had a particular dream in mind, but somehow it seemed to her she didn't even know she could have one, deserved to have one. Now why was that? Maybe Mike was right, maybe she should get some therapy. She didn't even know if there were therapists in Bishop. She would look in the phone book.

The way she figured, she was just like her mother, getting hooked when she didn't know what was what. Not that she didn't love Kevin, but that wasn't the point. She rolled on her side away from him.

What was the point? And what was her father doing in Big Pine?

She pushed at the pillow with as little movement as possible, tried to find a new place for her head. This was impossible, thrashing around; why was she so jumpy? It's not like her dad had called, it's not like he'd left a message that he saw her when she drove by, and she hadn't done anything. Just had a cup of coffee, a wonderful conversation. What was the big deal?

Her father had a cup of coffee in his hand, in front of the mini-mart, sauntering back to his car—that's how she thought of him, sauntering—he was a sauntering kind of guy, taking a swig of the coffee as she drove by.

She'd certainly had a good time; Mike certainly had things to say. A real view on things. She thought she also had a view on things; she wasn't so sure about Kevin. No, she did know about Kevin: he didn't have a view. He was kind of either-or, whatever anybody else wants, don't make a fuss. Sometimes she wanted to hit him. *What do you want for supper? I don't care, babe.* Like Saturday when she got so upset. *Do you want to eat Mexican? I don't care. I didn't cook, what do you feel like? I don't care. Kevin?* It made her teeth hurt. *Kevin? What?* Sitting there in front of that television like a big joke. He probably didn't even know which teams were playing; he probably didn't even care. As far as she knew he didn't care about anything. Did he care about her? She didn't even know.

Mike cared. Not about her, about things. Things in the newspaper, things on the news. Issues. It was exciting to talk about real things, to have a real discussion about something important, not about the garage door, or should they do the roof or shouldn't they, or what difference did it make if he didn't care what she made for supper. Really.

Okay, maybe Mike did care about her a little. He did seem awfully happy that she'd called, happy when she said she could meet him for coffee, happy to see her; he was. She could tell. She had actually lost five pounds, maybe even six, not that she had a scale or would even stand on one if she had it, but she could tell from her pants, the waistband of her good jeans, whether they cut into her when she sat. She'd put off calling him for nine days after he'd asked her at the library thing to go for coffee, not that it was for a specific day, he didn't say, *Hey, why don't we go for coffee on the eighteenth?* he'd just said, well, *Call me the next time you're down in Big Pine; we'll have a cup of coffee. I'd love to hear your ideas for the book drive.* Her ideas. And it wasn't like he'd asked anybody else who was there. He didn't ask Anna Marie, who was very good looking and skinny, although her hair was fried—he didn't ask her—or Anneke Neustadt, who had that terrific body from doing all that yoga and eating microbiotic or whatever it was that she did—he hadn't asked her. He'd asked Patty, and she'd vowed then and there to lose the weight. Five pounds—no bread, no cookies, not even bits of what the baby left in her high chair. And no macaroni, not with red sauce or with cheese, no noodles whatsoever. And no pie. Her passion was pie, but she'd held out, actually baked twice for Kevin, an apple and a chocolate cream, and she didn't touch one crumb. Five pounds, she thought, from the way her pants fit.

Three pairs of pants were in the running: black pants that went with her old suit, but they seemed too dress-up; some cords she had from before she was pregnant, but they were too short, no matter what she saw in the magazines, the cut of her cords was wrong to be that short; and her good jeans. She had to get into her good jeans; that was the plan. She didn't want to look like meeting him was terrifically important or like meeting him was the same as going to the grocery store—it had to be something in between, something simple but special, and she'd settled on the good jeans with a sweater, her only good sweater, and it was really not cold enough for a wool sweater but she thought it looked chic. Like something one would wear in the Bronx. Unfortunately, it wasn't black; she knew that's what most New Yorkers wore, black to everything; her sweater was navy and a little pilled in a few areas, but she'd worked on it with Scotch tape rolled around her hand. Thank God he didn't know that she was slick with sweat under the sweater, between the itchy wool and the coffee and the conversation and the excitement of just being out, and being thought of as someone that he'd even want to have a conversation with was very exciting. She knew her face was flushed. Seeing as how he was a teacher and all and had been to graduate school and had a master's and God knows what else. Well, maybe not exciting, but certainly the highlight of her week. Month. Forever.

The phone call had been hard. She wasn't sure if the number he'd written on the paper napkin was his apartment or some number at the Big Pine high school, and she wasn't sure if he was married. He didn't say he was married; he wasn't wearing a ring, and it shouldn't have mattered anyway, because it wasn't like she was a bimbo—they were only going to talk about the book drive—but she was a little nervous that some woman might answer when she called. She hadn't. He hadn't answered either, it was a machine, his voice on a machine, but he didn't say, *Hi, this is Mike and Martha,* or any two names, he just said, *Hi, this is Mike Britain; leave me a message and I'll call you back.* Not that she had left a message, because then he would have had to call her back. She'd just waited until after supper last Friday and told Kevin she'd watch a movie with him if he'd go get it, even if it had guns, and then she'd called as soon as Kevin took off for the video store. She'd tried to sound nonchalant. Like she was always running around having coffee with men.

"I'm going to be in Big Pine on Monday. I have to go to the doctor."

"Oh, I hope nothing's wrong."

She shouldn't have been so specific. "No, just a checkup, actually; it's my teeth." So why hadn't she said the dentist? She nearly dropped the phone.

"Hey, that's great. What time?"

"Uh, well, nine, or eight-thirty, I'm not really sure; I have to call." Oh for goodness' sake, she should have figured this out ahead of time.

"Well, I have a break at ten. I could meet you for an early lunch." He laughed.

She laughed too; she wasn't sure what to say so she'd laughed.

"How about ten at the Griddle?"

"The Griddle. Okay."

"You can tell me what you're reading."

"Okay."

"Great. I'll see you then."

He hung up. She wasn't even sure if he'd caught her good-bye. She went to the drugstore early Saturday morning with the baby and bought Judith Krantz's new book and Danielle Steel's too, because she wasn't sure which, and she'd ended up reading the Judith Krantz, but it had never even come up. There were too many other things to talk about. He was divorced.

Kevin moved, slid toward her, flopped his leg over hers.

Oh God, how could she lie in bed next to her husband and think about another man? She put her hand on Kevin's leg; he made an *um* sound.

And then it occurred to her. Did her dad have a woman in Big Pine? Is that what he was doing there?

Patty's eyes went wide.

Julie said it was L.A., that Daddy had a woman in L.A., she was sure of it, she said; but Julie always acted like she had all the information, and most of the time Julie was full of it. Miss Superior, Miss Authority, Miss Everything, like everything she said was gospel. If Julie told her one more time about how she was supposed to take the bottle away from the baby now, one more time about how she was supposed to begin with the potty training, she would hit her with the goddamn potty. Just because Julie had three kids didn't make her an authority on diddly-squat, because all babies were different; she'd read that. All those books she'd checked out from the library, all those professors from Harvard and Princeton, said the same thing—that your baby wouldn't necessarily do what other babies do at the same time. Like sitting up. Julie nearly made her crazy about sitting up. "She should be sitting up." "Not necessarily." "Oh, yes, she should." In that tone, as if there were something wrong with Patty Cake's spine, as if her only baby was going to be a cripple; she'd practically lost her mind. Running back and forth to the pediatrician, propping the baby up against a mound of pillows and watching her slowly slide to the side. Awful. The baby sat up when she was ready; she sat up just fine. And she should have known better; she knew how it was when her sister got that tone. Talk about having a view on things. *Hold on to your guns,* she had to say to herself when Julie started in.

Just because Julie was the oldest—where did she get off?

Kevin moved his leg off hers, turned over, pushed his butt up against her back.

And Julie's superior attitude about Daddy and what he did. Dad's having an affair; Dad's running around; Dad's cheating on Mom. Like she had proof. She had no idea what Dad was doing—unless she was following him around.

Patty sighed and turned onto her back. And where does Julie get off making it all his fault? That's not what the experts say. It takes two to tango; she certainly knew that, and she certainly knew about living with someone who has no point of view—it could make you want to bash their head in, make you do lots of things you never thought you'd do, and Mom is just like Kevin. Don't make waves; don't worry about me; whatever you all want to do is fine. You wanted to punch her. Maybe Dad just has to get away from her sometimes and be with people who have a point of view, who have real ideas and talk about them, people who have something to say. After all, he must miss work; he was always working until Grandma got really sick and Mom made him retire. Always in the drama. Now he had practically nothing to do. Sitting in that house listening to her—whatever anybody else wants, never mind about me—it could make your teeth hurt; it could make you want to scream.

Patty rolled back to her side, pushed at the pillow, and recrossed her legs.

And look how Mom had let herself go. She certainly wasn't giving up pie. And she wouldn't get her hair cut. It was too long and pulling her face down, and she walked around in those old pants and sneakers and never tried in the slightest way to fix herself up. Even when he took her to Tahoe for New Year's she looked like an old shoe.

And if Julie was right, if Daddy had been fooling around on and off since they were little, why hadn't Mom told him to leave? Why did she go on with it? Eleanor Roosevelt wrote: "If someone betrays you once, it is his fault; if he betrays you twice, it is your fault."

Patty turned over. She had to remember to use that in a conversation next week when she met Mike.

"For cripesakes, Patty," Kevin boomed from behind her, "I gotta be at the site at dawn, and you're rolling around like a goddamn pinball."

Linda

Charlie Eckerts pulled into the driveway and cut the engine. Linda stood at the top step of the porch. "It's okay, Buddy," she said to the dog's low growl. He looked at her, looked at the car, then sat back down.

The dawn was thick and soft, pink-orange streaks up into the lavender—a perfect dawn, as if it were the start of a perfect day. Linda held tightly to a hot mug. Charlie's long legs and boots swung out from the white Blazer; he unfolded himself from behind the wheel and stood up. He was wearing his hat. That's what got to her, that he was wearing his hat, that it was official; she must have moved her hand; some of the coffee splashed out of the cup near her foot. Charlie quietly shut the door of the Blazer as if there were still kids at home that he could wake; he adjusted the brim of his green Mono County Sheriff's baseball hat and hiked up his pants. Head down, he crossed the wet grass; he didn't look at her. She took a step forward; Buddy stood up again. "It's okay," Linda said softly to the dog. Buddy whimpered, stayed steady at her side, his eyes on the man.

"Linda," Charlie said.

She thought he was going to tip his hat; if he tipped his hat she would fall off the porch. "Do you know something? Have they found him?"

"No, ma'am," he said. She dropped the mug; it bounced off Buddy's back, hot coffee soaking the white fur; the dog whined and jumped and the mug made a thunk sound as it hit the wood. She lost it. Charlie took the three steps and reached for her; she collapsed into his chest. Buttons and the ice of his badge scraping her face; she was sobbing; Buddy was barking. "Come on, Linda, it'll be okay; it's okay," Charlie said.

"Where is he?" she cried into his jacket.

"We'll find him," Charlie said.

He opened the front door with his arm around her and moved her into the house. "I didn't cry all night," she said, wiping her face on her sleeve.

"Sit down," he said. "I'll get you a Kleenex."

"I burned the dog," she said, weeping into the flannel of Jack's plaid shirt. She had it on over her T-shirt, Jack's red plaid shirt.

"Linda," Charlie said, half pushing her onto the couch, "just sit down."

She'd been waiting for dawn, walking the house room by room, hoping she wouldn't have to dial the number, that Jack would call, that he would have arrived at Rachel Glass's house with a story, a big, fat story about what had happened on the road. Then the fear could slide up into anger, where it belonged.

Charlie lumbered off toward the bathroom. "I haven't been here since Jack burned up all those ribs." The Fourth of July; they'd had a big barbecue with a bunch of people the Fourth of July. Jack was always home for holidays, even if it was his week to go to L.A.; he'd move the trip forward or back, if it was a holiday for sure he'd be home. Thank God for small favors, she used to think.

Buddy pawed at the door from outside. Bella got up from under the coffee table and looked to Linda to let in her son. Charlie returned with a fistful of toilet paper, one end of it fluttering in front of his gun in the holster; he handed it to her. "No Kleenex." He gestured toward the door. "Should I let him in?" She nodded, mopped her face with the toilet paper, blew her nose. Charlie moved to the door. Bella relaxed, laid down, rolled to one side.

"Where could he be?" Linda held her fists hard against her face.

"Hey, we put out an attempt to locate—vehicle, plate number; it'll probably take 'em less than an hour." He chuckled. "He's broke down somewhere on 395, they'll probably hear him cussing before they make the plate." He opened the door for the dog. Buddy made a beeline for Linda, sat in front of her, and rested his head in her lap. "Poor puppy," she said, running one hand through the scruff of wet fur. "I'm sorry, Bud."

"He's fine," Charlie said. "They're both fine. This ain't no big hoohah, Linda, take it from me. You got us, Inyo County, Bishop Police, the H.P., I even talked to Beverly Hills; we're workin' the whole 395 corridor; we'll find him before noon."

Raising her eyes to his. "I thought you said it would take less than an hour."

He laughed. "Good girl, that's the ticket. You got any more of that coffee you threw at the dog?"

"I'll get it."

"Just sit there."

"Jack wouldn't do this, Charlie," Linda said to his back as he left the room, ". . . just disappear . . ." The toilet paper was a wet sticky mass; she wiped her nose with the back of her hand. "He'd call unless something is wrong."

"We'll just see what happens," Charlie yelled from the kitchen. A spoon jingled against pottery.

"Something's wrong," Linda whispered to the dog, "or your daddy would have called." Buddy raised his head from her lap, lifted his paw, and put it on her knee. Linda felt the sob rise in her throat; she swallowed it.

Charlie came back into the room, took a swig of the coffee, and sat down across from her in Jack's chair. "Hot," he said. With a tender smile, he put the mug of coffee on the table.

Then he took off his hat, ran his hand through his hair. "So, uh, where was he headed, good old Jack?"

She looked at him.

He folded his big hands around the bill of the hat and shrugged. "Down to L.A., I know, like you said . . . but where?" He looked at her, circled the hat with his thick fingers.

Charlie Eckerts had sweet eyes; wasn't that something, she'd never noticed he had sweet eyes.

"I mean, you gave me the name and all and Steve Thorne's gonna talk to the lady, but . . . uh . . ." He leaned forward. "Who is that Rachel Glass?"

Oh, and she knew it would come to this, oh, how she knew. She wiped her nose with her other hand.

Charlie balanced his hat on one knee, perfectly balanced it, the bill below his kneecap straight and still. He picked up the mug, blew into it, took a swig. "I gotta ask, Linda." He gave her the gentle smile again.

Linda kneaded the clump of toilet paper. Her head was a blur of words, a blur of lies that were worthless now in the light of Jack's being lost. There was no more saving face if Jack were lost. She let the tissue rest in the palm of her hand and looked directly into Charlie Eckerts's sweet eyes. "Why do you have to ask?"

"Could be something."

"You mean a clue."

"Sure."

How many investigations, how many times had she heard Jack go on about a case, rehashing all his clues. "You said you thought he was just broken down."

"I do, I do."

"You think something bad has happened to him?"

"Heck, no."

She was stalling; she had nowhere to go. She knew what it was to be a policeman; he would never leave it alone.

"Rachel Glass . . ." Charlie said.

"Rachel Glass," she repeated, looking at him, choking on the words but going on with it, taking a breath and saying it. "Rachel Glass, Charlie, is at the other end of Jack's trip."

He blinked. That was the only obvious reaction. He blinked and sat back in the chair, Jack's chair where he watched television, where he read his book. Charlie blinked, drank some of the coffee, and changed the mug to the other hand. He reached out for the dog. "Hey, Bud," he said.

Buddy stood up and eyed the sheriff. "It's okay, boy," Charlie said.

"It's okay, Bud," Linda repeated softly. The big dog took a few steps forward, sniffed the man's hand. The tears slipped down her face; there was no stopping them.

Charlie Eckerts rubbed the thick white fur behind the dog's ears. "I'm sorry, Linda," he said, without looking at her.

"I am too," Linda said.

He stayed for an hour, drank more coffee; he called in. No news.

He said he was sure Jack would be home for supper; he said he'd call Steve Thorne down in L.A., "Crank it up on the other end."

At the door, he shook her hand. Charlie Eckerts, one of Jack's oldest friends—who had eaten at her table, drank one too many in her living room, lost his temper playing poker on her porch, who had kissed her under the mistletoe on more than one Christmas, danced with her more than one dance, and as of this morning, held her when she'd cried—shook her hand. He lumbered down the steps and across the grass, Buddy galloping beside him. He nodded and pulled at the bill of his sheriff's hat as he backed down the drive. He did not smile.

Rachel

STEVE THORNE HELD out his cup. Rachel filled it with coffee, then moved back to the sink. She was not sure of the protocol, 8:00 in the morning; she was not sure in what capacity Steve Thorne was there. "Are you sure you don't want toast or something? An egg?"

"Oh, no, thanks." He laughed. "I'm tryin' to do that protein thing."

"Well, an egg," she said, turning to him, "that's protein."

He grinned, his round face pulling into a sheepish smile. "Well, then I got the cholesterol thing goin' on with the eggs." He shrugged. "You can't win."

She nodded, put the pot back in place, watched her hand shake, the pot shake as if it were doing the rumba as she tried to put it back into the machine; the bile of too much coffee and no sleep and she was trying to hold on to herself, just hold on to herself since he'd rung the bell. "I did a piece about that for a magazine, proteins and carbs."

"No kidding," he said. "So, who won?"

She stood there with her back to him and put her hands flat on the cold tile to steady herself, breathe. "Something's happened to him," she said, "something's happened to him and you're trying to figure out how to tell me . . . is that it?"

The cup in the saucer, the clunk. "Oh, no, ma'am, hey, we've put out a BLOC, you know, he's probably just broken down off the main road; they'll find him."

She turned, eyes questioning.

"Oh." He grinned again. "Yeah, sorry, be on the lookout." He lifted his cup. "BLOC, sorry . . . so, you grind your own beans?"

"Yes." Jack should have been here yesterday and they were talking about coffee beans; been here since yesterday—afternoon, night into morning, her breasts against his warm back, turning over into him, into the backs of his knees, the smell of his skin, smiling in the morning light that he was there, the touch of him under her hand, listening to him breathe.

"I asked Irene to do that," he said, "buy beans, but she says it tastes the same as in the can." He took another swig and shrugged. "It doesn't. She's got a thing for Folgers, I think, just like her Mom."

Rachel walked back to the table. "You think he's just broken down?"

"Yes, ma'am, I do."

"Please call me Rachel," she said, sitting in the chair across from him, picking up her cup. "I feel like I'm in an episode of *Dragnet* when you call me ma'am." She smiled; he smiled back. She didn't know him; had seen him once, talked to him twice, she didn't know much about Steve Thorne. The coffee was bitter; she thought she might be sick. "Wouldn't he try to get to a phone?"

"Well, you never know what might have come up."

"What do you mean?"

"He didn't call you again after you got home from the store?"

"No, just that once." He hadn't answered her question.

"And that was around?" He flipped the little pad of paper he had in front of him, flipped the pages, referring to his notes of what she'd already said.

"Ten-thirty, eleven, I wasn't really paying attention," because why would she pay attention, because how did she know that every moment would count, and why was he here, Detective Thorne, in her house at 8:00 in the morning if he thought Jack was only broken down, his round face across from her, waiting. "I'd just gotten home from the store," she said, "I was putting away the groceries, you know . . . walking around, talking to him on that phone." She pointed to the telephone. Her hand trembled in the air; she put it back in her lap, held on to it with the other one.

"Right"—looking at his pad—"said he'd passed Mammoth Lakes cutoff, said he might eat in Olancha, said he'd call you when he passed Jo's." His eyes up to hers, waiting.

"Yes . . . and I put everything away and . . . I made a meat loaf, I mean, I got it ready to put in the oven, and I worked . . . I write, you know . . ."

"Yes, ma'am," he said.

". . . and I took a shower . . ." Going over it in her head, over it again, out loud this time, like reciting a poem in school. "I didn't do anything really; I just waited for him to get here. . . ."

"Right, yes, ma'am." He looked up. His forehead was damp; she could see that it was damp, if you touched it you would feel that it was damp . . . hot out already, even this early, the Santa Ana doing her number but even so . . .

"Hey, Jack sure loves meat loaf, doesn't he?" The detective laughed, patting his notebook with his chubby hand. "Did you ever go to the Brighton coffee shop with him? Used to drag me there all the time; he loves the meat loaf there."

Her eyes filled, and her throat, and this rush of a sound in her ears, and what if she never saw Jack again. "Are you on duty?" She ran her hands across her eyes, inhaled, held it. "I mean, you and Jack are good friends. . . ."

"Partners eleven years," Steve Thorne said.

"Eleven years," Rachel repeated.

"Yep. Rode together eleven years until he retired. And you and Jack?"

Pink, his face was pink and damp and round, and she wanted to lie down, she wanted to lie down and weep, her cheek cool against the kitchen floor. "What?"

"You and Jack have been friends for . . . ?"

"Six years."

"Six years." He nodded.

Friends.

Quiet.

"Since that article you wrote, huh?"

She looked at him.

"Domestic violence," he said. "Yeah, I remember"—nodding his head—"you talked to him in the interrogation room."

"That's right."

"I remember," he said.

Quiet.

"Uh-huh," he said, and he closed the notebook. So much behind the tone—some smug conclusion, but he said nothing, put the pen in his shirt pocket, closed the notebook, tugged at his tie.

His collar was too tight, she could see that; he should tell Irene when she was out there buying up the Folgers to pick him up a shirt with a bigger neck size. "Well," he said, the scrape of the chair against the hardwood, "gotta get goin'."

"Is Jack considered a missing person?"

He stood, stepped around the chair, and pushed it back into place at her table. "Well, no, not now."

"No?"

"Well, not officially."

She waited.

"That has to come from the other end, you know." He actually cleared his throat. "The official request has to come from"—he actually took a few seconds before he said the words—"the wife."

"Of course," Rachel said. She thought she might run from the room. Crash through the French doors and run around the garden. Hit Detective Thorne with the coffeepot and then run. But it wasn't his fault; he was doing his job, wasn't he? It wasn't his fault. "Will you call me?" she said.

He looked at her. "Hey, *he'll* call you." He put the notebook in his jacket pocket. "Jack will call you," he said, with that pink smile. "Everything's in place; the word's out." He laughed. "He's probably eating meat loaf somewhere."

Blurry through the tears. "It's a little early for meat loaf," Rachel said.

The detective laughed as if she were really funny. She used to be funny, she remembered—yesterday. He walked back through her house; she followed him; he opened the door. "But will you call me?" she said.

Thorne licked his lips, pulled a handkerchief out of his back pants pocket. A cloud of cologne as the jacket was hiked—limes, lemons, a sweet limeade with a pink cherry face, all he needed was a sprig of mint. His shirt was wet under his arm and against his side, the white cotton clinging to the roundness. Thorne mopped his face.

"Could you please call me," Rachel said, "when you know something? You're my only . . ." His gun under his arm, his badge on his belt—a flash of Jack—and she was dizzy, her hand clutching the doorknob. He smiled. Returning the handkerchief, he adjusted his jacket, his tie, and smiled his cop smile, the reassuring one that suggested everything was just peachy. "Sure, Rachel," Thorne said with that smile, "I'll call you, sure thing."

Charlie

On Wednesday, September 20, 2000, forty-eight hours after no one had heard from him, retired Detective Sergeant Jack David North of the Beverly Hills Police Department was declared an official missing person by his wife, Linda Lee North.

Charlie Eckerts pushed back in his chair, took another sip of the cold coffee, and let his eyes scan the form. Jack David North: a fifty-four-year-old Caucasian male, five feet ten and a half inches tall, weighing in at approximately 191 pounds, with a stocky but not overweight build (described in the record by himself, Mono County Sheriff Department's Sergeant Charlie Eckerts, as healthy and strong), gray eyes, olive complexion, black hair with silver left temple (Charlie would have written gray, but Linda had said silver and she was watching him while he wrote), and one distinguishing characteristic, being a dimple in his chin (he'd written cleft, but Linda had corrected him, pointing out that Jack had a dimple that was very like Kirk Douglas's and different, she'd said, very different from a cleft; Charlie had erased "cleft" and written "dimple" over the smudge on #28; he was not out to make Linda any more upset than she already was).

Charlie leaned back a little too far in his chair; it rolled backward and he grabbed the edge of his desk. *Residence* was listed as: 5 Captain's Lane, Bishop, California 93514. *Attire* when last seen, question #40 on the Missing Persons Report, was listed as: blue Levi 501 jeans with no patches or holes; a black round-necked short-sleeved T-shirt; a black-and-white long-sleeved plaid shirt (make unknown but possibly bought at Bullocks Department Store, which was in Los Angeles but is no longer in business); white standard sweat socks (Costco or Kmart) over black thin thigh-high socks (make unknown) (wife says he likes to wear two pairs of socks, says he says it's more comfortable); black leather Reeboks with black laces; a black leather belt (make unknown, but bought by wife in some designer men's shop in the Glendale Galleria in the San Fernando Valley in Los Angeles where very expensive designer belts were on sale—she can't remember the name of the shop); and white briefs (six to a package, Hanes). Jack may or may not have also been wearing a gray sweatshirt (GAP) with no insignia that he kept in the car. No jewelry except for a chrome and brass watch with a metal snap band (Swiss Army). No discernible marks, scars, amputations, or tattoos. There was nothing listed under *Teeth,* #27, except a notation that he had just had his teeth cleaned by Dr. Mose Miller in Bishop, California, the week before. No cavities, just a cleaning and a checkup. Which, of course, was not necessary to write on the form, but Linda had her eyes on every letter of every word Charlie was writing, sitting across from him at her kitchen table; he swore the woman could read upside down. Number 42, the box for *Religion,* had been left blank. She began a whole song and dance with him about how she'd always felt that was part of the problem, that if religion had remained a part of their marriage, like it was with him and Marie, then what went on might not have went on, but he tried to move on to the next number as quick as he could. He was not about to become the poster boy for Protestants—he made it a point never to discuss religion or politics—and how much did he really need to know about Jack's indiscretions? *Indiscretion* not being a word he would usually use in such a situation, but that's what Linda had said. "Jack's indiscretions," she had called the other women, and even though she didn't allude to details, Charlie noted, there was definitely an *s* at the end of the word. He practically fell out of the chair. It was hard enough to be sitting there doing a Missing Persons on Jack to begin with: he'd been friends with the man for years—racing bikes, fishing, playing cards, getting shitfaced, and the four of them together, Jack and Linda and him and Marie—hard enough to swallow filling out a Missing Persons for someone you knew, and then on top of it, to realize maybe you didn't know them that well, because if push came to shove, Charlie had never suspected a thing about Jack on the indiscretion front. Not that Jack and Linda were especially lovey-dovey, but who was after all these years. There was talk, of course, about Jack goin' in and outta L.A. a lot, but Charlie had never been one for gossip, and Jack North had certainly never wiped his indiscretions on Charlie's sleeve.

Destination was listed as residence of Ms. Rachel Glass, 1602 North Elm, Beverly Hills, California 90210; Ms. Glass being the latest indiscretion, according to Linda. Steve Thorne, Jack's ex-partner, had described her as a looker, when Charlie had contacted him about the disappearance of Jack, not young or in the cradle or anything, Steve Thorne had said, a grown-up woman, but still looking good. Of course, Charlie had always thought Linda was a good-looking gal. Big breasts always got to him, and she had a big build, athletic, fleshy, with some meat on her—he liked that. But she was Jack's wife and Charlie didn't fool around with wives. He made a point of that too. No way. There were a lot of women in town who made sure you knew you could have them—not in so many words—but a look, a toss of the head, an innuendo, which was the way women said something without really saying it—and when that happened Charlie made sure he walked away. Just like he was saying the other day to Doc Filbeck, if you really took up the Ten Commandments, you could see that fooling around was covered twice: once under "Neither shalt thou commit adultery" and once under "Neither shalt thou covet thy neighbor's wife"—if you thought about it—and Charlie thought about it whenever a neighbor's wife started looking too good. Then there were also the women who were passing through. You're riding patrol, and they're going like a bat outta hell through Independence or Lone Pine or any of the towns up and down 395 in Inyo County's jurisdiction, like the signs aren't clearly posted as you approach town and leave—55 to 45, 45 to 35, and so on—and "Oh, Officer, I didn't see the signs," and "Oh, Officer," eyes all big and coy, a definite invite, a definite innuendo, like you would pull them over and take them by the side of the road, like that's gonna stop you from writing them the ticket 'cause they're flirting up a storm. As soon as you take that pen out and they see you're serious, all that BS comes to a halt. Charlie rolled his chair back and forth in front of his desk. Martha Grinnell, on the other side of the room, lifted a phone and said softly, "Inyo County Sheriff's Department, Martha Grinnell speaking. May I help you?"

The last phone call listed by Jack North's cell phone provider, AT&T Wireless, was made to Ms. Glass at 10:48 A.M. on Monday, September 18, 2000. No cell sites accessed since. He was last seen at the AM/PM Mini-Mart and Texaco on Interstate 395 right outside of Big Pine, California, at approximately 11:30 A.M. of the same day. He paid for 16.5 gallons of regular gas with his Pacific Century Bank VISA Card #6826 9042 5766 8093, expiration date July 20, 2002, and got a cup of free coffee from the coffee station by the register. The clerk, Miss Lucille Baines, nineteen, remembered Jack and his dark green Ford Explorer because he stops there, she says, maybe a couple times a month and always kids with her. "He always asks why we don't have flavored cream at the coffee station. French vanilla. Every time," she said, laughing. When asked if Mr. North kidded with her this time, she said yes. When asked if Mr. North appeared to be upset in any way, she said no. When asked if Mr. North happened to mention where he was headed, she said no. She added that Mr. North was "kinda cute but, you know, old enough to be my dad." Miss Baines appeared to be a nice, friendly teenager, forthcoming and reliable, but with a terrible skin problem that looked to be confined to her forehead and chin. She was their only witness thus far, and Charlie did not want to embarrass or upset her in any way; therefore, he made it a point to not let his glance drift anywhere near those pimples, but looked her right in the eyes. Somebody ought to give the kid some Clearasil or whatever they used nowadays.

Everything was in order except for #48 on the form, *Reason for Absence.* It was not clear to Charlie Eckerts or to Steve Thorne, both of whom were not only friends of Jack's but police officers who'd had experience with this sort of thing, and it appeared to also not be clear to Linda North or Rachel Glass, both of whom were women who supposedly loved Jack and were regular citizens who'd had no experience with this sort of thing at all. Number 48 was giving them all a really hard time. Either Jack was voluntarily missing, which didn't make much sense to Charlie, unless he had another indiscretion he'd gone off to see, running out on Linda *and* Ms. Rachel Glass—which was Steve Thorne's pick of a theory, but maybe Thorne was only trying to be funny—*or,* like Charlie thought, Jack had fallen into serious trouble along the way. Foul play, Charlie thought, some kind of foul play. A robbery gone wrong, or he'd stumbled onto something, stopped somewhere because something had caught his eye, his cop eye, and then he'd gotten entangled, gotten overpowered in some way. Or an accident, but, hell, they would have found the car, or a piece of it.

Charlie finished the last dregs of coffee and crumpled the paper cup in his hand. As far as the Inyo County Sheriff's Department was concerned, you would have to take a poll. Charlie thought it was trouble along the way that had taken a bad turn, and Ralph Crawley agreed; Warren Mosher in Lone Pine thought it was suicide, that Jack couldn't take the double life anymore—as far as Warren was concerned one woman was too much, two on a regular basis would make any man want to check out. B. J. Holland in Big Pine thought Linda had offed Jack, but he was in the minority, and Rich Shelly in Independence went along with Steve Thorne and what Charlie thought of as "the honey theory"—that Jack had another honey and he'd taken off with her. Charlie didn't buy the honey theory. Howard Saniger thought that some perp Jack had put away down in Beverly Hills had gotten out. "So the guy watches his pattern," Howard said, "sees Jack goin' up and down 395 once a month like clockwork, and he waits and takes him out. Does him and puts him down a mine shaft. Hell, we'd never find him then, him or the Ford Explorer." There were mine shafts big enough to drive a car into, Charlie had given Howard that, but somehow it just didn't sit right. Not with him. There were probably more theories than Charlie could even imagine, considering how many cops were involved.

It was an active search, no two ways about it, an active search by the brotherhood of police. The California Highway Patrol, Mono County Sheriff, Inyo County Sheriff, Mammoth Lakes Police Department, Bishop Police Department, and every police department for each and every county up and down the line—from Bishop to Beverly Hills—part of the routine for each patrol, part of the prodding at each roll call for each and every shift (where they had roll calls, because Inyo County didn't do roll calls; they just left each other notes or talked to each other on the radio). It was uppermost in everybody's mind—like one of those mottoes on a T-shirt—*Find Jack North*. Back and forth they reminded each other of past cases where somebody went missing, back and forth they theorized. There was the photographer who went up into the mountains to take desert photos and never came back down. His wife swore he went up the Sierra side, and so they're searching and they're searching the Sierra side and there's no sign of him at all. No sign of him because the guy'd gone up the Inyo side. Gone up, taken his photos, had a few wieners on his hibachi, and went to take a little snooze in his truck. Unfortunately, the photographer got himself all cozy, put the hibachi in the truck with him (maybe it started raining; you could get rain up in the mountains on a perfectly fine day—hell, you could get snow in June if you weren't lucky), closed all the windows, and carboned himself to death. Five days later they get a call from some hikers about a dead guy in a camper truck. Charlie ran his hand through his hair. Talk about a mess. Jesus. Five days, the guy popped when they took him out. Then there was the guy whose son-in-law shot him and hauled him away. They had the car; they had the blood and the fingerprints; they had the son-in-law. Means, motive, opportunity; they had all three. They just never had the body. The thing with Jack was they didn't have anything. No Explorer had turned up, no credit cards had been used, not since the day he'd disappeared, no sign of foul play, and like Warren Mosher pointed out, "Hell, we got no place to start." Where were they going to send the CHP helicopters? They were looking—it was true that they were looking—but how many miles, how many mountains; which way had Jack gone? There was no way they could use infrared, no way to send planes out with more than ten thousand square miles to cover—no matter which theory, there were no clues and nothing to go on—which way were the helicopters supposed to fly?

Charlie tossed the cup into the wastebasket. A little trail of sugar had escaped the packet and was caught in a fold of his shirt—he sat up straight in the chair and brushed it away. Poor Linda. He sure hated having to go over there to do the Missing Persons, what a godawful thing. But he was considered the contact; Linda's first call had been to him, and despite the fact that Howard Saniger was running the show because a missing person fell under the detectives' division, Charlie was considered the one. "Hell, you go, Charlie," Howard had said, "after all, you're Jack's friend." Marie had called Linda to go over right after, but Linda had said she didn't want company. Marie said she just couldn't believe that Jack North would drop right off the face of the earth and wasn't there anything Charlie could do. He shook his head, tried to release his neck muscles, release his fingers from making fists. Considering they were doing everything they could think of, every law enforcement officer from here to there and back again, and considering Marie darn well knew that, having been married to Charlie for twenty-six years and knowing that if a cop was involved the force darn well nearly killed themselves, it was a pretty dumb thing for her to say. Charlie put the form in the manila file, closed it, and set it squarely in the center of his desk. He hadn't said a word to her about Jack's destination, which also turned out to be his indiscretion; he hadn't said one word. He made it a rule not to discuss details of cases with Marie. Of course, it would get out—being as how every law enforcement officer in town knew that Jack North's destination was one Ms. Rachel Glass; somebody's wife would tell somebody's mother and brother and soon everybody would know. Including Marie.

He studied the photograph of Marie that he had pinned to his bulletin board. It was the one he preferred to look at, the one he'd taken when they'd only been married about five years, the one he'd taken of her on the boat; she was smiling and the sun was doing a reflection off her sunglasses and she was falling out of the top of her swimsuit. She looked a little easy, which she wasn't, but that's how she looked. The other photograph was from his son's wedding, done by some jackass photographer, and as far as he was concerned, him and Marie looked like they were stuffed, but she'd given him a fancy silver frame for it with a whole song and dance about how good she thought she'd looked that day because it was their anniversary besides being Andy's wedding day; there was no way he couldn't put the darn thing right there on his desk next to his telephone. After all, he was in close proximity to the market and the beauty shop and everywhere else Marie went—who knew when she might drop in. He hated the picture; he looked old. Or maybe it was because he looked like his dad. Either way. And he didn't think she looked so good in it either, but he had long ago made a point of not trying to figure out why Marie thought she looked good in one particular outfit and not in another or why when he thought her hair looked like it was painted on, she thought it looked good.

Charlie tipped the chair again, lifted his long legs, and put his feet up on his desk to the left of the Jack North manila file. His knees hurt. Of course, they always hurt; you'd think he'd be used to it by now. He had decided to think of it as a punishment for what he'd done. Not that he'd gotten his knees hurt when he was having his indiscretion, to use Linda North's word, his one indiscretion in twenty-six years of marriage, but his knees were really the only thing that bothered him, and he considered that to be pretty darn lucky, what with two guys he knew both getting cancer in the last six months, one prostate and the other some long name that amounted to leukemia, both younger than him—

he'd be forty-nine next June—so if that was all the good Lord was dishing out to him now, he'd take it as punishment for what he'd done.

His indiscretion.

Which was kind of contrary to who he was and certainly not the way he'd been raised, since you got married and that was supposed to be it, boy—and of course, fooling around was a sin, a big one, and didn't he know it, and hadn't he said enough *I'm sorry*s and *Please forgive me*s to the Almighty. And although he knew he had to be held accountable for his own actions, like it said right there in the Bible—not in so many words, but it said it all right, if you read between the lines—even though Charlie tried to hold himself accountable, he still felt kind of hoodwinked by what had gone down with him and Pat McCaffey. Charlie looked over at her—she was typing a tape, transcribing, the earphones jacked up like a little halo above all that red hair. Anything but an angel, but there she was, little pale nails clicking away. She tried to pull that hair up into some kind of a bun thing, but it was always slipping away, little wispy ringlets on her forehead, red strands of it uncurling out of the knot, unwinding across her uniform shoulder in soft spirals, like those things you throw on New Year's Eve. *Lead us not into temptation,* Charlie thought, and looked away. Sometimes it was hard to remember that Jesus Christ was the pathway to heaven and not Pat McCaffey.

Charlie concentrated on the photo of Marie in her bathing suit. He loved Marie. She was a good girl, a good mother, a good wife. Yes, sir. A man couldn't ask for better. It was baffling to him, therefore, that he'd done what he'd done, his indiscretion, that had kind of come out of nowhere. Sitting right there, the two of them, goin' over a case like they'd done a trillion times, Pat McCaffey with all those freckles and wisps and pink skin, all rosy; she smelled like coffee and Colgate and Chantilly—Charlie wasn't sure if it was Chantilly, but it was something soft and sweet that reminded him of high school, not like what Marie favored, which was something by some homosexual Italian that his mother would have said smelled like a whore. Only his mother pronounced it *hoor.*

A trillion times him and Pat McCaffey had been in the office alone. A trillion times, and there was nothing different about this time at all. Except that they did it. Up against a filing cabinet. Unbuckled and unzipped and standing, with their police boots on and their badges and their guns. It was lunchtime; Martha Grinnell had gone to get them all some Chinese from the Tiki Gardens, and anybody could have walked in. Charlie was so shook up he thought he might have a heart attack. Her face was as red as her hair and his probably was too; it's not like there was a mirror; he could see only her eyes. Soft and kind of slanty and kind of hazel, and it's not like it was easy with her being five-three and him being six-three; he was kind of holding her up and slamming into her, her feet couldn't have been touching the ground, but it never occurred to him that he had her kind of pinned up there against the metal until he heard the handle of his gun banging hard against one of the drawers. Like a drumbeat for a rock song. He'd never been so excited. Not in his whole life.

Charlie took his feet off the desk, then straightened some stacks of papers. He was getting a hard-on.

He looked at the framed photograph of him and Marie. He hated it; he really did. Pat McCaffey lifted the earphones off her head and set them on her desk. She rolled back in her chair, stood, yawned, walked across the room to the ladies, one hand tucking a scarlet spiral back up into the bun. Charlie watched her butt move in the uniform; maybe he was mistaken, maybe she wasn't even five-three.

The case they'd been working on that morning was a robbery, a lot of bags of evidence, and he and Pat McCaffey were tagging it—routine—in the file room, and she was teasing him about his handwriting and saying he should just slipknot the tags and let her do the writing because *What the heck did that say?* He was sitting at the long table and she bent over him to read what he'd written, laughing, and the tag slipped off the table, and she knelt down to get it, and her face was practically in his lap. She had the tag in her hand, but she was still kneeling, and he just wanted to touch those little scarlet curls and that expanse of white forehead, and the next thing you know he had her up against the filing cabinet, his mouth on hers. He didn't really remember the exact order; he more remembered the surge in his chest and that he was sweaty and he had his hands in her uniform and her breasts were bigger than he thought they were and she wasn't wearing panties but one of those skimpy things that rode the crack of her ass and she was wet. They didn't say much. They hadn't said much since. Pat McCaffey was married and had two kids. She didn't wear makeup; she wasn't even what you'd call pretty. Marie was what you'd call pretty. Marie had dark hair and light blue eyes and looked like she used to be something, like she had a past. She didn't, but she looked like it. She also looked like Elizabeth Taylor—used to, a little—at least to him. Now she looked like Elizabeth Taylor's mother. Charlie laughed out loud and the door to the ladies opened and Pat McCaffey stepped out and recrossed the room. She didn't look at him as she passed; she mumbled something to Martha Grinnell and they both smiled. He wondered if Pat was wearing one of those skimpy things under her slacks. They used to have lunch together, he missed that; the two of them used to have a lot of laughs. She had been his first female friend. And his last, by the looks of things.

Charlie sighed, looked around his desk for his coffee, and remembered he'd thrown it away. He'd never told anybody about him and Pat, no way; his indiscretion was between him and the Lord. He had prayed for forgiveness; he still prayed—each and every day—when he smelled the Chantilly by the coffee machine, when he watched her swing those hard little legs of hers in and out of the patrol car, that thing she did with her lips when she talked on the telephone, pursed them up like a little Kewpie doll's—*Lead us not into temptation but deliver us from evil,* Charlie prayed.

He lifted the Jack North file and reopened it; there wasn't anything in it except the Missing Persons Report. He read it again, carefully, his eyes lingering on the words: Ms. Rachel Glass. Charlie couldn't imagine having an affair, not a real one. He was sure what he'd done with Pat McCaffey didn't qualify. It couldn't count as a real betrayal; it was more like an accident, fast and furious, and it wasn't like they'd had a plan, gone to a motel or anything, and it wasn't like he loved her, for crissakes, he loved Marie. Charlie couldn't see jeopardizing your whole life and everything you'd worked for . . . for what? He didn't understand Jack North's thinking; he tried to put himself in Jack's shoes, but he just didn't understand. Rachel Glass, Thorne had said, was a little brunette with tight titties in her T-shirt. Those were his words. Oh, and a great ass, he'd said over the telephone, with a laugh, like him and Charlie were old pals. Thorne didn't even know Charlie, only laid eyes on him twice. Steve Thorne had been Jack's partner, rode with Jack eleven years until Jack retired, and that's how he talked. Of course, there was no way of knowing what Thorne knew, how much Jack had told him, and he sure wasn't about to ask. It was funny with partners—sometimes they were the best of friends and sometimes look out.

From what Linda had said, this thing with Jack and Ms. Glass had been going on for some time, since they'd lived in L.A., and as far as Charlie was concerned, if a man like Jack North would put his life and everything he'd worked for on the line, it had to be for more than tight titties and a great ass. Charlie looked over at Pat McCaffey; she was on the phone listening to somebody, she was doing that little bow thing with her mouth.

Besides the description of her physical person, Thorne had said that Rachel Glass lived in a fancy house in Beverly Hills with a swimming pool and a yard probably bigger than the Mono County golf course. There was no Mono County golf course, and Charlie knew it was a dig, but he didn't say anything, he just let Thorne go on. Thorne said that at this particular time he didn't suspect Rachel Glass's participation in any foul play; that as far as he could tell she'd been expecting Jack to show when he said he would and she was pretty well shook up. Charlie closed the file. He was hungry. He wondered what would happen if he asked Pat McCaffey if she wanted to go get something to eat. He wasn't going to; he just wondered.

He kept his eyes focused on Marie's picture. He wondered what Pat McCaffey would do if he were missing. He wondered if Rachel Glass was as shook up as Linda North.

Steve

IF IT WAS ELMORE Leonard, the wife and the girlfriend would have gotten together and bumped off the husband.

Steve Thorne put down the slice.

If he were a mystery writer, that's how it would go.

He replaced his feet on the stool rungs and checked the front of his pants. No matter how many napkins, he usually wound up with a nickel spot of pizza grease in his lap. Not that he cared about the pants; he only cared about Irene's finding it—she was like a detective when it came to sniffing out what he wasn't supposed to eat.

If the girlfriend and the wife got fed up enough, they could have taken the husband somewhere right off of 395. In a book, that is. Not on *Law & Order* or on *NYPD Blue;* both shows Steve tried hard not to miss because he really liked Sipowicz, his anger, and Briscoe's grumbling, but on those shows there was hardly ever any driving—murders took place in the city on foot—right on the street, in the middle of the traffic, or in some seedy subway station in the middle of the night. Steve took a bite, then swabbed a napkin across the pizza oil on his lips and mustache.

In a book, a girlfriend and a wife could take a guy right off the road at high noon. In California, that is. Maybe in New York State too, but Steve didn't know those roads, couldn't visualize it.

Like, say, the wife and the girlfriend decide they've had enough of it: the guy can't make up his mind between the two of them; they'll show him. They decide to have a confrontation. Steve coated the pepperoni with grated cheese. One of them drives up next to him; that would throw Jack. Here he is, goin' down to L.A. on schedule, everything hunky-dory, he thinks, everybody puttin' up with this setup, which only benefits him, and out of nowhere Rachel Glass pulls up in her little Beamer. Jack thinks—what's she doing here?

Steve lifted a hunk of pepperoni, popped it into his mouth.

She doesn't connect eyes. Then she passes him. Holy shit.

Steve chewed the pepperoni, wiped the back of his hand across his mouth. Jack would follow her for sure.

Steve could see it, his eyes on the Coke machine on the other side of the counter at Paulie's Pizzeria in Beverly Hills, but seeing only the scene. Jack's green Ford Explorer, the little Beamer, Linda waiting behind a boulder . . . and there they are. The three of them.

He doused the pepperoni and mushrooms with hot pepper oil, took a long swig of the Diet Coke.

The two chicks confront Jack, tell him he has to choose. Somewhere on a back road off of Interstate 395. Morning light, blue sky, snow-tipped mountains in the background, maybe even a stream. Fish in the stream if it were a movie, and the camera pulls back from the stream and the fish and the water and there they are—the three of them—Rachel, Linda, and Jack. And the music gets creepy. Steve folded the soaked slice of loaded pizza carefully into his mouth.

And then something goes down.

He chewed and swallowed.

Yeah, something goes down.

He wiped his lips, burped softly into the napkin, took another long pull of the Coke.

Okay. Let's say Jack picks Rachel over Linda, tells Linda he's gonna leave her for Rachel, and Linda loses it; she shoots Jack. Because his gun is there in the car and she knows it, Linda knows where it is, where he keeps it, and she goes for it—because Jack North doesn't go back and forth from L.A. to anywhere without his gun. No way, Jose—Jack's always got his gun.

Steve pressed his fingers to the leftover bits of cheese on the plate and ran them across his tongue. Of course, it was hard to think of Linda shooting Jack. Hard to fantasize. Steve wasn't as suspicious as Sipowicz on *NYPD Blue* or as hard as Lenny Briscoe on *Law & Order*. Of course, neither of them would probably have known the suspect like Steve did; she'd be a total stranger to them. On television the murder and rape and robbery stuff goes on with the guest stars, not with the regulars. On those shows, the wife and the girlfriend would be strangers to Sipowicz. Sipowicz wouldn't know about Jack and Linda's marriage; Briscoe wouldn't know the way Linda kind of doted on Jack. Steve tilted the Coke can to his lips.

He, on the other hand, knew everything. Well, not everything. He didn't know this thing was still going on with Rachel Glass. He knew when it started, when she'd sashayed in to interview Jack for that magazine thing, and then every now and then he'd hear the tail end of a phone call or her voice on Jack's line. He knew plenty. But not since Jack retired, he didn't know that, not since he left town. Not that Jack was ever one to talk about it when they were working together; he wouldn't, being a very close-mouthed kind of guy. And now they weren't as close as they'd been when they were together every day. Steve talked to him every now and then, less and less if he thought about it, because they were living such different lives. He saw him a couple times last year, more the year before. The four of them had had dinner when Jack and Linda came in at the beginning of the summer for somebody's wedding—was that the last time he'd talked to Jack?

Steve chugged the rest of the soda. He'd rode with Jack eleven years and they probably would have gone on if Jack hadn't retired. They got along pretty good. He bent the can until the top and the bottom were touching.

Lenny Briscoe was always losing partners on *Law & Order*—they all left the show—and poor Sipowicz on *NYPD Blue* lost the red-haired one who thought he could make it in the movies, fat chance, and then he lost his really great partner, Bobby Simone. That was terrible. Jimmy Smits was a great actor; Simone was a great cop. A real tragedy. But that was at least natural causes; the poor guy died of a heart thing; it wasn't like somebody blew him away.

Steve looked down at his pants, checked for spots. What if Jack were dead? He couldn't imagine. Jesus.

Linda couldn't have shot him; too hard to believe. He knew Linda. No way.

Goddamn it. Pizza oil between the knee and the pocket, a spray right through the goddamn napkins. Steve soaked a fist of paper napkins in his water glass and rubbed at his slacks. The thin paper shredded; threadlike bits of it clung to the round sticky circle on his tan slacks. He threw the wad of paper on the counter and smirked. If it was Steve's life, there was no doubt about it, Irene would have shot him for sure.

With or without help from the girlfriend.

"Hey, Steve," Danny said from the other side of the counter, "how's it goin'? How's crime?"

Steve laughed. "Crime's great, Danny boy."

"Yeah, that's what my uncle Paulie said all the way to the can. You ready?"

"You bet."

"Pepperoni and mushroom, yeah? Or you want to try the ricotta and arugula?"

"Ricotta and arugula? I thought that was salad."

"Right," Danny said, "soon they won't want crust. We got one now that doesn't even got cheese. Chicks think if it ain't got cheese it's more dietetic. I say if they're gonna diet, what the hey are they doin' eatin' pizza in the first place?"

"Right," Steve said, licking grease off his fingers. He loved this place; it was like takin' a trip, like goin' home if you were someone else. He wasn't from New York, but they didn't know that—Danny and his brother, Ganza, and their sister, Angela Christine, who owned this place—they had no idea. Nobody did, and he didn't tell them; he liked pretending. Steve Thorne wasn't from New York, he wasn't even Italian, but everybody always thought he was. Like he had an affinity. Like he was one of them in a past life. If you believed that crap. Irene did. Steve was really from Detroit, but he never told anybody; he always said he was from New York. Eating in this joint was like walking into *The Godfather* and Steve loved that, besides the pizza, which he really loved and which was a real piece of New York. He knew; he'd been to New York twice, eaten pizza at Original Ray's and elsewhere, and right here in the middle of Beverly Hills was a real piece of New York, a real taste—actually a real slice, right? Steve grinned, swiped the napkin across his mustache, studied the orange blur. A slice of New York was a play on words, a "double entendre" you called it, that you could use if you were a writer like Elmore Leonard or like, say, Rachel Glass. Danny slid another steaming slice of pizza on Steve's plate.

"There ya go, Detective. Another Diet?"

"Thanks, Danny."

Steve put a fresh layer of napkins on his lap. The stain was beginning to resemble the state of California going up and down his leg like that.

Rachel Glass could have done it. If it wasn't Linda, and he couldn't believe it was Linda, it just didn't smell right—but what about Rachel Glass? Divorced with all the trimmings—the house, the car, the luxury setup, posh. Two kids—one married, one in college. Writes that crap Irene reads in the magazines. That must pay her pretty good besides what she gets from the ex-husband. Good-looking. Steve thought she was good-looking; he liked that type. Dark and wiry and compact; he liked that.

Steve picked up the cheese and the pepper oil and took turns shaking each across the slice of pizza in a precise layering effect. Rachel Glass looked like she could explode. Linda looked okay, but like a wife, like she'd lost her magic, like it had dimmed. But then you had to think—a dame like Rachel Glass could have anybody—so what was she doing with Jack? And if she was with him, and it sure looked like she was with him, like they were still an item—then why would she shoot him? Nah, it didn't make sense.

Danny popped the tab, put the Coke in front of Steve, and moved down the counter.

"Thanks, Danny."

"Yeah."

He'd had things since he and Irene were married; nothing that amounted to much. A shtup every now and then—that was enough. All you needed was something to get you out of bed in the mornings, something to look forward to. A little something. An affair was an altogether different thing, and he wasn't interested. You let a piece of tail get too close to you and the next thing you know she's whining about love and why don't you leave your wife and kids and do the whole thing all over again with her. Better to just give them a shot and move on, say adios.

As far as Steve knew, Sipowicz on *NYPD Blue* had never had an affair while he was married to either wife, not the chubby drunk or the good-looking one who got shot in the court. Killed actually, not just shot, and poor Sipowicz had to deal with both those deaths in one season. The partner and the wife.

Steve shook his head, put down the cheese and the oil, and studied the slice.

Briscoe on *Law & Order* had been divorced lots of times, but Steve couldn't remember the history of his character and if his divorces had come from affairs. As far as he could remember, there wasn't one cop on any cop show who had had a long-term affair.

In fact, as far as he could remember, there wasn't one cop that he knew from real life who had had a long-term affair. Not like this.

Because it wasn't just the affair; it was the goddamn knowledge—both chicks knew. That was the corker. That's what took away from the "chick gets pissed off and shoots the guy" theory. It would be different if Linda North had just found out that Jack was cheating, different if Rachel Glass had just found out that Jack was married. If it was a new thing, a surprise, but it wasn't—this thing had been going on for a long time. Both chicks knew and both chicks put up with it. Steve Thorne studied the slice.

Boy. The shit that women put up with. Boy oh boy.

He lifted the warm, beautiful triangle with both hands. Both chicks knew and both chicks put up with it. Boy, you had to hand it to old Jack North.

The weight of the cheese and pepperoni and mushrooms drowned in hot pepper oil and extra sauce had no regard for gravity. The entire mess slid off New York's finest thin crust into Detective Thorne's lap.

Rachel

SHE COULDN'T SLEEP; she couldn't eat; she couldn't sit there. Rachel watched the cursor blink silently on the blank screen, on and off, on and off, like neon. Write something. Do something. Do anything. Move. She picked up her date book and threw it across the room. It took a dive halfway to the bookcase and made a soft plop on the rug. Nothing spectacular. She put her head in her hands, covered her eyes with her fingers, and inhaled. Furniture wax. 409. Cleanser.

"What are you doing?" Grace had asked, the third time she'd called that morning, making sure Rachel still had her wits.

"Waxing the dining room table."

"Uh-huh."

There was no need to explain the comfort of waxing to Grace. What one did during calamities, what one turned to in times of stress: Rachel cleaned and polished; Grace cooked. Not just cooked—lost herself. The first time Dickhead copped to having *another* woman: beef Wellington for ten smeared with slivers of mushrooms and foie gras, baby peas with little onions creamed and spooned into artichoke heart cups, potatoes au gratin squeezed through a cake decorating device until they became perfect little cups, and for dessert a tiramisu, because at that rate you don't care if anything matches, a tiramisu along with ladyfingers, because making ladyfingers would take another hour and at that rate perhaps you could bury yourself in enough butter and cream and flour to forget who you are and what is happening to you. Grace lost in the hum of her KitchenAid classic mixer, Rachel drifting off in a cloud of French wax. Back and forth with the grain until her arms ached, but it didn't matter, nothing mattered; it had been a week.

Monday to Monday. Not leaving the house, not taking the chance to miss the call. His call, her call, anybody's call. Please call me; somebody call. Not even walking down to Grace's house, only walking from room to room. Stalling. Stuck. Horrified. It had been a week.

Rachel got up from the chair, silently padded across the rug on bare feet, picked up the date book, and held it to her chest. Pushed it into her breasts under the peach satin. Walking around in a nightgown at noon; she'd never done that except when she had the flu. The first few days she'd dressed with the dawn, ready for anything, ready to go to him when he called, because he would call, absolutely, he would call. He would tell her the story of how he'd driven off the road and into Brigadoon, how he'd been abducted by aliens and spent the last week circling Earth. *They didn't have a phone, baby, can you imagine those little green guys didn't have a phone?* The last two days she'd been in the same nightgown; or did today make three? Grace's mother's nightgown from Grace's mother's trousseau; peach satin from another time graced with coffee stains from now. Rachel held fast to the date book, dug her toes into the rug.

She'd called Steve Thorne twice; he'd called her back both times. Friendly, open, warm, like his sweating face, but with all his *hi, how are you*s, he had nothing to say. There was no sign of Jack or his car. Nothing. No sign.

"What do you do now?"

Send me a sign, Jack, please send me a sign.

"We keep looking, ma'am. Nothing stops that; it's an active search."

She was back to ma'am. Rachel after their tête-à-tête in the kitchen and now somehow she'd slipped back to ma'am. No, please like me, please call me Rachel, please tell me what you know. Fingers clenched around the spirals of the phone cord; no, don't worry yourself about the small stuff; listen to what he says. *An active search.* Images in her head of uniformed cops turning over bushes and cactus plants in search of Jack. "Where's the baby, where's the baby?" she would coo to Ben-oh, and he'd fling the little pillow from across his face and shriek, "There he is." Hours of reciting *Where's Spot?* "Is he inside the piano?" Ben-oh wiggling on her lap, pudgy fingers patting her arm in anticipation, five-year-old Dana leaning against her side, smiling at her mother—she already knew the hiding place of the illusive puppy. "Is he under the staircase?" mother and daughter together for baby Ben. "Oh, my goodness," said Dana, mimicking her mother. "Where is that old Spot?"

"Where's Jack?" Ben had asked her when he'd called an hour before. "It's been a week. Are you two still at it; is old robo cop still there?"

Nothing, no words except the neon of *It's been a week,* flashing in her head. Monday to Monday.

Ben laughed. "Is he washing your car, Mom?"

She'd stood with the phone at her ear and her mouth shut. Missing? Is that what she should say? How about he went back early? How about he didn't come down after all? Right, give that boy the freezer and the trip to Paris. "Washing the car," she'd repeated in a daze.

"No, shit. He's really washing the car? Hey, Mom, I'm clairvoyant."

"He's missing," Rachel had managed to get out; that's what she'd said. Missing? What happened to the writer? What happened to her choice of words? She had avoided telling Dana all week, acted as if she was too busy to even talk, hanging up on her daughter for fear of saying the words. Trembling now, rigid and trembling, elbows tucked into her hipbones so she wouldn't fall. Hold on to rigid, kid, try to find the words for what is happening here and tell Ben, explain to your boy how people can disappear. Tell him when Jack was supposed to arrive and when he didn't and what has happened since, tell it like a story that has nothing to do with you, not laden with emotion but precise and detailed. Hold on to yourself, tell it all the way down to this morning, only leaving out the phone call a week ago to Linda North. And the cleaning thing; no need to burden your son with the news that you've turned into Lady Macbeth.

A week ago. Rachel studied her bleeding cuticles as if they didn't belong to her.

"Jeez, Mom."

You could practically hear his heart beating. Because what did he know, her boy, from bad things? There was no *missing* in his life; there had been no airplane crashes, no gunshot wounds, no bad guys. Once upon a time when he was twelve some big guys had hassled him for his Walkman in the mall, but they were *big* guys, not *bad* guys, and when a security guard happened to step off the elevator, they'd run.

"Jack couldn't just disappear," Ben said.

Nothing, no words.

"Jeez, Mom, he's a cop."

No words to comfort; she had lost all words. She would have to put out a *be on the lookout* for her words.

"You mean, like they didn't find anything, like there's no trace?"

So informed, so on top of it with the lingo, maybe he would write mysteries some day, her son. "No trace," Rachel had whispered. That's it: she didn't need words of her own; she could just repeat what everybody else said.

Quiet, and then Ben, solemnly, "Do you think he took off?"

Her gaze danced around the orange tree. A bird, a dove, two doves, that particular sound of their flutter, bees in the blossoms, Rachel leaned forward at the open window until her forehead grazed the screen.

"Took off where?" There you go, three words strung together all by yourself; good girl.

"I don't know . . . ran?"

Jack running across the desert in a shirt and pants, with a jacket, with a baseball hat, with a gun—Jack running with his gun out chasing criminals, Jack running without his gun away from criminals, Jack in trouble. Look, Spot, see Jack run.

"You know . . ." her son went on, "like running from the situation, you know?"

Jack running from Rachel as she guns her BMW; she takes off after him in a cloud of dust. Rachel in her BMW and Linda in her Honda, they chase him, trap him like one of those poor wild horses in *The Misfits.* They lasso him between their cars.

Rachel moved her forehead against the screen. Silver-gray, the Honda Linda drove was gray like Jack's eyes. Rachel had seen it once, she had driven by their place in Santa Monica before Jack had retired. A day of madness, missing him, a Sunday, because on Sundays they rarely got to speak. Sundays were for families, he used to say, on Sundays it was tough to get to the telephone, and one Sunday when she couldn't seem to stop herself she'd driven down their block. Linda's silver Honda in the driveway behind Jack's green Ford Explorer, her bumper bumping up to his, and Rachel shamefaced that she had done such a thing, driven past his house as if she were in high school.

A cloud of exhale, stale breath and coffee—where was she, what was she thinking? Rachel moved back from the screen.

"Mom?"

"Yes, Ben." She folded where she was, sat on the rug. The satin was ripped, where her knee hit, where it cut on the bias, there was the start of a rip.

"Hey, I don't know . . ." Ben had said, "I was just, you know, tryin' to figure it out. He probably wouldn't do that, Jack, run . . . I didn't . . ." Ben stalled. "I didn't mean to make you feel worse. . . ."

She nodded.

"It was probably just something . . . I mean, like, you think he crashed somewhere? Jeez, Mom."

Speculation, conjecture, theory. How many times had she and Grace conjectured this week? How many times, how many theories, how many sitting up in the bed, flying up out of a deep sleep, shocked awake as if shot out of a gun?

"I mean, Mom, he has to be there. If he didn't run, he has to be there . . . unless somebody took him, but who would kidnap Jack? It's not like he's Donald Trump or something."

She pulled at the peach threads. Ah, the kidnap theory, she'd done the kidnap theory; alrighty then, let's stop him now. "Ben?" Rachel said.

"I mean, people don't kidnap people unless they're gonna get something in the end . . ."

"Ben . . ."

". . . unless they stopped him, you know, pretended like maybe they'd had a flat or something so that he would stop, you know, he'd pull over, not him but any guy, a random guy, so that they could roll him . . ."

Roll him, look how he knows the words.

". . . maybe they just needed some cash. And then Jack, you know, because he's a cop and all, you know, maybe he got tough . . ."

"Ben!"

He stopped. Her finger was poking through the satin; how did that happen? Now you could see her knee.

"Mom?"

A breath, and then, clipped and quiet, "I don't know the answers. I've been through all the questions and I don't know the answers. I don't know where he is; I don't know what happened. I don't know." Enough, shut up.

"Oh." Her sweet boy forming his sentence so that it wouldn't hurt her more. "So, like, what are you doing?"

She felt her cheeks pull into a smile. "I'm waiting, Ben."

"Mmm," said her son.

Rachel could see him so clearly, as if he would gallop down the stairs: the slam of his door, the thump of those big shoes on the hardwood, and he'd throw himself into the sprawling wing chair in her office, wafting soap and shampoo, jingling his keys. *Hey, Mom.* Nikes on her desk, his grin to the right of her computer screen. *What's up?* Oh, Ben.

"Does Dana know?"

"No, not yet."

"Oh."

"I'll call her. I have to call her."

"Hey, you want me to come in? I could, you know, it's not like I have to be in class every minute; it's not like I've missed any. I could get a ride next weekend or I could come in now. I mean, I couldn't get a ride now because it's Monday, but I could come in Friday, huh, Mom?"

You could just rip a whole new hem with your finger; sit quietly on the floor of your office and rip someone's trousseau into shreds. "Oh, sweetheart, I think I'd just feel better if you stay where you are." Rachel stood up.

"Oh."

"I think I want to be by myself."

"Oh," said Ben.

"But, thank you," Rachel said, and took a step, and six inches of peach satin fabric floated quietly down and around her ankles, trapping her on the run.

"Free-floating anxiety," Grace said, "is another story altogether."

Rachel leaned her head back against the refrigerator—maybe the steady hum of General Electric would lull her to sleep. Sitting on the floor of her kitchen, legs stretched out in front of her, she watched Grace pace.

"Oh, to not know what's bothering you, to not be able to pinpoint which of life's heartaches is messing with you, only the privileged get such a gift. I, on the other hand, am awake at three as if I'd been hit." She stopped and eyed Rachel. "You look like shit. Is that my mother's nightgown?"

Rachel nodded.

"Mm-hm. You know, one little Valium and you could sleep the sleep of princesses. I would stay right here next to the telephone; I would wake you if anybody calls."

Rachel shook her head no.

"I promise."

"No, Grace."

"This falls under the same heading as why you won't take anything on an airplane even though you're white-knuckling it all the way to New York—in case the pilot is senselessly stricken from a bad piece of airplane food and you have to land the 767 while he's throwing up?"

Rachel smiled.

Grace smiled back. "Uh-huh. I thought so."

She sat down across from Rachel, leaned back, and lay flat on the kitchen floor. "Well, when you wake up tonight at three-thirty, four, you can call me; I'll probably already be baking a cake." She flexed her feet, crossed her legs at the ankles, and shut her eyes.

Rachel arched her back against the refrigerator.

"So," Grace said.

Rachel watched her.

They were quiet.

"Do you think about her?" Grace said.

She didn't get it.

"The missus," Grace said, turning her head to Rachel. "I don't know . . . you and her, what's going on . . . the two of you . . . both waiting . . ."

Head spinning.

"I just . . . oh, who knows with me—that you talked to her, you know, and that it's the two of you, it was in my head."

Rachel had sometimes thought about what Linda was doing, feeling—were they feeling the same things?

"How long were they married?"

Heart thrashing, eyes on Grace. "*Were?* You said *were*."

"Are. I'm sorry. Are. Are. I meant are." She sat up.

"You think he's dead."

"I do not."

"Oh, boy."

"Rach, please, I don't. I don't know what to think, but I don't think he's dead."

They sat there. "And why did you ask me that?"

"I'm sorry," Grace said. "I don't know; you know me, I'm crazy."

Rachel ran her hand through her hair.

"I meant *are*."

She wanted to run from the room. She wanted to run to him; that's what she wanted.

"Rach . . ."

"You don't have to stay with me."

"I know that."

Jesus.

"Please, Rach."

"Okay."

"I'm sorry."

"Okay."

"Okay," Grace said. She exhaled. "I'm sorry." She kept looking at Rachel. Catching their breath, resettling, like feathers falling to the floor.

"Do you want something to eat?"

"No."

"I could make my famous grilled cheese."

"No."

"With pickles."

"Uh-uh."

"Okay . . . do you want to take a little walk or something?"

Rachel didn't say anything.

"Okay, okay, we won't do anything. We'll just . . . wait."

Rachel took a breath.

"Waiting for Godot," Grace said, trying a little smile.

A deep breath.

"It's nice and cool in here. Your house stays cooler than mine, don't you think?" Grace lay down again, flat on her back, raised her arms above her head, and stretched her fingers, *"Waiting for*

Godot," she murmured, "*Waiting for Lefty*—did you ever read that?"

Rachel got to her feet. "Godot and Lefty never showed up."

Grace turned to her.

You could actually hear the kitchen clock.

Charlie

THEY FOUND THE Ford Explorer on Monday night. Well, Monday around five o'clock, if you wanted to be correct, and the Sheriff's Department didn't find it, two hikers did. Spotted it hanging from the side of the canyon off Glacier Lodge Road and called it in on their cell phone; hung up on rocks and a piece of tree, teetering like it was a toy car, about a thousand feet down. Two German hikers whose English was about as good as his German, B. J. Holland said. B. J. got the call; he was working the substation in Big Pine.

Charlie had just come out of the bathroom, about to clock out and go home, about to call Marie and say he was leaving so he wouldn't have to hear her carry on later about how his being late had messed up her lamb roast. He didn't even like lamb. Not that she ever asked him, but he could spend the rest of his life without ever eating any more lamb. "I can't hear him," Martha Grinnell was shrieking. He'd never heard Martha raise her voice; he crossed the office in three strides, grabbed the phone.

" 'Deutschland, Deutschland über Alles' is about as far as I go," B. J. was yelling, and you could hardly hear him, what with the thunder and lightning that was going on. " 'Auto, auto,' the guy was yellin' at me in German." B. J. was trying to catch his breath. "Hell, that much I know, 'auto' . . . about four to five miles in, in the switchbacks right off Glacier. Jesus, he musta gone right over the ledge . . . no way we coulda seen him, no way; the goddamn Explorer hung up there on the embankment, brush and trees and shit, shakin' in the wind like James Bond."

"Is Jack in the car?" Charlie said.

Martha's eyes were as big as plates; Ralph Crawley had just come in; his uniform was plastered to him like he'd taken a shower with all his clothes on.

"What?" B. J. yelled.

"Is Jack in the car?" Charlie yelled back. He was shaking; Pat McCaffey put her hand on his arm. "Is Jack in the car, B. J.?" he yelled.

"Hell, I don't know; it's rainin' like a son of a bitch. You can't see squat."

"What's goin' on?" Crawley said, and took off his hat.

"Jesus," Charlie muttered, and there was a solid crack of thunder, and B. J. yelled, "Tell Nick he's gonna need a Huey from Lemoore; he's gonna need an I-don't-know-what to get to the car."

"What's goin' on?" Crawley said, and Pat McCaffey said, "Jack North."

". . . must have rolled two, three times . . ." B. J. was screaming. Ralph Crawley ran his hand through his hair and shook his head like a big dog, spraying them with rain.

". . . like a tooth hangin' out of my kid's mouth . . . why it hasn't gone the rest of the way down beats the hell out of . . ."

"Get Nick Rowlands," Charlie said to Martha, and she flew across the room to another phone.

They met on the baseball diamond at the high school in Big Pine. That was the command post. All of them, it seemed like to Charlie; everybody had shown up. On duty, off duty, didn't matter. Because it was a cop, Charlie figured, because it was one of them, they'd all come in a big hurry as soon as they'd heard. Warren Mosher looked to still be eating part of his dinner; the tail end of a wedge of pie was in his fist. Just the crust; you couldn't tell if it was apple, the fruit was gone. B. J. was right; it was raining like a son of a bitch, coming down practically sideways, but it was the mountains and it would clear, just like when he took Marie to Hawaii—one minute it was raining and the next minute the sun was drying everything. Charlie pulled at the slicker around his neck, stomped his boot against third base, and then they went up.

It was about four and a half miles into the canyon and nearly all the way down the side of the mountain—Jack's Ford Explorer was hovering like a dandelion in the wind. Nick Rowlands was the Northern Patrol Search and Rescue supervisor, everything was his call, but it was clear once they got there that there was no way they could rappel down to the vehicle, even if the rain stopped, even if it wasn't getting dark and would soon be black as pitch and in the middle of a goddamn thunderstorm; they'd never make it down. And an airplane wouldn't either, not with the wind coming up the valley, not with the up-and-down drafts. B. J. was right about that too. Only a helicopter could make it through the little windows, the little pockets, of storm, only a helicopter could land the rescue personnel close enough to the car. But the Navy rescue helicopter from Lemoore was out—B. J. was wrong about that. It would take an hour and a half just for the Huey to get to them, and it would need a bigger area to land—or perch was more like it. The Explorer was hanging, ready to roll the rest of the way down. Up at the top of Glacier, Charlie stood bent, pushing himself into the wind, trying to get a better look.

"I told you," B. J. said.

"Jesus."

"You can say that again," Warren Mosher muttered.

It was crowded. There was sheriff personnel and search and rescue personnel. There were vehicles, and there was gear. Rescue gear to pull up the Explorer, rescue gear to pull up Jack—or Jack's body, depending on which way you went.

"He's a goner," Warren said.

Charlie pulled his hat lower. "Maybe he crawled somewhere."

"And what? Is still breathing? When do you think he went over the top?"

"Hell, he didn't crawl anywhere," Rich Shelly said. "He pushed the darn thing over himself a week ago and is long gone . . . probably sitting with some honey in Las Waygass having a drink."

"You're full of shit," Charlie said to Shelly.

"Hey . . ."

"Hey, both of you," B. J. said, "cut it the fuck out."

The black-and-white-striped HP helicopter had taken only forty minutes to get to them, and it was shuttling the rescue team down the crevice of the inside of the mountain two at a time. Like bright orange balloon dolls, Charlie thought, in their orange gear against the side of the black mountain; balloon dolls like those the clown made at his kid's birthday party years ago—rabbits and lambs and the squeak of the balloon as he twisted it, and the kids' eyes all big, scary that it would pop. Hunter-orange balloon guys with lights coming out of their heads; lamps shining out of their crash helmets through the wet and the dark, orange rain gear over cargo pants, seat harnesses around their waists and legs and through the crotch, tied and roped and setting anchors as they made their way down to Jack's car. Tied in case they fell; anchored so that when they made it to the car, they wouldn't go down with it if it decided to roll. When it decided to roll was probably more like it, Charlie thought.

The rain had diminished now into a soft sprinkle, thick inky clouds, a couple of stars here and there in the pockets of clear sky.

"Anybody got a cigarette?" Charlie asked.

"You quit, Charlie." B. J. laughed. "Last Christmas."

"I should have seen him when I was doin' forest patrol," Warren Mosher said.

B. J. put his fat hand on Mosher's back. "How could ya, Warren? You woulda had to dangle yourself off the side of the goddamn mountain to see him, for crissakes."

Warren worked at the beak of his hat. "They'll probably have to cut him out of the car."

"If he's in there," Rich Shelly said, and he was grinning. Charlie wanted to rip Shelly's goddamn head off and piss down his throat.

"They won't be able to bring him up tonight," B. J. said, "unless he's alive."

"No way he's alive," Ralph Crawley said, coming up behind them. "They gotta tie and anchor the vehicle. They'll get in the car and bag the body. It's already after eleven; they'll sleep down there and bring him up at light."

"He's a goner," Warren Mosher said again. "Poor fucker."

Charlie walked away. He didn't want to hear it; what difference did it make?

"Let me know what you got," Nick Rowlands was saying into the walkie to the rescue team, low like it was a chorus, "let me know what you got, let me know what you got." Doowah, doowah, as if he were a backup singer for Gladys Knight, as if he were one of the Pips. The two men exchanged looks. "Shit," Nick said.

Charlie kept his eyes on the little orange balloon men; he could feel his pulse thump in his neck.

They would know right away. They would know before they touched him: the angle of the body, the lividity—the blueness of the lips, where the blood had pooled. They would know if Jack was dead.

Linda

IT WAS THE first time she'd been alone. Patty and Julie taking turns, coming and going, with and without the babies, with and without the husbands, the front door banging, the asking, the over and over of the asking since she'd told them Jack was missing—for a solid week: "Have you heard anything? Have you talked to them? Mom, did they call?" Both of them devastated, both of them needing, and how much more could she give? And Tony had a game—oh, he was pitching in the play-offs, his team had made it to the play-offs, if only Jack could see. And Patty's baby had a fever; Kevin's voice sounded high on the phone: "I don't know, Mom, I can't read the darn thing, but she sure feels hot to me." She'd sat both girls down and told them they had to go home.

"Go home and sleep in your own beds, take care of your children . . ."

"Mom, we're not . . ." Julie had said with the look and the set of the shoulders, and Linda had cut her off. "You can come back tomorrow."

Patty's face was all quivery.

"I mean it," Linda had said, her eyes on the two of them, seeing them as if they were little: *Where's Dad? When's Daddy coming? Friday;*

Dad's coming Friday; now go clean up your rooms. Jack busy being a cop in L.A. while she was the cop at home. *I said now*—trying to be tough like him, the tone, the force, the presence—*go clean up your rooms.* Their stubborn retreat—the stomp of Julie's little tennis shoes, the swing of Patty's hair.

"Go home," Linda said now to her grown daughters, "I said go home."

Standing on the porch waving as they pulled out of the driveway, she had actually sagged with relief. Putting on a front, trying to stay strong for them, she felt like she was in a show. That's what the whole thing felt like—some show. The lights would come up and the people would clap—Jack would clap, delighted and surprised at how good she was—never suspecting she could have been an actress all along.

She sat at the kitchen table, her arms bent across the newspaper, the crossword letters blurring under her wrists. Bella turned over on her back near the refrigerator, her paws up against the wall. Buddy padded across the linoleum, moving through the house again and again to sit by the front door. Waiting for Jack. They were all waiting.

She had paced at first. Paced and then raced, whipped into some kind of frenzy, as if she were getting everything neat and tidy for his return. The ironing, the dusting, the fixing. Sitting on the kitchen floor in the middle of all her pots—"Mom, what are you doing?"—not looking up, not needing to look into her children's eyes: "I'm rearranging these." If she could get the pots in the proper order, Jack would come home. If she could iron the collar without those tiny creases near the tips, Jack would come home. If she could make it all be the way she thought he wanted it, Jack would come home, then spend a half hour in the shower, filling the bathroom with steam. *Linda, where are my moccasins? Linda, did you see my glasses? Hey, Linda, how about some ice cream?*

Linda lifted her arm and studied the long gray smudge of newsprint on the soft flesh from her elbow to her hand. What if he never came back? What if he did? The constant back-and-forth of reassuring herself he wasn't dead and telling herself he surely was. It would be easier if she knew one way or the other—or would it? The pictures in her head. Eyes closed, eyes open, the pictures of Jack dead. Buddy whined; Linda turned.

Quiet.

She felt like she'd become a vampire: her ears able to hear sounds regular people couldn't—tuned to his car in the driveway, his step across the gravel, his breath in the night—her eyes able to read shadows; she saw Jack now in any dim light, a hazy ghostlike presence of him in the corner of a room as if he would emerge and morph into flesh and blood like in one of those silly movies Tony and Carey had dragged her to. The fuzzy presence of him in the house terrified her. "Mom, why are all the lights on in here?" "Because."

In the few times she had left the house it had only been to go where she knew he might be. Stationing one of the girls next to the telephone, returning in less than twenty minutes, she'd made her rounds: the auto parts store, the parking lot behind it, Markie's Hamburgers, the place above Mustang Mesa where he liked to shoot, the China Club, the other side of the lake near the picnic tables, the grove at the schoolyard where he'd watch Tony pitch and coach him, crouching, the glove between his knees, his look to the boy, the nod, "That's it, that's it," the smack of the ball into the leather. "You got it, *all right*." As if he would return and appear in one of these places, forgetting they were all looking for him, waiting for him, forgetting he was supposed to come home.

Linda studied the jug of roses on the table in front of her. Patty had such a way with flowers, such a way with pretty things. She put her hands around the cup of warm milk she'd made—it was cold.

Didn't her mother give her warm milk when she was little? She wanted to call her mother. She touched one of the yellow roses, pink in the middle, beautiful. She should go to bed. Try to lie there without thinking. "You just clear your mind," Marie Eckerts had said, "empty it, just like you do the garbage." "It's meditation," Angie Saniger had chimed in. The two of them with their tuna casserole and Angie's famous yellow Bundt cake with the powdered sugar as if Jack were already dead. Linda had held tight to Buddy's collar; she'd wanted to let him go, watch him charge them backward off the porch, watch them topple, Angie's big bottom stuffed into those Capri pants, Marie's perfect hairdo collapsed over her face. She didn't even let them in, said she wanted to be alone—Jack would have laughed that she'd said it—like she was Greta Garbo in that film. "Speak your mind, for crissakes, Linda, what do you care what people think?" But she'd never been able to live her life that way. As if her mother were still alive. *Be a good girl* and *Mind your manners* and *Watch your mouth, miss.* Until now. "I want to be by myself," she'd said to them. Mrs. Greta Garbo North.

She had no idea what any of them knew. Not that she cared because what difference did it make now if Rachel Glass was the topic of conversation over breakfast at the Ham and Eggery or a shampoo at Esther's Cut and Curl. No one had let on anything, and they'd been coming all week—Lucille, Ralph Crawley's wife, whom she hardly knew; and Angie Saniger, who really looked like one of those horrible squatty dogs, those yippy-yappy fat things that get under your feet; and Marie, who'd burst into tears the first time she came before she'd even gotten one foot in the door, carrying on about how she just didn't know how Linda was dealing with it, if it was Charlie who was missing she'd be losing her mind—did Marie think she wasn't?—and Marge from Wicki's with a bag of fruit, most of it so ripe she'd probably taken it from the half-off bin, "Just dropping this off," she'd said, Walter waiting in the car for her with the motor running, eyes averted, head down, probably because he didn't know what to say to her; and Judy Beckson, whom she hardly knew from the library, and her moron of a husband who'd brought a bottle of wine as if they were coming over for supper instead of a . . . disappearance. What should one take to a disappearance? What does one say about a disappearance? No time for anybody to write to Ann Landers, and Ann Landers herself probably didn't even know.

Linda fingered the tiny white pill Julie had left in the saucer: "You're not going to become a dope addict, Mom; it's just to help you sleep." As if she wanted to be in some drugged nightmare when he called. Linda slipped the little pill into the water with the roses, slid it right under the deep green leaves.

After the cleaning and the fixing and in between the rounds of visiting his hangouts and people dropping in with food, she had searched for clues. After all, she'd been married to a detective for thirty-five years; she knew what to do. Hiding from Julie and Patty, she dipped her fingers in and out of Jack's pants pockets, in between his handkerchiefs and his papers, and through his toolbox, as if there would be a tip-off in a pair of pliers, a hint in a can of shaving cream, shaking her head at the insanity of thinking he had left her a sign of where he'd gone; she even shook his shoes. Weeping into his shirts, appalled at what she was doing because she had promised herself years ago she would never do it again—search Jack's things for matchbooks, scribbles of phone numbers, as if he would have come home with a handkerchief bearing a lipstick smear, as if she would learn the name and whereabouts of another "someone else"—wiping her face on his shirtsleeves now, sick at the thought that she was doing it again but for something far more horrifying, sick at the thought that he was gone forever. Smelling Jack, seeing Jack; he was everywhere, and he was nowhere at all.

She turned the pages of his address book; his left-handed scrawl made her sick with fear. There was no Rachel Glass on the *G* or the *R* page. Maybe there was another book in his car. Maybe there was no book, because he'd memorized the telltale pages; maybe there was nothing to find; maybe there were no clues, because he wasn't really missing—he was in L.A. hiding under Rachel Glass's bed.

Linda got up from the table. She stood there for a minute, her hand flat across her chest, then straightened her chair.

Her chair, his chair. His place at the table. His cup. His towel. His pillow. His toothbrush. There was no place to go.

She relived that last night, the night before the morning he left. Nothing. No clues. No fights, no anger, no loving, nothing at all. Meat loaf and mashed potatoes and canned peas. Ice cream with peaches. TV. He got into bed before she did. She washed her face and put on under-eye cream; she tweezed her eyebrows, then sat on the toilet lid in her nightgown and filed two broken nails. She didn't understand how anybody could garden in gloves. She brushed her teeth, turned off the bathroom light, and got into bed. He had his back to her; she pulled the blanket and sheet up over his shoulder and kind of tucked him in. She studied the ceiling and thought about what they should get Carey for his birthday—what did you want when you were eleven? It was so hard to know with boys. She turned off the light, rolled in the same direction as her husband, and moved closer in to him. The steady rhythm of his breathing, his warmth, her arm over his hip; she remembered having a little fit of coughing, and he mumbled, "What?" and she said, "Nothing," and they turned over together, facing the other direction, his arm sliding now over her hip, his hand grazing the blanket where it touched her breasts, and that was it.

She relived that last morning—where she was when he pulled out of the driveway. In bed. Dreaming. His tires on gravel had opened her eyes, but the fact that he was leaving meant nothing in particular, because it wasn't for sure; even though she'd had an inkling he was going to L.A., it wasn't for sure—he could have been off to breakfast or to pick up something or fix something or any of a thousand things. She didn't want the inkling to be real, so she reached for the dream, tried to hold on to it, fall back into its cocoon. It was a good dream: she was in a park like the one Mom and Daddy used to take her to when there was nothing to do on a summer night except take a drive, and there was a pond—or was it the lake?—there were ducks, and little Emmie, only somehow she was bigger or maybe Emmie was Patty, and her dad—wasn't that her father? She reached for the dream, but it was like holding smoke: the images drifted out of her consciousness and re-formed into the pieces of furniture in their bedroom. She could close her eyes and try, but she knew it was hopeless. She felt herself smile, stayed where she was for maybe five minutes, then sat up. There was only the pleasant feeling of a good dream, the crease in her cheek from the pillow slip, and the smell of Jack's shower as her feet touched the floor.

She didn't know for sure that he was going to L.A. She didn't want to give in to that, didn't want to think about him and Rachel Glass, how she pictured it in her head: see Rachel Glass waiting for him, see Jack's car in her driveway. She didn't want it; she wouldn't have it; she would hold on to the dream.

Breakfast, she ate a big breakfast, too big, and she'd just said to herself that she wasn't going to do that, that she wanted to lose five pounds, ten. The condemned man ate a hearty breakfast—isn't that what they said? She checked on the roses and the mildew, and the squirrel had gone through the geraniums as if he thought they were a smorgasbord, and somewhere around ten, ten-thirty, she knew.

Linda circled the kitchen table. She'd gone over it a million times; there was nothing new to learn, no clues. Buddy stood poised in the doorway, ready to follow her, if only she knew where to go. Could Jack have called Rachel Glass and told her he was coming when he really wasn't heading there at all? The dog cocked his head. Linda watched him, listened. Nothing.

"Sit, Buddy."

Jack wouldn't do that; it made no sense. He'd called Rachel Glass because that's where he was going. Then what happened? Slamming into the wall again, the wall at the end of her thoughts and her clues and her searching, her desperate attempts to be a detective all slamming into the same wall, and she slammed the chair, his chair, as she circled; she grasped Jack's chair with every bit of her strength and her anger and her hopelessness and slammed it into the table and into the table, the cup turning over, the milk sloshing, the jug of flowers Patty had picked and put in the center of the table falling, the water hitting the table and her shins, and the smell of the roses; she picked up Jack's chair and ran with it across the kitchen as if she were one of those pole-vaulters and slammed it into the wall. A sound came out of her, more like a laugh than a cry; Jack would be shocked. *Linda, what the hell got into you?* A chunk in the plaster, a gash from the chair leg across the wall; maybe someone would have to slap her; maybe this was hysterics like in the movies; maybe he would never see it because he would never come home.

Buddy was barking and the phone rang. She slipped on the water, wrenched her back as she slid on the water, grabbing the receiver. "Hello? Hello?"

"Linda? Do you have your scanner on? They found Jack's car right outside of Big Pine, up Glacier Lodge Road."

She didn't even know whose voice it was; the phone fell from her hands and she ran.

Charlie

SHE WAS STANDING on home plate. Somebody had thrown a slicker over her: you could tell she didn't even know it was on her; she wasn't holding it or anything—it was just teetering on her shoulders like she was a piano or a chest of drawers or something someone had left out in the rain. Nobody was standing close to her, nobody was even talking to her, like she had some communicable disease. Or maybe nobody knew what to say. Charlie put one arm around her. She didn't turn into him like she did that day when she cried on the porch, that first day when this whole song and dance began. As soft as Linda was in Charlie's mind's eye, she appeared now to have been transformed from a big luscious woman into a block of something stiff and hard. Her hand was icy as he took it, her cheek cold. She wasn't crying or shaking or falling apart as far as he could tell; she was just . . . like a big Popsicle, Charlie thought, a peach Creamsicle, if they still made those.

"Is he dead?" Eyes front, looking straight into his.

He pulled himself up to his full six feet three. "They didn't get to the car yet, Linda. Who called you? Somebody who heard it on their scanner, I'll bet. You shouldn't be here; you should be home."

She turned. "I'm going up."

"Hey . . ."

She walked away from him; he followed and grabbed her arm. "They're not gonna let you up there."

"I'm going up," she said, shrugging off his hand. "Either you can take me or I'll drive myself."

"Linda . . ."

"I'm going to see Jack, Charlie."

He let go. He felt kind of shaky. "I'll take you," he said.

Linda

HIGH ON THE edge of the mountain, around and around the slick curves; she kept her gaze fixed on Charlie's hands on the wheel.

"Everybody's listening to police business on their scanners; it's just not right, I'll tell you. Scanner land, B. J. calls it," Charlie said. "You know B. J. Holland, don't you, Linda? Out of Big Pine."

Her own hands were shaking, but she didn't feel cold. Or was it her arms? Or was it all of her? She clasped her hands together, pulled her elbows hard into the sides of her chest, intertwined her fingers into a ball. What had Jack been doing on this road?

"Where does this road go?"

"Mmm?" Charlie didn't look at her. "Is that how you heard we found the car—on Jack's scanner—is that how you heard?"

"Where does this road go?"

"Mmm?" he said again.

"Charlie . . ." It was all she could do to sit there. "Could he be alive in the car?"

"I don't know, Linda."

"He could be."

"Depends."

"But he could be."

"Depends on when he went down."

"But he could be."

He didn't look at her. "Could be. Sure."

He could be; he was alive in the car. She would hold on to that; he was alive in the car. "Where does this road go?" she asked again.

"Around."

She wanted to hit him. She put her lips together carefully. "Around?"

"Around and back out again; it's where the hikers come, hikers and campers." He gave a little shrug. "A loop, kind of—you never been up here?"

She didn't answer.

Charlie nodded, even though she hadn't said anything, nodded and kept his eyes on the road and around another curve, and he stopped short in a mess of vehicles. She reached for the door, pushed it, and was surrounded as soon as she got out of the car.

A blur of men and night and lights: she'd seen it before, a crime scene, she knew what it was; and later, when she tried to remember, it was like film that goes out of whack, too fast and off the track—someone named Nick with a walkie-talkie, and they wanted to take her away, keep her apprised. No, she said, no, they were yelling and struggling, Charlie was pulling her arm, the sky so clear, a star, where had the rain gone? *The baby is in the bath,* the only clear thing that she could remember was that. *The baby is in the bath,* the voice said loud and clear over that radio, and Jack was dead.

Charlie

THEY BROUGHT HIM up at dawn. The body. And there was this piece of Charlie that had a hell of a time believing that it was someone he knew. Maybe it didn't matter how many years you saw stuff, because leaning out over the incline, watching them carry the bag strapped to the miller board, it was a hell of a hard thing to swallow that the body inside that bag was Jack's.

The team had slept down there, rolled out mats and caught some shut-eye, 'cause it sure didn't make much sense to try it in the dark and, of course, the pressure was off as soon as they got to Jack and knew he was gone. Everybody just slept right there, kind of finding a place for themselves, settling in. He didn't sleep, just walked around, had some coffee, ate one of those Balance bars that he got from Warren Mosher; it tasted like shit. They had to cut Jack out; the Explorer was crumpled around him like a tin cup. They got in and cut, bagged him, and eased him out—God knows what he looked like. Charlie was happy to have missed that.

The sun coming up sent red streaks across the sky, red and pink and what he thought was called magenta—at least he thought that's what it was called—he didn't know a hell of a lot about colors, and it sure wasn't like him to notice a sunrise or how beautiful the damn thing could be, but the idea that it was happening like a goddamn painting in a museum sure didn't seem fair. He had to hold on to himself. Here they were strapping Jack to a board and hand-carrying him up the side of a goddamn mountain with the helicopter waiting, blades turning and catching the sun all orange like it was on fire, and this kind of biblical thing was going on in the sky with yellow coming out like beams, like Jesus was going to step off a cloud and say welcome to Jack or something, with His arms open, the way He always is in the pictures, and Charlie thought he was going to lose it. He took off.

The coroner would meet the helicopter at the baseball diamond to pronounce, and he wanted to be there. He was officially off-duty, but he wanted to be there. And he didn't want to go home; no way was he ready to deal with Marie and her badgering him with questions, and she'd cry; she'd fall all over him crying and carrying on about Jack. *What if it were you? What if it were you?* A cop could get shot in Philadelphia or buy it in Nebraska and she'd start in with the *What if it were you?* And Jack's being a cop and a friend of theirs on top of it, it wouldn't matter how he'd died; he could hear her *What if it were you?*

Charlie ran his hands through his hair. How Jack had died was the business at hand for all of them, the talk of the mountain, how Jack had died. Charlie put his hat back on.

He looked like shit, like he'd been run over; he needed a shave. He'd dozed about an hour in the car, but that was after all the business with Linda North. And talk about timing—driving her up and not knowing what to say and hang it if she doesn't take three steps out of the car and the goddamn walkie goes off in Nick's hand and a rescue guy is yelling, "The baby is in the bath." The baby is in the bath, of course, being code for the fact that they had gotten to the body and Jack was dead. In the bath versus out of the bath. Dead in the water versus alive. Talk about timing, and who would have thought she'd know what that meant? It's not like it was the 10 code. Come to think of it, he didn't even know what a dead body would be in the 10 code: 10-89, 10-98? Couldn't remember. He slipped on his shades, planted his hands firmly at ten and two o'clock on the wheel, and took the curves down.

She'd slipped right out of his hands, didn't faint or lose consciousness, just slipped to the ground like someone had walloped her, let go of her strings. And then carrying on that she wanted to stay until they brought him up. Jesus. They sent her home with Pat McCaffey, of all people. Howard Saniger with that drone of his, boy did he have a way, just waltzed her right into the car. *We're gonna take you home, honey; we're gonna call your girls. Linda, come on, honey, we're gonna take you home.* Hell, he didn't even see Saniger get there, didn't even know he was on the scene.

Charlie ran his hand across his mouth.

From the prelim it looked like no foul play, no perp taking him out, no gunshots or anything visible—not till the autopsy. Charlie held his hand in front of his mouth, exhaled and breathed in. Where the hell were the goddamn Tic Tacs? So far it looked like the only one of them that could be right on cause of death would be Mosher, who'd pushed the suicide theory, but that would only be if Jack had left a note, in the car or on his person; a note being the only way that he, Charlie, would ever believe that Jack had bumped himself off, taken himself out by driving off Glacier.

Charlie searched the seat next to him, then pushed one arm in between the seats behind him and searched around on the backseat floor. That would mean that adultery would be the cause of death, if you thought about it, if you went with the suicide theory: Jack was so despondent over this having to pick between two women that he drove himself off a cliff. Adultery as the cause of death, being at the root of the suicide. But how could that be? Hey.

Charlie found a peppermint in the glove box and unwound the cellophane using one hand and his teeth.

He just didn't think so. Hell, he'd just seen Jack two weeks ago. Had a beer, a burger, played some pool. He might not be a head shrinker, but he sure knew if a man was broke up enough to drive himself off a cliff.

Charlie rolled the peppermint around in his mouth. Of course, it did happen. Like that guy in Vegas a couple years ago—respectable guy, a wife, two kids, works in a bank, falls in love with another banker, a teller or something; they have a thing, he leaves the wife, she leaves the husband, they take off. Holed up in Wells, Nevada, in a Holiday Inn. Lyin' in bed, everything fine, just fine, making plans, and outta nowhere he says, "I can't do this. I can't stand what I've done to my wife. I love you, but I just can't do this, Amy," or Susan, or whatever the hell her name was; then he lowers his hand off the side of the bed into his valise, pulls out a thirty-eight, and blows his brains out.

Charlie sucked on the peppermint and tilted the visor to deflect the rising sun. Well, adultery was sure the cause there.

And Doc Filbeck told him about some crazoid they'd brought into the ER once who'd cut his penis off with a hacksaw. Lusted after his neighbor's wife. That was the whole thing—lusted after his neighbor's wife, couldn't stop himself, and went for his saw. Told the docs Jesus told him to do it. Charlie shook his head. Poor fucker. Every blade of that thing twanging on his pecker. Hoo-ha.

Charlie ran his hand across the stubble along his jaw. He oughta carry a razor in the car.

He took the last curve and stepped on the gas.

He couldn't buy it. No way. If anybody was gonna take himself out over this goddamn love affair, it would have been one of the women. Not Jack North. No way.

Charlie chomped down hard on the peppermint. He should have bet Warren Mosher fifty bucks that Jack's death was an accident, that there would be no note.

Rachel

When she woke up, she didn't remember. It had always been that way. Her eyes would open and for just that one instant, she would forget the bad thing. If she had a bad thing to remember. Then it would seep over her like fog.

Rachel rolled to the other side of the bed.

Like syrup. Today was Tuesday, yesterday was Monday, Monday had been a week. Jack was missing a week—how was that possible?

She ran her arm under the pillow, repositioned her legs on the crumpled sheet. Jack's side of the bed. When she was married to Henry it was her side of the bed. But Jack had stretched himself out on that side the first time in this house in this bedroom and she'd never said a word. She'd relinquished all rights to sides. When he was away, she took the middle.

Rachel's eyes followed the outline of the window through the lace. Quiet. Gray changing to blue. Morning. She rolled on her back and straightened the cover on either side of her body. Her father said morning was the purest time of the day. "Everything settled," he'd say through his mustache, showered and shaved and shiny, sitting at the dining room table cutting through his poached egg. A poached egg on rye toast, perfectly placed, a glass of water, two cups of coffee—no more, no less. Six-thirty in the morning, every morning except Sundays, dipping the corner of the toast into the last bit of yellow—Ben Rosenthal, in suit pants, a starched white shirt, and a paisley tie, his jacket hanging perfectly squared on the back of his chair. "Everything fresh, my love, everything ready to begin again," he would say as she'd wander through, mumbling about school and why did she have to leave her bed and her dreams, and there he'd be, all chipper, rinsing his plate, rolling down his sleeves, inserting his cuff links. Rachel hated mornings. By 6:00 her dad had already gardened for an hour. Sometimes she would stir in bed and hear his clippers in her sleep, hear him puttering around snapping branches, running the hose. A morning man, her mother said, "He is the dawn and I am the dusk," and it was true. As much as Rachel couldn't stomach the romance of the line or her mother's delivery, it was true. Lady never got up with him, never said good-bye except what she might have mumbled to him from their bed, but she was always ready with a V.O. and water when he got home, a V.O. and water for him, an apricot sour for her that she actually mixed in a silver shaker, olives in a side dish, tiny pickles, smelly cheese. Lady was big on the cocktail hour; Lady would have preferred dinner to be hors d'oeuvres. Their house circled around the cocktail hour, which Rachel thought was quite Gentile considering they were Jews.

But in the mornings, Ben Rosenthal had the house to himself. With a sleeping wife and daughter upstairs, he made and ate his breakfast, rinsed his dishes, and left them neatly stacked. He donned his jacket and hat—pinstripes and fedoras in the winter, seersucker and panamas when the heat set in—and leaving a cloud of crisp aftershave in the downstairs hall, he would fold the newspaper under his arm and walk to the El. One muggy August morning, the summer Rachel turned sixteen, he crumpled at the station as the train came in, never saying a word, suffering a massive heart attack and dying approximately six minutes later, fellow commuters reported to the authorities, who then told her mother, the *Chicago Tribune* still neatly folded under his arm.

Rachel watched the lace move at the windows, rearranged the pillow under her head.

Lady Rosenthal never remarried. Ben was forty years old when he died and Lady was thirty-eight. Her mother had lived without her man longer than she'd lived with him. She'd dated after Ben, but nobody had *bowled her over*—her expression—she had also been heard telling Ben-oh, her grandson, that the reason she had never married again after his grandfather was that nobody since him *rang her bell.*

Rachel had never had a man like her father. Maybe they didn't exist; maybe she remembered him better than he really was. *Dapper* was the word that came to mind, elegant; Ben had a certain elegance, a certain savoir faire. Rachel rubbed her eyes, lifted her knees under the blanket. Maybe it was the cuff links. Even Henry couldn't pull off cuff links. And Jack—there was no way to picture Jack in French cuffs. Or a panama. Or a paisley tie.

The phone rang. Unaware that she had thrown back the covers or let her feet touch the floor, naked, standing, she grabbed the receiver. "Hello?"

"Checking," Grace said.

Heart racing, sitting back on the bed, slumping back across the pillows. "Oh, hi, Grace."

"I figured you were up."

"I'm up."

"Did you sleep?"

"Yes."

"And no?"

Rachel shrugged.

"Uh-huh . . . so, you okay?"

"Yeah."

"I'm poaching chicken breasts."

"Grace, it's not even seven."

"Madam, this is your lucky day. For lunch you are having a divine chicken salad. *Don't say no.* With pecans and Gorgonzola." She made a little "wsst" sound with her mouth. "I'm also considering grapes. But it's so Midwest."

Tears catching her unawares, Rachel nodded. "Oh, Grace."

"Do not *oh, Grace* me. I'll be there at noon, high noon. So, with or without grapes?"

"Without."

"Good choice," Grace said. "I will set the table with finery, veddy first class, we may even go so far as to have mint in the ice tea."

"I like mint," Rachel said, smiling, and carelessly lulled by the sweet talk of the conversation she forgot the bad thing again, so when the call waiting clicked on the line she assumed it was Dana and told Grace to hold on.

"Hello?"

"Ms. Glass? Uh, Rachel?"

"Yes?"

"Steve Thorne."

"Yes?" Standing again.

"Hi."

Knowing by the tone in his voice he'd heard something. Winded, as if she'd been socked.

He cleared his throat.

Knowing by the gap between his words that what he had to say wasn't good; her legs going numb. "Yes?"

"Uh . . . Rachel . . ." And knowing the language was cop talk, knowing what he meant when he said it, losing her footing when he said it. "Rachel . . ." It took the Beverly Hills detective several seconds to get it out. "Rachel . . ." As if saying her name would make it easier. "Rachel"—and then his voice went wobbly—"I'm sorry for your loss."

Patty

HER FATHER WAS dead. She said it to herself over and over, but it made no sense. Her father was dead and she had to change the baby, her father was dead and she had to make supper, her father was dead and she was taking a shower and she was washing her hair—how could she be washing her hair? How could she do laundry? Fold the sheets? Her father was dead and she had actually laughed at something on television, laughed out loud, walking across the room, and Kevin had it on and it was *Everybody Loves Raymond* and she had laughed out loud and then been shocked and embarrassed that she could laugh, that such a sound could come out of her when her father was dead. Kevin had to take the baby out of her arms she was sobbing so hard. Life goes on, he'd said, and she'd wanted to slap him. How could life go on as if nothing had happened? How could that be?

Her father was dead and she had to find a dress. Patty pushed through the rack of hangers, passed by what would be inappropriate—anything that wasn't black, anything that wasn't simple, anything that wouldn't fit. Was everybody a size six? Was she the only woman in the world who ate food?

It was her third store and she was getting nowhere and Kevin was at home alone with Patty Cake, which was making her crazy because it would take her a while to drive back, but where could she have gone but Reno to find a nice dress? Carson City? Julie said she had a dress, Julie had everything, Julie spent a lot of money on clothes, and Patty couldn't bring herself to ask her mother, the idea of asking her mother made her sick. Can I borrow something to wear to Daddy's . . . no. There was nothing in Bishop, nothing, and she couldn't drive all the way to L.A., so here she was in Reno, not exactly the fashion capital of the world.

Look at that—seventy-nine dollars and it wasn't even lined, it wasn't even anything; maybe she was in the wrong store.

Kevin would probably give the baby a beer and pork rinds for lunch and make her watch the Jets game; he'd probably forget to warm up the macaroni and cheese, forget to feed her, forget to put her down for a nap.

Here's one that's plain, but the fabric is shiny—no, it's too skimpy in the bust.

She'd never had a black dress. Julie had a black dress and a black suit, but Julie went to work. She, on the other hand, didn't go anywhere. A little black dress that you read about in the magazines—but a dress like that is supposed to be for romance.

Her throat filled.

She had seen her father last. From what her mother had told her, from what the police reports had said, they all thought that it was the little checker in the mini-mart, but they were wrong. She hadn't told a soul—not Kevin, not her mother, not a soul. It was all she had, she thought, her special something, a memory that would have nothing to do with anybody else, just her.

She played it over and over in her head: his step, the way the light caught the black of his hair; he had a kind of smile and then he'd raised the cup of coffee to his lips. Jeans and a black T-shirt and a black-and-white plaid shirt over that, with the sleeves rolled up. She loved that she remembered that, that the sleeves were rolled. She knew it was him from the back, before she got even with him, before she'd passed him in front of the mini-mart. That was special, that she knew it was him. Her dad had a specific walk. Julie always said it was because he was a cop; Patty didn't think so. It was just him. Confidence. And handsome still and kind of crusty and so . . . alive.

"May I help you?"

She couldn't do this. How could her father be dead?

"Miss?"

The saleslady was older, older than her mother, and her glasses hung from a pink plastic chain across her big breasts, and her feet hurt—Patty could tell that the lady's feet hurt from the way she stood. She ought to sit down; she ought to be home watching soap operas with her feet on some stupid stool.

"Can I help you find something?"

What was going to happen to her mother? Her mother had been with her father since the beginning, since she was a girl. What would happen to her mother?

"Miss?"

What would happen to her if anything happened to Kevin?

How could it be that a dress you could buy for romance could also be worn to a funeral?

"Are you looking in the right size?"

How could her father be dead?

"Miss?"

How could it be that the very day her father died was the day she'd had coffee with Mike? How could it be that the secret she had about seeing her dad in front of the mini-mart was all mixed up with the secret of where she'd been? Because if she hadn't been in Big Pine meeting Mike for coffee, if she hadn't felt funny about doing that, she would have stopped—oh, yeah, she would have, she would have stopped when she saw him, pulled over—*Hey, Dad,* she would have said, waving. *Hey, Dad, what are you doing down here? Hey, Dad.*

"Miss, are you all right?" The saleslady extended her hand to Patty, touched her arm.

She could have stopped him; she was the last one to see him; it was her. If she had pulled over she could have changed his mind, changed his route, changed what happened to him—he wouldn't have driven up Glacier Lodge Road; he would have followed her home. Or maybe they would have gone to lunch at the Whitney, split a piece of coconut cream. Or maybe they would have talked, spent the afternoon just being together, talking about life. Whatever they would have done, none of this would be happening, everything would be the way it was; he wouldn't be dead.

"Miss?"

If she had stopped, he wouldn't be dead. Patty nodded blindly at the saleslady and ran from the store.

Steve

IT WAS ONE hell of a funeral. Or it was going to be, Steve thought. Five cars from L.A.—two black and whites sent from the department, official, driven by uniforms (which Steve thought was pretty good considering Jack had been gone a couple years)—then him and Irene in his Camry with the Silkas (Paul Silka made detective along with Jack); then Dauer (their old boss, retired five years with so much hoopla that they'd retired his badge number along with him, which was a big deal) and his wife, Midge, and Ault (the new boss) without Jeannie Ault, who was too pregnant to make the haul, the three of them in Dauer's Infiniti, which didn't look to Steve like it was worth any thirty, thirty-five grand (and wouldn't it be nice to have a rich wife); and then Barcay and Mandavia and Lawrence Freedman (who'd been in the department with him and Jack from the get-go) bringing up the rear in Freedman's old Chrysler with no wives because they were going to head up to Mammoth afterward and fish. A parade of Beverly Hills P.D.

They lost the black and whites right after Mojave. The plan was to make it a procession, but that was over pretty damn quick—if one of the wives wasn't flagging them down to make a pit stop, then somebody else needed something to eat. Or coffee. Or gas. Not him, because he'd gassed up before they left and why everybody else hadn't was beyond him. Ellie Silka wanted to stop at Manzanar, because she'd read about it in some book—that was a good forty-five minutes that he hadn't planned on, with everybody putting in their two cents about America's dragging her own off into internment camps and Silka's wife going on about what it must have been like to have been born Japanese in America in 1941. And that set Barcay off, because he'd been in Vietnam and probably shouldn't have said what he said about gooks, because she went ballistic; Steve had a hell of a time getting everybody back in their cars. Then Midge Dauer had to eat as soon as she shot up her insulin, so they had to stop for lunch at some joint in Independence, even though they'd already stopped for breakfast in some joint in Olancha, and as much as he wasn't ready to sit around and listen to everybody figure out what they wanted on their hamburger, there was no way to say no. It was a good thing they hadn't left the morning of the funeral; they would have missed the whole damn thing.

They split up when they got to Bishop and checked into their motels. Irene wanted to stay at the more upscale Best Western at the far end of town, the guys wanted to stay anywhere cheap, and the Silkas and the Dauers were staying with Midge's mother. Steve didn't even know Midge Dauer was from up here. Her mom ran some kind of ranch or camp or something that had belonged to her great-uncle with plenty of room for them, but Irene wouldn't budge. She had some half-assed idea that this was some kind of vacation, and she wasn't going to stay in anybody's house. The whole thing made him crazy. He and Irene had been together a long time, and they pretty much kept it at an even keel, but the idea that she wanted to make Jack's funeral weekend into some kind of escape-into-a-honeymoon paradise pissed him off no end. He'd followed her through the air-conditioned room with the king bed and the mints on the turndown and the fake flowers, and it was all he could do to not give her a shot. She'd locked herself in the bathroom. He walked around the hotel, bought a beer in the bar, and took it with him outside—they had a nice pool and a kind of meandering creek that went around the grounds.

The ducks had come up on the grass with their babies, all fuzzy, and Irene would have liked that, but he wasn't going to tell her; she could just stay in the goddamn bathroom and stew. She could look at herself in the three-way mirror and be happy he hadn't taken out a tooth.

Steve watched the mother duck feed her babies and took another swig of his beer. It wasn't that Irene didn't like Jack, because she did, or she *had*—and that was a tough one—trying to remember that everything now with Jack was past tense. They'd had some good times together, the four of them; it had nothing to do with Jack—it all had to do with Irene's refusal to deal with death. Not just Jack's, anybody's. When somebody died, she didn't want to talk about it, like it was catching. Don't talk about it; you make too much of it, she'd say. Like last year, when she'd accused him of being a romantic when he went on about the bagpipes that had played "Amazing Grace" at Ramos Sanchez's funeral, about how beautiful it was, because this kid, this cop, twenty-five years old, talk about your whole life ahead of you, and the whole family there, rows and rows of little Mexican women wailing with that lace shit on their heads, little old men in crummy suits with their shoulders low, and the pipes and the flag, and how beautiful it was, which was the truth, because he'd nearly lost it, crying and all; it was a good thing he'd had on his shades. *Bagpipes at a Mexican motorcycle cop's funeral,* she'd said, *were ludicrous.* He'd had a hard time unclenching his hands. He had no idea if they were going to have bagpipes at Jack's.

And something about the fact that she'd accused him again of being romantic about funerals, when she was the one who wanted to be romantic while he was about to bury his partner, just made him want to spit.

Steve took a deep breath, drained the beer, and laid the bottle gently on the grass. He'd promised the shrink that when he felt this way he would get away from her: *Get separate from her,* Dr. Turner had said, *disengage.* Steve resettled himself on the white lawn chair. Disengage, he'd like to disengage all right, he'd like to disengage a few teeth from her mouth with his fist. Kissing him like a whore because they're in some goddamn motel room. Goddamn.

Irene would probably stop to go to a cocktail party on her way home from burying him. Or maybe she wouldn't bury him at all—she'd probably let someone else do it, relegate it to his lawyer or something; she'd probably be out shopping with his pension money stuffed in her purse.

"Do it with a lawyer," she'd said when he'd tried to talk about his death and what he wanted funeralwise, her face all white.

"What? Is it supposed to be a surprise? What if I want you to take me back to Detroit? What if I want you to sprinkle my ashes over Lake Michigan? You gonna read my mind? What if somebody blows me away?"

"Please, Steve," she'd said, and actually walked out of the room.

"Please, Steve," he said now, out loud in the lawn chair, imitating her. The mama duck eyed him but held her ground.

"Hey, duck," Steve said.

Jack was gonna have the works, he figured. Knowing Linda, she'd see to it. He, on the other hand, better find somebody who would see to him. He pushed at the empty bottle, rolled it back and forth on the wet grass. Sunny was hopeless, hardly ever talked to him, caught up in that San Francisco scene with all the other fruitcakes; he could just see him coming back with his significant other to bury dear old dad. His fag son carrying his ashes out of a church filled with uniformed cops—just what he needed—oh, yeah. Steve kept his hand on the beer bottle, his eyes on the ducks. He should have had more kids. That's what was missing; he should have had them with somebody else. He should have had somebody else all these years. Like Jack.

It had been hard with Rachel Glass, hard making the phone call because her loss was his loss too, and that had never happened to him before—delivering the news of the death of someone close to him to someone he hardly knew. Backward. And hard going over there. Not that he had to officially, not on behalf of the department or anything, but he thought he should. For Jack. He figured Jack would have wanted him to make sure she was doing okay or as okay as could be expected. She wasn't. And he wasn't any good about death, in the knowing-what-to-say part to make somebody feel better; he didn't know jackshit. And besides, Jack was his partner; he was having a lousy time too, but he went anyway, swung by. He didn't stay very long—just sat across from her for a little while, had some coffee, left. She mostly had questions, and he told her the answers, and that was about it. Except for the big one. *Why did Jack have to die?* because that's always the question no matter who it is who dies, who or how or when, no matter whether they say it out loud or not, ask it, and she didn't. It's always the question—*Why?* And why is 'cause *That's the way it is,* which nobody wants to hear, that's for damn sure.

Steve let the beer bottle roll down the little hill of grass to the walkway; it clattered when it reached the cement.

She wasn't okay, Rachel Glass. Linda probably wasn't either.

He had to call Linda, tell her he was here. He'd called from L.A. a couple of times and talked to each of her girls—nice, regular girls, married with kids of their own, right there taking care of their mom the way it should be. The other time he'd called he'd got the machine and that was creepy: hearing Jack say "Hi," and leave a message and everything—knowing he was dead. He had to tell them to fix that.

He raised his legs at the knees and planted his heels in the chair rungs. He wanted another beer. What a shame they didn't have roving waitresses crossing the lawn. In dinky outfits. The doc said he needed to lose ten pounds, twenty maybe, all right, twenty really, and he wanted another beer. And he was going to have one. There was no way to know; you could watch your cholesterol and run a goddamn mountain every morning and lift weights and shit like Kipper did, Mitch Kipper, his old pal in the Hollywood Division, and then cancer comes and knocks you on your ass. Maybe it wouldn't come back, maybe they'd caught it in time, but how many times do they say they got it all and back it comes? Kipper has a great attitude, but who knows what goes on in his head; he's probably scared even with the jokes. Because you never know. No matter who you are, no matter how much you got, it don't mean shit.

You come in, and as soon as you know enough to understand, you know you're going out—but you don't know when and you don't know how. That's the deal. No negotiation. And the older you get, the more you cling to everything you got here, but it don't make any difference 'cause sooner or later you go. Newman on that plane, him and the wife take a happy anniversary to Hawaii, and down she goes. One minute you're pouring the little bottle of scotch over the ice and watching the movie and the next thing you know you're pieces in the water and your baby girls haven't got a mom or a dad. Sam Poncher keels over in the line at the bank, and now you gotta make yourself get up the nerve to go over there and visit. You talk, but he doesn't answer, sits in the chair drooling with his hand all curled up, and the wife traipses in and out with the cookies and talks to Sam in a loud voice as if he's deaf all of a sudden or become a foreigner who can't understand what she says. He must have ate a dozen cookies the last time he went over there, and he doesn't even like macaroons. Tommy Smith takes it in the head from a drive-by right in front of First Christian with his wife and the minister and the whole goddamn congregation watching. Good morning to you, Jesus, thanks a lot.

Steve flattened his legs against the lawn chair, looked around: the sky was darkening; the moon and the sun trading places; the ducks were gone.

Or you could be Jack. Back and forth between two broads, everything copacetic, both of them loving you, and you drive off a fucking cliff.

Steve put a leg on either side of the lawn chair. Two women mourning for Jack—hell, he wouldn't even have one.

Julie

THERE'S NO REASON to tell her."

Julie didn't look at him; she kept her eyes on the road, the sky, the fields, the trees; he'd already told her that about a thousand times.

"No reason," Brian said again.

"I'm not going to."

"But you're thinking about it."

She didn't want to cry; she was all cried out; her head hurt.

"What's the point?" he said.

"You mean because it doesn't matter now? Because he's dead?"

"Honey . . ."

"Don't honey me."

Brian didn't say anything, just slowed the car as they approached town.

"I hate that," she said.

"You're upset."

"I'm upset; that's a good way to put it."

"It doesn't matter if you weren't talking to him."

"Okay."

"It matters to you now, but it doesn't matter in the long run—you and your dad were really close." He circled the lot behind the movie theater and pulled into a space. "He was really tight with you. You know that."

She didn't say anything.

"He wasn't talking to you either."

"Is that supposed to make me feel better?"

He ran his hand through his hair, then killed the motor. "Jule? It wasn't the first time you and Jack had a set-to."

"A what?"

"I don't know—isn't that a word?"

Her throat filled; she couldn't look at him.

"Anyway," he said.

She sat there.

"You knew what I meant."

She didn't look at him.

"Never mind," Brian said. He exhaled and tapped a little beat with his palms against the steering wheel. "Do you want me to do this for you?"

"No."

Her head was full, jumbled. And she was being mean to him, mean to Brian, who was trying so hard, but she couldn't help it. She had to be mean to someone, and she didn't want it to be the kids; she'd yelled at them at breakfast; she'd actually made Emmie cry. She'd even been snippy with her mother. Oh, God, she had. It wasn't that she wanted to tell her mother that she hadn't been speaking to her dad; it wasn't that.

Two times she'd been with him and all the times she hadn't, all the days when she could have called him, seen him, said something since she'd said what she'd said—accused him of being a liar, accused him of having an affair—is that what he thought of when he thought of her? Is that what he thought of her when he died? Did he think of her when he died? Her and Patty when they were little? Just her mother? All of them? She had no idea if you could even think during the pain of a heart attack. She had no idea about anything except she wanted to take back what she'd said. She wanted to apologize. *I'm sorry, Dad. Oh, Dad, I'm sorry.* How many times had she said it in her head?

"Julie?"

"What?"

"Do you want me to do this for you?"

"I said no."

He looked at her; she turned away.

"I'm gonna go get a Coke at the market then; I'll meet you back here."

She didn't want him to look at her sweetly; she didn't want him to be nice.

"Are you sure you don't want me to go in with you?"

She did, maybe she did, she didn't know if she did; she wanted to hit her head against the dash.

"No."

"Okay, then." He got out of the car and shut the door quietly. She watched his back as he crossed the grass—hands stuffed in his pockets, head down.

She had to apologize to him too. She had to apologize to her sister for being pushy; she had to apologize to her kids and to her mother. But most of all to her dad.

She opened the car door and got out.

And she had to do this by herself. She had no idea how he would have wanted it, because it had never come up; her father was not the kind of man that would ever discuss this, but she would do it the best way it could be done. That's why she had asked her mother—because somewhere inside of her she thought it might count, somewhere inside of her she thought maybe it could be her *I'm sorry, Dad.* She would take care of everything; she would make her father's funeral arrangements alone; she would do anything and everything to lessen the burden for her mother and, despite the fact that she was not spiritual and she was not religious, she prayed with all of her heart that if she did this, somehow and somewhere he would see, he would hear her, he would know that this was her saying *I'm sorry, Dad.*

Linda

SHE WAS TOTALLY shocked when the guns went off, as if she'd forgotten where she was. She stood up. Hand to her mouth, purse falling, the rustle of two daughters—"Mom, what are you doing?"—and her heels were stuck in the sod. The minister eyed her, gave her a nod.

She knew what this was—a policeman's funeral—she'd seen it before.

Seven uniformed police officers, twenty-one shots. So straight across the sky, loud, and the sun, and the smoke, and the tips of the rifles against the blue, hot, and the white of the special dress uniforms glinting in her eye like an ad for Clorox; she wanted to hold up her hand. Taps—she didn't even know they had brought a trumpet—eight uniforms lifting the flag like Irishwomen lifting the wash, sheets catching the wind as white as the uniforms, like Japanese ladies folding the origami into perfect thirds; Stars and Stripes forever folded into perfect thirds; they were pushing the flag into her arms. She took it. She thought of raising it to wipe the sweat from her lip, slipping her captured feet out of the shoes, toes in the grass.

Linda clutched the wedge of red-white-and-blue warm triangle that had been over the coffin—how could he be in a coffin?—and it was done.

A maze of faces and it was done.

Whatever the minister had said and it was done.

The sparkling white gloves of the honor guard; the smell of Patty's perfume; Tony sobbing against his father, all grown-up and still a baby in his stiff new suit; Carey burrowed into his mother; Julie's hands shaking as she wiped Emmie's nose; Emmie hiccuping into the wind.

Hot and dry and the smell of dirt and the sound of shovels.

The children leading her to the car.

Little Patty Cake looked up at her. "Grampa?"

Linda sat now on the ottoman at the foot of Jack's chair. The baby's eyes were big; she held her pudgy arms up to her grandmother. Linda lifted her from the rug.

"I got her, Mom," big Patty said behind her.

"It's all right." Linda held tight to the baby and pressed her nose into the damp curls. Patty Cake laughed and clapped. "Patty-cake, Grampa."

"Your song, huh, kid? She's all mixed up," Jack had said, pushing his face into the baby's middle while she shrieked. "I'm *Grampa,* you silly shrimp boat, there's your *grandma* over there." He grinned at Linda as he left the room, the baby tucked under his arm like a football.

"Patty-cake, patty-cake, baker's man . . ." The baby's chubby hands in her big ones.

The din of people.

Cops laughing in the kitchen, telling jokes in the kitchen, hanging around the sink and the scotch and the sandwiches; you could hear them laughing as they swapped shop. *Jack and I this* and *Remember when Jack that.* She knew what this was.

"Bake me a cake . . ."

"Can I get you anything?"

Get me Jack flashed like neon, but she said nothing, just smiled up at whoever it was.

"Pat it and roll it . . ." People on the porch and in the den and sitting on the front steps drinking coffee and dropping crumbs.

"Linda?"

Charlie Eckerts without his hat.

"Mark it with a *B*"—poking her finger softly into the baby's middle—"and put it in the oven for baby and me."

A row of wives across the couch watching her, happy that it wasn't them; she knew what they were thinking, with their egg salad sandwiches cut into triangles like the shape of the flag.

Steve Thorne's eyes.

The minister's hand was sweaty.

"Again," cooed little Patty Cake. "Again, Grampa."

Grampa.

A funeral, a wake, a wife, a widow. An empty blur. Linda sat on the ottoman at the foot of Jack's chair.

"All gone," the baby said, holding her arms above her head.

All gone, she thought. And it was done.

How could that be?

Dana

DANA CLOSED THE magazine and tried to reposition herself without moving too much; Rachel had fallen asleep. Their heads shared the same pillow—Dana had been lying on the spread next to her mother, reading some stupid article aloud about eating according to your blood type in order to lose weight, which Dana thought was insane and hysterical and would surely make her mother laugh. It hadn't. Neither had the joke she'd heard in the pickup line at the preschool. Neither had her rendition of Chris Rock talking about the differences between men and women. She was running out of material. No matter what she tried her mother's look slid off her face and over her shoulder into nothing land—glazed.

Dana could smell her mother's hair—not Rachel's usual scent of French soap and crisp shampoo and conditioner—just the smell of hair. Unwashed hair. Her fastidious mother had hardly left the bed. Her impeccable mother wasn't eating. Her perfect mother was . . . broken. That was the word that came to mind. Broken. Wrecked.

She'd thought her mother was Superman.

Her neck hurt; she needed to move it, but she stayed where she was.

She wasn't alive when her mother's father had died; she was too little to understand what was happening when her father's parents had died. She didn't know about death or grief or people being broken. She was lucky; she hadn't known that she was lucky until now. Steady breathing from Rachel, in and out. Let her sleep, Dana wished, let her be better. "All better," the baby said, when she'd gently pulled the Band-Aid off her knee. All better. She wanted to make her mother all better like Sarah's boo-boo, but she didn't know how. Grace was better at this—where the hell was Grace? She never should have let her go to the store.

She remembered how Rachel had coated her itchy chicken pox with pink lotion, crooning to her not to scratch, cradling her when she'd creamed her leg riding her bike into a tree; Rachel's cool hand holding her head over a toilet bowl, Rachel's cool head when the kitchen curtains at Lady's house caught on fire, Rachel's open heart to all of Dana's boy-girl high school drama, Rachel's acceptance of Dana no matter what. Unconditional love—that's what they meant by that—unconditional love. When Dana had needed her mother she always got her, until now.

She'd thought her mother was indestructible. Wonder Woman. A ship sailing through choppy seas. She had seen her mother lose jobs and regroup, lose dreams and regroup, lose a husband and regroup, practically lose a mother (because Lady in her dementia was certainly lost to the outside world) and regroup. She'd never seen this; she had no experience.

Rachel moaned in her sleep, frowned. Dana reached out and tentatively pushed her mother's hair back from her forehead. Warm, damp—did she have a fever? She couldn't remember ever reaching out to touch her mother; it was always her mother reaching out to touch her. Rachel sighed, then rolled to one side, and Dana turned with her, putting her hand gently on her mother's hip.

She didn't know that this could happen.

She held her mother, her breasts pressed into Rachel's back, her knees tucked into Rachel's. She was struck by the fact that her mother was thinner than she was, smaller—a tiny Wonder Woman, she thought, a fragile Superman, a broken mother. Dana's eyes filled. She breathed in the smell of Rachel.

This was all new to her, this swapping of places.

She had never been a mother to her mother before.

Rachel

GRACE DID NOT ask her how she felt, didn't expect her to speak, just sat with her. "I'm here," Grace would say, "I'm with you," Grace would say, "I love you," Grace would say, and hand her a bowl of rice pudding or sit across from her quietly, holding her hand. Grace, who reviled any display of affection said, "I love you," and held her hand.

"How are you?" was the chorus of Dana and Ben. How are you, Mom? Frightened eyes, wanting her to be okay, wanting her to be regular, wanting her to be like before. *I'm fine. Just fine. Okay. You bet.* Because what could she say? Not the ribbon of words that nobody wanted to hear, because then the asker was left with no comeback.

"How are you?"

"I'm out of control."

"Oh. Alrighty then." And there they stood.

The ticker tape of words that rotated depended upon nothing; it was as arbitrary as what room she was in at the moment they smacked her, swept up and shocked her. Shock, Rachel typed onto the screen. Panic. Empty. Terror. Numb. Lost. Alone. Her fingers moved across the keys and then stopped; she bent her head. Well, nobody wanted to hear those words.

And because their connection, the Jack-and-Rachel, Rachel-and-Jack connection, had been committed but tentative—oh, to say the least, tentative—and to most a secret, most didn't even know. "How are you?" from Woody in New York, who had been advised by Grace on behalf of Rachel that Rachel had been hit with a really bad case of a mysterious virus, or was it a puzzling allergy, or was it a rampant flu? "I'm better," she'd mumbled after dodging weeks of calls from Woody about the piece she hadn't sent in on the ten best whatever-there-was for *Allure*. "You poor thing," Woody had drawled. "Are you better?"

"Getting better," Rachel whispered, squeezing her hand shut, so tight that her nails left a row of indented scallops across her palm. Because what was the point in telling—now? *Oh, I have this boyfriend and he died on his way to me . . . and I never mentioned him because he has a wife.* Had. *Had* a wife. *Had* this boyfriend. *Had.*

Panic. At 9:17 in the morning on this particular Tuesday—*panic* is the word.

She lifted her fingers from the keys, then pushed the chair away with the backs of her legs as she got up and circled the room. What made her think she could work? What made her think she could go to the grocery store? What made her think she could open the mail?

Was he alive before he went over the edge? Was he alive on the way down? Was he alive when the car rolled and hit? Bad words. Words not in one's daily vocabulary.

She knew very few of the details; only what Steve Thorne had told her when he'd returned. From the funeral. A word she couldn't fathom and had not yet asked him about. First things first—heart attack—a heart attack just like her father had. Not in those words, but in words that Detective Thorne seemed to have memorized from a form. Cold words. A myocardial infarct—no, a massive myocardial infarct, to be specific. The wall of the ventricle—no, the wall of the left ventricle, which was probably the size of a silver dollar, he had said, curving the first finger of his left hand to meet his thumb in a circle about the size of a silver dollar, his eye peering through the circle, and had he used his left hand because it was the left ventricle, the thought occurred to her, but she didn't open her mouth.

"Jack didn't know what hit him," Detective Thorne said.

"How do you know that?"

"The pathologist."

She waited.

"Because of the size of the bruise."

"Bruise? Do you mean from the fall? From the car going over the edge?"

"No, sorry. The bruise in the heart. When the blood dies it looks like a bruise, he said. It was a big one."

When the blood dies. A big one. The only way to stay upright in the chair was to stare at his tie.

"It was fast."

"He wasn't in pain?"

"Oh, no, I mean, it was fast, they said, with an attack that big, it had to be fast . . ." He shrugged, lowered his chin. "But there had to be pain."

Pain. A word she hadn't fully understood the first time out, her first dealings with death—the pain of losing her dad had been overwhelming, but maybe something about being just sixteen and not fully formed, or something about the details that Lady had kept from her or the fact that Lady had smothered her with love to make up for it, or that her life changed in so many ways at the time of his death and soon after—high school, boys, college—life opening to her with all its promises, all its hurts. Rachel looked at Steve Thorne, wrapped her arms around her rib cage under her breasts, and held on . . . not a hurt like Jack must have felt in his arm, in his chest; she didn't know what it could feel like except what she had heard or read.

She had taken the news, asked some questions, watched Thorne drink coffee, and gone upstairs to her bed. The cave of her bed had become her sanctuary; sleep had become her best friend. Grace had let him out. Grace had done everything—lured her out of the bed a little longer each day with warm pots of macaroni, warm wraps for her shoulders, warm baths. Dana came and went and hovered; she didn't bring the baby. Frightened, you could see it in her eyes. Ben-oh came home two weekends in a row, brought his laundry and lay around, talked to his sister in whispers, sprawled next to Rachel's bed in her little yellow flowered chair, humming, wearing his Walkman, his eyes closed, his big shoe tapping her spread. They watched for her to rally. As if the mysterious virus had really happened and would soon disappear, as if this wasn't about Jack's being dead.

Her pain now was deep and constant, different, a vast emptiness, an aching hollow that couldn't be filled. It ran her. Propelled her. Leveled her. It was everywhere.

She hurt. But not like Jack's being hit with a massive myocardial infarct—she would never forget those words.

"Do they know when it happened?" she had asked Thorne that day he'd come to call.

"Pardon?"

"The heart attack. Before he went over?"

"Oh, right . . . no, they don't know."

She'd watched him.

"Probably before," he said, lifting his coffee cup. "The way I figure it, the heart attack caused him to lose control."

She'd nodded.

"Of the car."

Glazed. Numb.

"That's the way I see it," Detective Thorne had said, and took a discreet slurp of coffee, "in my head."

Jack's going over a mountain was not what she wanted to see in her head. Slumped against a wheel, losing consciousness, gasping. She'd stood up fast.

"Hey," he said. "Are you okay?"

Panic. Horror. Devastation.

"I'm fine," Rachel had said. Give 'em the old razzle-dazzle. She'd looked right at Steve's friendly face. "I'm fine."

He'd called every now and then since that visit to hear her say those words. He'd described the funeral beautifully—without her even asking; she didn't have the strength to ask, the courage to say the word *funeral*—the sky, the guns, the honor guard, only leaving out who was there. As if she couldn't make it because she'd been ill. All she could visualize was Jacqueline Kennedy and the short black veil, mixed up with a combination of every funeral of every soldier in every movie she'd ever seen—which made no sense but was probably better than trying to imagine the real thing. "So, you need anything?"

"Oh, no. Thanks, Steve."

"You just call me."

"Thank you."

"You sure you're okay?"

A frozen smile into the telephone. "I'm fine."

The routine of mourning, the rules: they ask, you say you're fine, and then they can happily hang up because they're off the hook. They can go to work and walk the aisles of the grocery store and slice open their mail. All the things you can't do because your new job is to imagine. Jack in pain, Jack's hands slipping off the wheel, grabbing his chest, the tires slipping over the edge, dangling and plunging over the edge, the big car hurtling down. The fat Explorer tumbling and turning as it hit the rocks, with Jack bouncing across the interior like a rag doll, held inside the bending, breaking metal can by a seat belt. Did he know when the car caught on the rocks and stopped? Was he conscious? Was he still alive?

The phone rang. She was in the house alone. It had been a month and she had to work and she had to face facts and she had to function and she'd told Grace to go home. She had to do this herself, no one could help her, no one could understand—because *isolated* covered all the other words. Isolation was the word that was different. No one understood. This was not about watching someone die of cancer or AIDS or any of the mean deaths that took their time, any of the mean deaths that people knew—the slow, evil deterioration of the body and the spirit until the person succumbs. Preparation, the gift of preparation. Not this time; no one understood the sudden emptiness, the surprise, and the swift pain. The only one who could understand the instant death of a person you love was her very own mother, and Lady didn't even know who she was. "Mom, what did you do when Daddy dropped dead? How did you go on?" Rachel stood across from the answering machine imagining the conversation, Lady smiling at her and speaking in "mumbo jumbo," which is how Ben referred to his grandmother's dementia.

Rachel counted the rings, then listened to the recording of herself from the old days. "Leave it at the beep," said the happy Rachel who used to be fine.

"Hey, Mom, it's me, Dana. You must have gone out. That's good. You have to get out of the house. Really." A breath. "Maybe you went with Grace for a walk. I'll call her . . . anyway, please call me, Mom, really, I want to know how you are. . . ."

Sinking. Sad. Furious. Panicky.

Not fine.

Rachel grabbed her keys and her purse and was in the garage before Dana had told the machine good-bye.

She had made the run three times without him, meeting him partway up. A holiday for two to change the routine—a rendezvous—twice in Lone Pine, tromping around for three days, up and down Mount Whitney, eating in all the local diners, shooting at tin cans across a sweep of green field, shooting pool and drinking beer in the one bar; once they'd met in Independence at an old hotel that was full of rooms and empty except for the two of them. And the only restaurant was closed for dinner so they ate bologna sandwiches in the room. Sitting cross-legged on the frayed bedspread spreading the mustard with her finger until he'd handed her his pocketknife. Slices of white bread falling out of the plastic, salt on his mouth when he kissed her, the smell of nectarines, the clunk of the mustard jar rolling across the floor. Independence was as far up as she had gone. Anything north of there would have been too close to Jack's other life; he'd made that clear. Other wife, other life; Rachel lowered both front windows, she needed more air.

"Next time let's meet in Big Pine." After the sex, after the shower, the two of them in the steamed mirror.

"It's too close."

"No it's not."

Her eyes on him in the mirror, the set of his jaw.

"It's only a few more miles," she said.

She waited.

"Jack?"

"No."

She turned to him and fluffed her hair with the towel. "*No* is all of it?"

Gray eyes lowered, tanned square hands buttoning his shirt.

"Jack?"

"Rachel?"

"Big Pine isn't much farther."

Strong fingers off the buttons and lightly circling her wrist. "I said no."

"Don't talk to me that way. I'm not a baby."

"If you want to go to Big Pine, go by yourself." He walked out of the bathroom, through the hotel room; she heard his car keys. "Jack?" Out the door. She turned back to the mirror, heart racing. She got dressed and ran with her purse and duffle down to the parking lot, hair wet, pants half zipped. His car was there next to hers, the motor running, Jack behind the wheel. She stood at his open window and studied the loose ties of her sneakers on the concrete.

"What do you want, Rachel?"

"Weren't you going to say good-bye?"

"I'm still here, aren't I?"

Sometimes it was like that. It was best not to make waves.

A gray day in October like Jack's eyes. Too cool to put the top down, and she was too afraid. He had admonished her bravado about wheeling around *in this day and age with all the goddamn crazies that could jump in with you, Rach,* but she'd never listened until now. Perhaps she would never again put the top down; perhaps her daring had gone over the edge with him.

A gray sky and a highway past some outlet stores, past subdivisions that ended ruler-sharp against burnt fields. A gray sky and the anticipation of the road that lay in front of her. She was fueled by her goal, possessed with the going, obsessed with the idea that she might be able to breathe easier if she could see where he'd been. If she could see it, maybe she would stop waiting for him. If she could see it, maybe she could get closer to believing he was really gone.

She got coffee in Mojave at the Chevron.

"How you doin'?" from the lady in stripes handing her back her credit card.

"Fine, thank you."

An exchange of smiles.

She did not slow down where he'd spun her the story of the ghost ship; she did not look out across the salt flats that softened into the horizon; she did not replay the conversation in her head.

She did not stop in Olancha. She knew the place; she knew the gravy, the little bits of sausage in the warm beige gravy that he liked to splash over his eggs. She knew the waitresses—unattractive twin sisters who bickered with each other as they sloshed ice into big green plastic glasses of Coke. He used to flirt with them. "You sure look good today, Raylene; that color becomes you." Rachel hiding behind a page of newspaper, Jack's foot on hers under the table, until he'd get the older one to blush, the younger one to smile. "I like your hair like that, Corinne." "Oh my goodness," Corinne would purr. Rachel passed the place, slowing only because the speed limit was posted, keeping her eyes front.

She stopped in Lone Pine. She did not go to the Whitney Portal where they used to go. She sat at the counter of the seedy luncheonette and had two scrambled eggs. She didn't eat the hash browns, just the eggs and the buttered middles of both pieces of toast. Grape jelly on her fingers. Sweet coffee. The place was filled with workmen and the smell of fried grease and sweat.

Two drunks sprawled on a bench where she'd parked the car perked up as she unlocked the door.

"Hey."

She turned. Tanned as if they'd just returned from Maui. "Yes?"

"You got any change?" asked the girl. Rachel opened her purse; the girl stood and staggered, held out her hand. Smoke curling into her eyes, she took Rachel's dollar and grinned. She was probably Dana's age; she was missing two teeth. "Thanks." Sour beer breath, dirty fingernails on the stub of cigarette, and the toothless smile.

Rachel's eyes filled; she wanted to hold her. "You're welcome." She had to call Dana and tell her where she was.

"Nice car," the boy drunk said, and kind of saluted her, his fingers up to his sticky hair.

She took off. Twenty-five to 45 to 65, the BMW hugging the straight stretch of road. Green on either side and then mountains, huge purple things like picture postcards capped with snow. The sun came out; she tilted her visor and pushed the automatic dialer on the car phone.

"Grace?"

"Jesus, Rachel, where the hell are you?"

"I'm sorry; I should have called."

"You sure the hell should have. Dana's here."

"I'm sorry."

"You're crackling . . . didn't you know we'd worry . . . where are you?"

"I had to make the trip."

"What trip? What?" Static and then Grace said again, "What trip?"

"I have to see where he was when it happened."

"For crissakes . . ." You could hear the sigh of disgust through the interference. "Here's your daughter . . ."

"Mom?"

"Dana, I'm fine." It was the first time in a month that it was nearly true.

* * *

She did not look at the big hotel where they'd stayed in Independence or relive his anger in the room or her anger in the parking lot or any anger at all—or any happiness—she tried to stay in the moment and not get bogged down.

She reached Big Pine and crawled through town, seeing it for the first time; the whole thing was about three blocks long. And then across from a school and a baseball diamond she saw the sign for Glacier Lodge Road. She pulled over, let the motor idle, straightened her back against the seat.

She took the turn slowly, trying to imagine Jack's making the turn from the other side of the road, calling her from somewhere a little north of the turnoff or maybe earlier; there was no way to know. She had memorized the conversation, repeated it so many times that she was sure there was no way to glean from it what might have made him make the turn. He was on his way and then he wasn't.

The eastern slope of the Sierras. Steep and beautiful. The further in you drove, the higher the altitude; the further in you drove, the sharper the curves. But beautiful. Breathtaking. All words that had to do with majesty applied and somewhere in the middle of this daunting beauty Jack had suffered a massive myocardial infarct and gone down. Steve Thorne's words. Four, five miles in, before or after, but there was no way to know. Had she expected a marker? A bit of yellow tape drifting in the wind? Rachel drove to the end—the park and the campgrounds—turned around, and came back. Taking the curves slowly, hugging the edge—what had she expected to see? Chalk marks indicating where the tires had slipped? A sign? Did the altitude make him disoriented? Was he backing up to turn around? Had the car gone over frontward or backward? And where? She drove it again. What had she expected? And again. What had she hoped for? And again. There was nothing there.

* * *

She began to get shaky during the second drink—before that she'd been fine. Okay, not fine, but functioning. Enough to have driven to Bishop, gotten a room at the Best Western, called Dana and Grace to explain that it was too late and she was too tired to drive home. Fine enough to buy a toothbrush and toothpaste and have a talk with the maid in the hallway about where to eat. Fine enough to walk to the restaurant.

A small town at sunset, cars slowing on Main Street, one movie theater, a JCPenney, competing hardware stores. Picture-perfect. The rose and orange of the sky trading places with the black night, stars as big as your fist, crisp mountain air, clean and sparkling. People hustling home to supper. Norman Rockwell and white bread.

The waitress was overtly kind, as if she'd never served a woman alone and didn't want Rachel to feel bad that she had to eat by herself. Lanky and tan—everyone in town looked tan—and yes, she could give Rachel a small salad in place of the fries, even though it already came with a salad, and yes, she could hold the gravy and the mayo and the butter and the sauce that usually came with it. "Are you on a special diet?" she'd asked, giving Rachel the up and down. Rachel shook her head and tried to smile.

She lifted the olive from the martini. Too many questions and no answers, and even if there were answers they wouldn't change how she felt. Even if she'd seen the exact place where it had happened, it wouldn't change how she felt. He was on his way and then he wasn't. She would never see him again.

She imagined Jack in town. Walking into this Hickory House, sitting across from her eating baby back pork ribs, which is what she figured he would have ordered. Rachel ate the olive.

They weren't finished. She had things to say and she couldn't say them to him. She had things to do and she couldn't do them with him—he was gone.

She would never get to say good-bye.

She would never see him again.

She twisted the toothpick through the paper napkin, in and out, like stitches in cloth.

The waitress put two salads down in front of Rachel, one on either side of a plate of grilled chicken.

"Plain," the waitress said, one hand on her hip, beaming at Rachel. "See?"

Rachel stared at the food and lifted the second martini. She took a drink and picked up her fork. She sat there. The only other person who could understand what she was going through was Linda North.

Linda

THERE WAS NEVER enough Tupperware. Or plastic wrap. And the freezer was full, and what would she do with all the food if she kept it?

Linda shoveled the entire pan of lasagna into the garbage disposal, then mashed the heavy foil container into the trash. The smell of sauce and cheese was staggering; she ran her hands under the water. She held the note that she'd ripped from the top of the foil: *Lasagna (from* The New York Times Cookbook*): Bake at 45 minutes in a preheated oven at 325 degrees. Ralph and I are thinking of you. Lou.* Was Lucille Crawley from New York? The blue writing blurred under her wet thumb; she ripped the paper to shreds, the shreds into confetti, and reached for the next offering.

That's how she thought of them, as offerings—left on her front porch with the newspaper, handed with whispers through the opened screen door into the arms of one of her girls, like little orphans left on the doorstep, like little dead mice that Buddy brought in when he was a puppy, dropping them at her feet: cakes and pies, Pyrex dishes of baked macaroni, a parade of endless casseroles, cookies with sprinkles. Who would send her cookies with sprinkles? Linda pulled at the card stuck to the plastic wrap with a used red Christmas bow. *Hope you're feeling better. Love, Marie Eckerts.* As if she'd been sick. And with her last name as if there was more than one Marie dropping off store-bought cookies rewrapped to look like homemade. And without Charlie's name, just Marie, as if she were alone. Linda dropped the cookies one by one into the whirling disposal, some of the red and blue sprinkles shooting up and sticking to her hands. Marie had probably had them in the cupboard since the Fourth of July. And next week was Halloween.

She was aware of that, that next week was Halloween. She was aware of how her girls were pushing her to be alive, bringing the kids over to show her their outfits for the parade and trick or treat. Carey's hair slicked into spikes, the ends pink, he was wearing somebody's old golf sweater, a white shirt, cuffed pants, and glitter on his shoes. "I'm a Backstreet Boy, Grandma."

She nodded.

"It's a rock group."

"They suck," Tony said.

"They do not."

"Do too."

"Shut up."

"That's enough," Julie said.

Tony, all smirks and grumbling about how he was too old; he'd walk the little kids, but he wasn't wearing any g.d. costume. He said the initials, not the *goddamn,* one eye on his mother, his fingers grazing Linda's shoulder. He'd stayed close to her this past month, come over on his bike after school when he didn't have practice, polish off a quart of milk and talk about football; he'd even tried some grown-up conversations with her about girls. And once when she hadn't realized he was in the house, she'd passed the living room and was stunned to see him sitting quietly in Jack's chair, his arms settled on the indentations left in the leather by his grandfather, his fingertips just a few inches short of the mark.

"Look at me, Grandma, I'm a mummy." Emmie, pushing in front of Carey for Linda's attention, turning slowly so Linda could take her in.

"I see that."

"From Egypt," Emmie said.

"You'd think she'd want to be a fairy," Julie said, "something pretty . . . never . . . she only wants to be dead." She stopped, went white. "Oh, God, Mom . . ."

"It's okay," Linda said, smiling at Emmie, feeling the soft strips of white sheet Julie had sewn together for the mummy costume, cupping Emmie's little bottom and Emmie snuggling up, sliding into her grandma's lap, her mummy face wrapped in gauze, with poke holes for eyes and nose and mouth, against Linda's breasts.

"Are you sad 'cause you miss Grampa?" the child mumbled through the gauze.

"Uh-huh."

"Come on, sweetie," Julie said, reaching for her daughter. "Mom, come home with us for supper."

"I already said no."

"Please, Grandma." Emmie tugged her hand.

"I can't, honey, I already told your mommy, I have to stay home."

"Why?" Tony said.

"Because I have to."

Jack's eyes repeated in her grandson's face. "Why?"

"Tony," Julie said to her son.

"What?"

"Leave your grandma alone."

Linda looked at him and put her hand on his arm. "Because I have to learn how to be here, honey, by myself."

"Mom . . ."

She stopped Julie with a look.

"Like a big girl," Emmie said, "like when I have to go to sleep with the light off, like a big girl."

"Like a big girl," Linda repeated, "that's right," and holding tight to Emmie's hand, she'd walked them to the door.

She stood at the sink, took a breath—exhausted, as if she'd climbed a mountain. She had to go to the store and buy candied corn for next week, for the cowboys and ballerinas and goblins that would knock on the door. That was one thing to do, and she had lots of things to do, yes, she would remember, she would make a list. She was washed by an image of Jack with Julie and Patty on this kitchen floor, this very kitchen floor right where she was standing, newspaper under the huge pumpkin, piles of squash and seeds, the three of them covered in orange pulp, carving the jack-o'-lantern's smile.

She had to stop remembering. She couldn't make her way from one room to another without being hit with a memory, ten memories, twenty memories, each overlapping the other in complete detail. Was there a way to stop that? She would put that on the list, go to the library and see if there was a book. How to cope with the knowledge that your husband was . . . say it . . . the struggle to say the word. Her grandmother Stella used to say *passed.* "He passed," she'd say in that light wavery voice of hers, all high up and shaky, her hands fluttering around like hummingbirds. Passed. Linda reached for another wrapped container and ripped off the envelope taped to the top; slanted loopy handwriting in black ink: *Dear Linda, Hope you're doing okay. We're praying for you. Michele and Warren Mosher.* She lifted the foil. A sweet potato pie, slightly caved in in the middle, the pinched edges of crust burned. Michele Mosher needed to pray for her oven; it was off.

Sweet potatoes and pumpkin. Halloween and then Thanksgiving. Thanksgiving and then Christmas. There would be no more carving of pumpkin smiles or turkey close to the bone. "And this big old leg for your mother . . ." Lifting the drumstick to the platter, his eyes averted, the sly smile. Patty piping up, "No, Mommy likes white meat." "Ah, the breast, that's right, Mommy's got the beautiful breasts," the kids paying no attention, gray eyes to hers across the cranberry, the yams, the stuffing, a secret message, husband to wife, over the tops of their children's heads. A caress, a promise of what would be later. Could be, would be. The quiet of late afternoons on a holiday was always theirs. The kids playing with toys, falling asleep over Christmas wrappings, or rushing off with their friends, the house suddenly empty, and she'd be scraping plates, up to her elbows in a sinkful, and there he'd be. "How about a little lay-down?" into her neck and her ear, behind her, his arms coming around, his hands up under her shirt, tugging at the buttons, turning her toward him; he'd pull her from the kitchen. "You'll finish it later. I'll help you." "Yeah, sure."

Stop it; she had to stop it. What good would it do?

We're praying for you, Linda read again; she crumpled the note into a tiny hard ball and slammed it into the trash.

She'd prayed plenty the week he was gone, the week before they found him. What would she pray for now? She slid the pie out of the pan and under the running water, squashing the pieces in her hands. Buddy scratched at the door. Wiping her wet hands on her pants, she crossed the kitchen and let him and Bella out into the yard. It was beautiful, cool. Her favorite—October—her best time.

Jack raking the leaves into huge piles, Patty watching from her lap, Julie jumping on them with shrieks and squeals.

Linda stood at the open door, her eyes on the dark sky. She didn't know how to put up the Christmas lights; she didn't know where they were. She didn't know how to take down the screens and put up the storm doors. She didn't know how to change the filters on the furnace. Or did he just clean them? She didn't know. She didn't know when her car was supposed to be serviced. She didn't know how to do that thing he did when the idle was too high and it got shaky at a stoplight. She didn't know how to barbecue. She didn't—she was always in the house making the potato salad, chopping the cabbage for the coleslaw, rinsing the strawberries, icing a chocolate cake, she'd never even opened a bag of coals. Linda studied the yard and the fence and the sky without seeing them, turned, and closed the door.

She'd left the water running. She should finish this in the morning; she should go to bed.

She couldn't eat alone, set the table for one; she couldn't do it. She had taken to eating in front of the television set. On or off, it didn't matter, just so she wasn't sitting at the table by herself. Sometimes it was just easier not to eat, then she didn't have to think about where or what or any of it. Any of it. Like why there was no one next to her in the bed. Even if they weren't touching, weren't speaking, there was his breathing, the presence of him in the bed. The knowledge of that other person she had lived with for thirty-five years. She'd taken to sleeping on the living room couch, the one closest to his chair. How long would that go on—not wanting to face the bed? The phone rang.

If it was one of the kids and she didn't answer it, they'd come driving over to see what was what.

"Hello?"

"Mom, you said you'd call me before you went to bed."

"I was going to, hon, you beat me to it."

"Are you okay? What are you doing?"

"I was throwing the ball for the dogs."

"You ought to go to bed; it's late and you're rattling around there—did you eat supper?"

"I had some of Lou Crawley's New York lasagna; it was very good."

"Are you sure you don't want me to come over?"

"Patty, I'm fine. I'm going to let the dogs in."

"Will you call me when you're in bed?"

"I'll call you in the morning."

A few seconds of hesitation. "I love you, Mom."

"I love you too. Buddy's barking, honey."

"Mom?"

"Patty, I'm fine, stop worrying, I gotta go."

She hung up, stood at the counter motionless, studying Jack's bowl of change that he kept next to the phone and the calendar.

She missed the phone calls, the "Hey, babe" in the morning, the "How'd it go today?" in the night. Every day when he was away, even when he was down there with her, he would call. Not twice, not at any special time, but he'd call. Sometimes she wouldn't answer; furious, standing next to the answering machine holding her breath, she'd listen to him leave some half-assed message not mentioning where he was. As if she didn't know.

If he wouldn't have gone down there, this wouldn't have happened. If he wouldn't have gone down there, he would be home.

Part of the horror was the fact that she continued to listen for him: his car in the drive, his "Hey, babe" as he opened the door. All the years when she was up here and he was down there—driving home nearly every weekend to be with her and the kids, jamming a marriage and chores and raising the kids together into wedges of time; she was used to segments alone, pieces until he would come home, with a list and a plan: mow the grass, change the oil, fix Julie's bike, make love to her.

Linda stared at the quarters. Stop it; don't remember; do something else.

The trick was to pretend she was doing okay, that was the only way any of them would leave her alone.

"Why don't you take a night class at the high school, something to fill your mind . . . you could learn to speak Spanish, or what about computers?" Marie Eckerts had said.

"I don't have a computer," Linda had said.

"Oh."

Fill her mind. Is that what she'd said? The same woman who once upon a time had said, "Don't you worry about Jack running around down there in Beverly Hills with all those movie stars?"

"What about the gym? You could do aerobics or one of those salsa dance classes. Oh, we could all go—wouldn't that be fun?" Angie Saniger, practically clapping her hands, with her fat face and that big can of hers, pushing Linda to join a gym. Linda, who had always been the jock, the cheerleader, the center on the girl's basketball team, and Angie, whose ankles were like tree trunks, waddling around in tight pants and high heels. Angie'd have a heart attack if she took a salsa class.

Linda scooped a handful of quarters out of Jack's change bowl and held them in her hand.

A heart attack. Charlie had explained to her about the heart attack. Should she hold herself accountable for not cooking more fish? Letting him eat ice cream, roast beef, sausage, butter stacked on his bread? Leg of lamb? Coffee cake? "Make that thing with the cinnamon."

"Jack, it's loaded with butter." "I know, that's why I like it." The smile and, of course, she made it. Her gifts of food, her own offerings of love to him, that's what she did.

"A heart attack from his cholesterol?" she'd asked Charlie. "He walked every day; he walked the dogs before breakfast and after supper; he was in good shape."

Charlie's head was down; he circled his hat in his hands. "I don't know, Linda." Of course he didn't know. Nobody knew; nobody had any idea. Did Jack have the heart attack before the car went down, or did he have the heart attack after the car went down? Was it from the meat loaf she'd made for supper the night before?

Did it matter?

Did anything?

"What if we would have gotten to him sooner?"

"I don't know, Linda. The doc thinks when the car hit he was already gone."

Charlie's hands circling his hat; Jack's hands on the wheel, broad nail beds, bigger than you would think because he wasn't that tall, but beautiful wide hands, the scar across the top of the left one where he'd been burned. Jack's hand pulling the razor, Jack's hand opening the top cabinet, popping a beer, moving bike parts, holding the soap, holding one of the babies, holding her. Gone. Stop it now.

Lou Crawley thought she should take a trip to some place she'd always wanted to go, like Egypt. She'd actually said Egypt. It was all Linda could do to not laugh in her face—the image of taking Emmie with her to Egypt in her mummy costume.

She released the change; two quarters missed the bowl and fell to the floor. She picked them up and put them in her pocket. She would like to wrap her face in gauze, then no one could see what she was thinking. Buddy scratched at the door to come back in. It was nearly midnight; what was she doing? She should go to bed. No, to couch. That's right; it was hard to know whether to laugh or cry at all of it, hard to know. Linda moved to the sink, stared at the running water, at the containers still sitting there. As if learning how to speak Spanish would help her forget about Jack, as if going to a salsa dance class—didn't you need a partner if you went to a dance class?

She reached for Angie Saniger's Bundt cake. You knew it was a Bundt cake from the shape and you knew it was from Angie. She must make a gross of Bundt cakes a week; she ought to go into the Bundt cake business—this one actually looks like her ass.

Linda ripped the foil from the cake, holding it in one hand, sick at the smell of rum and sugar; she faltered, then stopped.

Breathless at the sink, drained by the senseless act of throwing away food that had been lovingly brought by other policemen's wives, aware of what she was doing, the ridiculous anger, the futility of the envy, she dropped the cake, holding on to the sink and feeling childish and stupid as her legs got soft.

She'd expected Jack to die when he was a uniformed cop. Oh, she had. She had actually learned the differences in sirens when they'd lived in L.A.: ambulance, police, fire, and when it was police she could feel her shoulders raise, a tightening in her gut and her neck and her jaw, a wave of panic, and she would wait for the phone to ring. As if the siren was a warning. They were living in Santa Monica and Jack was working in Beverly Hills, two separate places, and a police siren in Santa Monica had nothing to do with what was happening in Beverly Hills, but she still got antsy; pictures of bad guys floated in her head. When it was just her and him, she'd been more easy with it, but once the babies were born, it had changed. How could she take care of the girls if Jack got killed? Could she make a living washing heads in Frank and Wilma's Beauty Salon like she'd done every summer in high school? In those days they had one-man cars, and Jack would come home and tell her how he'd stopped someone, how it was a matter of walking up to a car with nobody covering you. She knew the stories, what could happen; a uniformed police officer was a target, she knew.

She'd expected him to die when he was a detective. Detectives left the area; they searched for suspects wherever need be, east L.A., west L.A., South-Central, knocking doors down, guns raised to whatever was on the other side. She knew. Jack had been involved in more than one shooting, more than one "Halt. Stop," and when they didn't, more than one gun going off. He'd killed a man on Ninth and San Pedro Street. He had. A standoff like in some movie—the guy had a rap sheet ten miles long and Jack had a faster draw, but it wasn't a movie, it was her husband, stunned by what had happened, slumped in his chair.

Linda let go of the counter and sunk to the floor.

She had expected him to die when he was in uniform, and she had expected him to die when he was a detective; she had never expected him to die once he quit.

She'd let her guard down.

She had expected him to be with her forever. Like a fool.

A fool sitting on her kitchen floor in the middle of a mess. Linda chewed a hunk of sweet yellow cake. It was delicious. It was. You had to hand it to Angie Saniger—rich and moist and delicious. She put another piece in her mouth. She was so tired of crying, so tired of waiting for this to all be over, as if it were some bad dream. What was she supposed to do now? What was she really supposed to do?

"How do you feel about a job?" Charlie Eckerts had said, moving that hat between his fingers.

"A job?"

"Sure."

Buddy lumbered over, slid his head under Charlie's hand; Charlie set his hat on his knee and ruffled the fur behind Buddy's ears.

"I haven't had a job since high school."

"So?"

"So . . . I can't imagine."

"You're smart; you could do anything."

"Like what?"

"You could work at Wicki's. Marge is always looking for somebody to help out."

The whoop of laughter was a surprise. "Wicki's? With Marge and Walter—have you lost your mind?"

"Probably," he said, laughing with her. "I couldn't think fast enough."

He was sweet, Charlie Eckerts; she couldn't imagine what he was doing with Marie.

Linda licked her fingers, then picked up another chunk of cake.

What was anybody doing with anybody?

Marge and Walter fought around that grocery store as if it were their living room, pushing each other with words, rotten put-downs and such nasty comments it could make your head swim. It didn't matter who was standing there. Lou Crawley said she saw Marge throw a peach at Walter once. Marge was checking Lou out and Walter said something to Marge and it must have been the straw that broke the camel because Marge just picked up one of the peaches she was bagging for Lou and threw it right at Walter's head. And yet when Marge had her surgery, there he was. He even closed the store, which was a first, since if it was up to Walter he'd keep Wicki's open 24-7 if it meant selling another can of soup. There he was at Marge's side, sleeping in a chair next to her bed, his arm extended in between all the tubes and wires, his fingers surrounding hers. Linda had never seen Walter so much as touch Marge before. She went by the hospital one afternoon and Walter was spooning Marge little bits of pudding as if she were a child, the moment so intimate that Linda turned and left before they heard her at the door. But once Marge was on her feet and back at the register, they were just like they were before.

Why did they stay together?

Why did anybody?

There was talk about her and Jack, that Jack fooled around, that she should leave him; she'd heard it, pieces of conversations; she knew. As if other people knew what was best for her. Or anybody. Like what Marge was doing with Walter, or why Charlie was with Marie. People always having an opinion. Well, even she had an opinion, she had to admit that—Charlie Eckerts, so sweet and goofy, all legs and arms and kind of tender, or maybe it was just plain nice, and Marie Eckerts so pushy.

Linda took another bite of cake.

Too pushy for her own good. Marie's opinion was *the* opinion as far as Marie was concerned, and she had an opinion on everything. She didn't stop when she was with Charlie, but he didn't seem to notice. Or comment. Marie'd say something and he'd just nod as if he were thinking about it, and go on where he was as if he'd made his peace with it, the way she was. Marie was all over him in public, holding his hand, sitting real close, snuggling up as if they were kids. Charlie didn't seem to notice that either.

He'd been so nice to her these past weeks, coming over to see if she was doing okay, talking to her about things. She liked him.

She needed a glass of milk.

She had a sudden fantasy picture in her head of Charlie leaning forward and kissing her over Buddy's head.

What was she thinking? She pushed herself up, washed her hands under the faucet. What was she thinking? Where was her head?

She needed Jack.

She'd spent her whole life waiting for Jack to come home so she could talk to him about what she should do—about the kids or if they should go somewhere or who did what to whom. About a plane crash, a breakup of two movie stars, whether he could fix the refrigerator again. About politics, about some historical thing, about anything. She laughed under her breath. What would he say about her working at Wicki's?

What would he say about her eating a whole cake? Well, half of it, three-quarters anyway—there wasn't that much left on the floor. What on earth was she doing thinking about Charlie? Buddy was scratching at the door and barking. Is that the way it starts? One day you're friends with someone and the next day it turns into something else—one kiss and everything is different, one kiss. Doesn't anybody think about the stakes? About what could happen? About who could get hurt? The phone rang. Julie checking on her, she was sure. Linda lifted the receiver. "I'm fine, honey," she said. "I'm going to bed."

Quiet on the line, no daughter saying, "Hey, Mom." Some music in the background, like in a restaurant, a bar.

"Hello?" the woman said, and then she took a second; the woman on the other end of the line took a second. "Linda? It's Rachel Glass."

She felt her fingers at her mouth, didn't feel her hand move, just her fingers where they stopped against her lips.

"I'm in Bishop."

Bishop.

"I need to see you."

It must have been a bar; you could hear the song change, people laughing, that sound.

"I guess I should have started another way . . . but"—she took a breath—"I need to see you. I need to talk to you."

As if there were something to say. What was there to say?

"Linda?"

Buddy was going to break down the door. All she could see was that woman's face; all she could smell was cake.

"I know this is . . ." Rachel Glass faltered. ". . . I don't know the word . . ."

"Unusual?" Linda said.

She laughed, a little laugh. "Yes, I know it's terribly late . . . yes, and unusual . . . I just"—she hesitated—"couldn't stop myself."

And Linda had no idea where the words came from. "Do you know how to get here?"

An intake of breath, and the music. "No," Rachel Glass said.

Rachel

SHE WASN'T USED to the dark, not this kind of dark, this expanse of black sky, this lack of streetlights, this great stretch of dark road. The house sat back from the road and the driveway behind a maze of trees. She didn't need to check the scribbled directions on the napkin, she had seen the house in countless photographs. Never in person; she'd only driven by the place they'd had in Santa Monica; he'd never let her drive up this far. Her heart was beating hard; she could hear it, or feel it, she wasn't sure which—crickets, cicadas, her heart slamming, and the dogs; she could hear them from inside the house.

She could pull away; she could forget this.

Rachel turned into the driveway and the porch light came on. She killed the engine, opened the car door, and the front door of the house opened; she saw the figure of a woman in silhouette.

Rachel got out of the car; Linda North pushed open the screen door and stepped out of her house. She held the collar of a huge, white dog; he had stopped barking.

"Are you afraid of dogs?"

"No."

"It's okay, Buddy," she said quietly, bending to the dog.

Rachel took the steps up to the porch. Linda North straightened her shoulders; they faced each other in the glow of a single yellow light.

It was amazing to her that her first thought would be about looks, about how Linda looked, could it be so trite, this sizing each other up as if they were in high school? She was prettier than her photographs—no, not pretty, she wasn't a pretty woman, but she had a good face and lovely eyes. The camera wasn't kind to her. She was taller than Rachel or bigger or stronger, or maybe it was just that she seemed calm. Rachel certainly didn't feel calm, quite the opposite—speedy and shaky, as if she might explode. She had an insane thought that she would like to walk into Linda North's arms, put her head on Linda's shoulder, and hold on. Out of her mind, she must be out of her mind.

The smudges under Linda's eyes were the same smudges as under hers, the downward lines at the sides of the mouth, the look of exhaustion that told all. Rachel was suddenly so tired she thought she might collapse, just slowly fall over onto the porch floor in front of the dog. "Is that Buddy?"

Linda nodded.

It occurred to Rachel that she knew the dog's name, that she hadn't hidden that fact—could it matter now? Would they still keep secrets now that Jack was gone? She bent to the dog. "You can let go," she said to Linda. The dog smelled her face, her hair; he was beautiful.

"Come on in," Linda said, and turned; she held the screen door open into Jack's house. Rachel took a step, the dog at her side, his weight against her leg as if she were a sheep he was tending.

Yellow and green and the furniture was tacky, or maybe the word was affordable, or maybe the word was worn, or maybe the word was lived-in, or maybe the word was loved. Her eyes were moving faster than her brain could take everything in—fabric she never would have picked, stained and faded now, but in a yellow floral that didn't go with the green of the chair; the shape of the lamp shades, which were wrong for the tables; the wall-to-wall carpeting in what she thought was an ugly gray-green; and bad paintings, the kind you buy at a parking lot fair. A chewed tennis ball under the coffee table, a framed photograph of Jack and Linda, the kind taken by a photographer in a department store, in color, with a red frame. Red candles in candlesticks. A red glass candy dish with a lid. Another big white dog across the room on a beat-up piece of rug; the dog lifted its head and eyed her but other than that didn't move. Stacks of magazines and reading glasses on every surface, half-empty coffee cups, balls of used Kleenex, a vase of dying flowers, an upright piano coated with dust—you could actually write your name in it with a fingertip—plastic squeeze bottles of hand cream, and Jack's chair. Rachel knew it was his chair; they had talked about it. She had teased him. "A BarcaLounger? One of those awful things that tilt back, that fat guys sit in and drink beer? You don't have one of those in your living room." "Oh, yes I do, Miss Smarty Pants, yes I do." Faced with the creases in the leather, the dark indentation where his head had rested, his arms, his hands, Rachel was hit with a wave of nausea; she stumbled into the dog.

"Do you want coffee?"

What was she doing here?

Linda's stare. "Coffee?"

"Okay."

She didn't want coffee. No, maybe she did; maybe that's what she needed—a cup of coffee, her mother used to say, would fix you right up. A cup of coffee and she would probably shoot off like a Roman candle right out of this house—Jack's house, Linda and Jack's house. She felt as if she were trespassing, as if she should tiptoe, not touch anything, not sit down. "Sit down," Linda said.

She sat on the edge of one yellow sofa. Buddy positioned himself in front of her, watched his mistress go into the kitchen, returned his gaze to Rachel. Big, black eyes, black like his nose, like coal for the face of a snowman; he sat at attention like a guard at his post. Maybe Linda had given him a silent command—stay with her; watch her every move.

What was she doing here?

She had wanted to see it all and now she was seeing it all and she wanted to run.

She got up. Buddy got up. She took a few tentative steps toward the kitchen; he moved at her side.

Linda was standing at the sink, her back to Rachel, filling a Pyrex pot with water. The kitchen was busy, things everywhere, stacks of papers and boxes, and wrapped packages of what looked to be casseroles lined the countertops on both sides of the sink. Had Linda been cooking this late? Kids' photographs held up with fruit magnets were all over the refrigerator—Rachel had never allowed that; she liked the clean sweep of stainless steel, her spotless, shiny kitchen, and now she suddenly felt as if she'd made a mistake. Why weren't there pictures of Ben and Dana and little Sarah stuck up with happy magnets of plastic fruit in her house? Why could she never let a dent stay in a pillow? Why did everything have to look as if photographers were coming to take pictures for a magazine?

Linda poured the water into the Mr. Coffee, put the pot in place, and pushed the switch. She crossed the room and sat in one of the chairs at the table. She looked up at Rachel standing in the doorway.

Her eyes were brown, not dark brown like Rachel's, but a golden brown with dark pupils, astonishing.

You could be flattened by reality; you could be frozen, stunned in your own tracks—to be standing in Jack's kitchen in Jack's house. "I don't know how I got here," Rachel said. It was the truth; it was as if she hadn't driven from the restaurant, as if she'd been transported, beamed in. She steadied herself, her hand against the door jamb.

Linda moved her back against the chair.

"I didn't plan this."

"I didn't think so," Linda said.

Rachel waited.

"People don't usually drop in in the middle of the night."

"No."

"You can sit down, you know."

She came into the room and sat across the table from Linda and then it occurred to her that maybe that was Jack's place. For years she had tried to picture it—picture him in the house, picture him having breakfast, having a sandwich, having dinner—and now here she was.

Buddy made his way to a water bowl and took a big, noisy drink. He made a real production out of it, splashing and slurping. The room filled with the smell of coffee and the sound of the dog. Linda slid her chair back and walked to the sink, took two mugs out of a cabinet, then filled them with coffee. The sugar bowl was already in the middle of the table alongside a water glass filled with teaspoons. She moved to the refrigerator and came back with a carton of milk, put everything on the table between them, and sat back in the chair.

They busied themselves with the coffee. Rachel remembered a play she'd seen once that was all about a tea ceremony, or maybe it was called *Tea Ceremony,* she couldn't remember which, or any of it, except that it was all about fixing a pot of tea. The ceremony of making the tea, the ceremony of two women sitting across from each other who loved the same man. Maybe they should have had tea instead of coffee. Maybe she should have gotten drunk in the restaurant and gone back to the hotel. She felt an overwhelming desire to lay her head on the table. She took a teaspoon.

Linda took a sip of coffee.

Rachel stirred in the sugar, then put down the spoon.

"You wanted to talk to me," Linda said.

"I did."

Linda's mouth pulled into a half smile. "Not anymore? You changed your mind?"

Rachel felt her own mouth pull, a bit of ease; she tried to relax her shoulders. "It just seemed clearer before I got here."

"I guess so."

There was no way to say it except to say it; she'd thought about it all the way into Bishop. "I went up there . . . you know, up Glacier Lodge Road. I drove up without a plan; I just kind of took off this morning. . . . I thought if I saw it . . ." She looked at Linda. "But I don't get it . . . why he went up there."

Linda recrossed her arms.

"Do you?"

"No."

"Did he leave a note?"

"No."

"Nothing?"

"What are you getting at?"

"You don't think he killed himself?"

Incredulous, the beautiful eyes mocking. "You're kidding."

"You don't think he drove off?"

Linda laughed; this choke of laughter came out of her that was so startling Rachel nearly toppled her cup.

"He had a heart attack," Linda said.

"I know that, I just thought . . ."

"You thought my husband would drive off a cliff?" Linda studied her and picked up a spoon. "Then you sure didn't know Jack."

"I knew him." Oh, wait, be careful.

"Not like I did."

"No, probably not."

She felt like a little bomb had gone off, a small explosion, but all the pieces were settling now, floating back down.

Linda put two spoons of sugar into her coffee, stirred it, let the spoon clank against the porcelain, then placed it on the table. "You weren't the first."

"Is that supposed to hurt me?"

"Did you know that? That you weren't the first?"

Rachel couldn't keep her thoughts straight; they were running into each other making everything mud. "I loved him."

"That's nice to know." Linda circled the mug with both hands. "So did I."

"I know that."

"So there we are." Linda took a sip of the coffee.

The clock above the stove was the same clock she had in her kitchen; the same painted clock that Jack had bought her was in Linda's kitchen. Could that be so?

"Okay, I want to ask you something," Linda said. "What did you think when he'd come down there?"

"What do you mean?"

"Did you think he would stay forever? Did you think he wouldn't come back home?"

"No."

Linda took a moment. "He wouldn't have fit in, you know."

She would hold on to herself; she would get up and go.

"Did you think there was no one up here? That when he drove away to come to you he was only leaving the dogs?"

"No." Had she thought that this would be easy? Had she thought at all?

Linda put down the mug. "You knew about me."

"Yes."

"Then how could you do it?"

"I don't know how to answer that."

"You never asked yourself how you could sleep with someone else's husband?"

The tone in her voice, the expression. Words, what were the words?

"Talk about letting yourself off the hook."

"You don't understand how hard this is."

"I sure don't."

"I don't have what you have; I'm out of the loop. No information, no one to talk to. Don't you see? I'm cut off down there. I'm alone."

"You were always down there alone. And why should you have what I have? Equal rights for girlfriends? Are you doing an article about it for a magazine?"

"Are you always this mean?"

Linda repositioned herself in the chair.

"I thought we could talk," Rachel said.

"About what?"

"I don't know now."

"Did you want to compare notes? Talk about Jack?" The scrape of the chair against the linoleum; Linda stood up.

"I just thought we should be together."

"I don't want to be together. I shared Jack with you plenty when he was alive. I'm not about to share him with you now."

"That's not what I came here for."

"What the hell did you come for?"

"I'll go."

"Oh my God," Linda said. "Did you want me to make you feel better?"

"I'll go," Rachel said.

"That's it, isn't it?"

Rachel crossed the kitchen in front of Linda, into the living room, moving fast, Linda behind her, loud. "I thought you came here to say you were sorry, tell me you were sorry—that I should help you deal with this takes the goddamn cake."

Rachel stopped short, turned. Linda was right there; they nearly collided. "I came here to see you, to see what it was . . ."

Linda so close to her, right in her face. "See what? Why he loved me?"

"He loved the two of us. I thought we'd have something in common."

"Don't tell me that. We have nothing in common; we have nothing to talk about."

"Okay, okay." Rachel scooped up her purse, her keys. "I didn't come here to apologize."

"Fine."

"Is that what you want from me?"

"I don't want anything from you. I didn't ask you here."

"Then why did you let me come?"

"I wanted to see if you had the balls to get out of the car, to walk into this house and look me in the face!"

"I'm looking at you, aren't I?" The flush, the heat, the sound of her own voice.

"Did he ever tell you he was going to leave me?"

"No."

"Did he ever say he was going to marry you?"

"No."

"Then how do you live with yourself?"

"You think you had nothing to do with this, that the whole thing is my fault?"

"I sure do."

"Oh, really? Then where were you the last six years—out to lunch? Why didn't you stop him? Why did you let him come back and forth?"

"Jack did what he wanted. I never told Jack what to do."

"You didn't tell him anything! You never had the courage to tell him that if he left again you wouldn't be here when he got back."

Motionless, the two of them, close enough to smell each other; stopped, caught.

Linda steadied herself against the arm of the couch. "No, I didn't."

"Well," Rachel said, catching her breath, "neither did I."

They talked some after the fury, the two of them across from each other, each on a yellow couch. The dog lay between them on the rug. They didn't talk about Jack, really; they talked more about their children, about how each of them felt.

Rachel got back to the hotel at 4:30 and lay across the bed in her clothes. She pushed off her shoes, then pulled the spread up and around her. She felt better; she wasn't exactly sure why.

Linda North had walked her to the car. They didn't touch each other, there was no shaking of hands, no hug. There would be no contact; they would never see each other again. This night, this encounter, this girlfriend and this wife ensnared, caught in the web of this man, his love, his death—an uneasy alliance was all they had.

Rachel studied the gray light making its way around the edges of the hotel drapes, the inevitable dawn.

Thoughts and words drifting—if she knew anything it was some sense of relief, some yielding inside. She would go home when she woke up; she would make the drive, call Ben-oh, see if he'd come home this weekend, call Dana to come over with the baby—they would talk. She would see what was going on with her children. She knew that much. She turned on her side, jammed one hand under the pillow, yawned. She would see what was going on with her children. Rachel closed her eyes. And she would write.

Linda

BUDDY CIRCLED THE yard at full gallop, ears flying, mouth open, tail up—Bella and Linda watched from the porch steps. Bella gave Linda a look as if to say all young boy dogs were insane, then lowered her big head into Linda's lap. Linda switched the coffee mug to the other hand and smoothed the fur on old Bella's head.

The first light had been gray and it looked like it would stay that way. Frost across the branches, her breath making little clouds. She would go in, have breakfast; there was always the possibility she might freeze to the steps.

Linda moved and Bella raised herself and hobbled to the door. Buddy, on the other hand, was not interested in settling inside near a heating vent; he continued to make his morning loops. She decided she would have to break her girls from their morning loops, their phone calls to reassure themselves that she was still alive, morning, noon, and night. The calls were making her nervous; she decided they would have to stop hovering and let her be.

The sink was still lined with casserole dishes. Her eyes moved around the room, rested on Rachel Glass's coffee mug on the table, the lipstick smear at the rim. She picked up the mug and set it in the sink.

Rachel Glass might be prettier than she is, but she wasn't as strong. That was about all she felt, that was her sum-up if she had to weigh it in her head, the two of them, if she had to figure out the way it was. She didn't know if she would have liked her, if things had been different, if they had met under different circumstances; she didn't know how she would have felt. Not that it mattered; she would never see her again. Maybe it was too early for breakfast, maybe she'd have a little lay-down.

She crossed the kitchen, opened the door, and gave Buddy a whistle. His fur was cold against her leg as he brushed past.

Linda followed the dog into the living room and eyed the couch closest to Jack's chair but didn't sit down. She walked through the room and down the hall into their bedroom. You could still smell his aftershave, or maybe only she could; maybe it was in her head.

She slipped off her Keds, lay on top of the spread, and pulled up the folded afghan at the foot of the bed. Buddy watched her until he was sure she was really staying put and then stretched himself out on the floor along the side of the bed, end to end, as if he thought she might roll off and he could cushion her fall. Linda settled herself on the pillows, pushed her hand into her jeans pocket, and pulled out Jack's wedding ring. She held it in front of her, turning it until it caught the light.

First had been the fight about whether she should see the body, her and Charlie carrying on.

"There's no reason, Linda. You don't need to see it. I saw what there is to see."

"I have a right. Take me."

"Hell, it's not about rights. You're his wife, and I'll let you do whatever you want, you know I will, but why put yourself through this?"

She'd sat there in his car, clutching her hands so tight her fingernails had left marks.

"It's not a pretty picture," Charlie said.

Her mind conjured up pictures of Jack that she couldn't stomach.

As a cop's wife, she knew; she'd seen plenty of pictures of people dead. And someone who'd been dead in a car for a long time . . .

"You hear what I'm saying?" Charlie said.

"Yes." She tried to breathe, tried to think it straight.

"I'll take care of it," he said. "Make sure it's right." He looked at her. "I'll bring you everything, Linda, I promise."

And he had—Jack's clothes, his wallet, everything that was in the glove compartment of the Explorer, including his gun. She had opened the bag at the kitchen table, letting the contents slide across the wood. In the middle of his T-shirt and his pants and his socks and his everything was a smaller sealed bag.

"Jack's watch," Charlie said.

"Mm-hm."

She lifted the bag, felt the weight of it in her hand.

"You okay?"

"Yep."

Charlie's frown. "I'm glad you didn't go. I'm glad you didn't see him, Linda."

She didn't know if she was glad or not, but it was too late now. She pulled open the plastic seal of the little bag, let the watch drop into her hand, and behind it slid the ring. Her chest locked as if someone had walloped her hard.

She put the watch on the table and held the ring in her hand. The scroll of the gold, the little curve the band made to hold the diamonds; she remembered the two of them picking it out—how she had wanted plain, a plain gold wedding band, she'd said, and Jack had liked fancy; the ring had been his choice.

She lifted her eyes to Charlie. "Where was this?"

"Huh?"

"Jack's ring." She took a breath. "Was it in the glove compartment?"

"No. Why?"

The words of the fight after he'd told her it must have fallen into the bike parts, fallen somewhere, lost, that he'd lost his wedding ring; the way he'd stood with his back to her washing the oil off his hands.

"Where was it?" she said to Charlie.

Charlie's shrug, as if she were being silly. "On his finger, Linda, where else?"

On his finger.

Linda sat up, tucked her feet into the afghan so they were totally covered, and lay back down. She slipped Jack's ring onto the third finger of her left hand next to her gold wedding band and studied it, her hand above her face up in the air. She turned her hand and the ring fell off her finger and onto her chest; no sound on the crocheted afghan, just a little thump in the middle of her breasts. The ends of her mouth lifted into a slight smile.

The palm of her hand clasping the ring to her chest, the other hand on top, she yawned. She would sleep and then she would call her girls, maybe go watch Tony at football, maybe have all of them over to supper Sunday, maybe not. Maybe she'd get a job at Wicki's, maybe she'd stop being mad at everybody, maybe not. Maybe she'd buy a computer. Maybe she'd go to Egypt. Linda laughed out loud. There was no reason to tell Rachel Glass why Jack was on Glacier Lodge Road; it was nobody's business but her own. Her husband was making the curve to come back to her; he'd put on his wedding ring to come back to her. He'd made up his mind. Linda closed her eyes. She knew and that was enough for her—Jack was coming home.